MEANS TO AN
END

SHERRYL D. HANCOCK

Published by Vulpine Press in the United Kingdom in 2018

ISBN 978-1-83919-275-3

Cover by Claire Wood

www.vulpine-press.com

Also in the *MidKnight Blue* series:

CHAPTER 1

Joe called Midnight right after he'd spoken to Donovan, and she was at the hospital at dawn the next morning. By the time she arrived Joe had been informed that Randy was improving after her brush with death. When Midnight walked into the room, Joe actually smiled at her. Midnight grinned and leaned against the wall in relief. She had been half afraid that Randy would die in the time it would take to get down to the hospital.

Joe told her what the doctors had said, and then asked if they could take a drive together. Midnight agreed happily, glad that he was finally ready to leave the confines of the room. She wasn't as happy a little while later. Joe was very quiet on the drive. He looked tired, sitting behind the wheel of his Porsche; they'd arranged for it to be driven to the hospital from the accident scene the same night as the crash.

As he headed almost automatically toward the beach, he played Def Leppard's *Slang*, a rather dark-toned album with a lot of references to death, anger, and hate. Midnight knew Joe didn't actually like the album, just as Rick didn't—it wasn't Def Leppard's usual upbeat, rock'n'roll style of music—but he was listening to it now, which meant that he wasn't feeling cheerful. Midnight wondered what was going on; she had a sixth sense when it came to her partner, and she knew he was gearing up to tell her something she probably wasn't going to like.

1

"So what's up, Sinclair?" she asked lightly, but she watched him worriedly.

Joe looked over at her, his light blue eyes devastated and blood-shot. He narrowed them for a moment, then turned away again. It was as if he were trying to gauge her, to see how she was going to handle what he wanted to tell her.

"Joe..." Midnight began, but stopped when he shook his head.

They reached the beach a few minutes later. He parked at the curb overlooking the ocean, and they stared out at the sea for a long while. At some unspoken cue, they both got out of the car. Joe waited for her to precede him down the long wooden stairway that led down to the rocks below, which stood like sentries over the pristine shore-line of La Jolla. Once seated, Joe looked at his partner of over thirteen years.

"Midnight," he began solemnly. "Last night was... the worst night of my life." He closed his eyes for a long moment, then pinned her with a look so pained it made her wince.

"I know, Joe. I'm sorry I wasn't there. It must have been..." She trailed off as she shook her head, unable to fathom it.

"I lost her, Night," Joe said, as if he needed to emphasize it. "She died—she was gone. I felt so sick I couldn't even think." His eyes said volumes about what he'd been through. Midnight knew it had been hard on him; she'd been devastated when he called her.

They were both silent for a long time. Joe was the one to break it. "Look, Midnight, I wanted to talk to you. To tell you..." He hesi-tated, drawing in a deep breath, looking pained. "I'm leaving," he said finally.

Midnight's mouth dropped open in shock, her cat-green eyes

shining in the morning sunlight. "What do you mean, leaving?" she asked calmly, even as her mind reeled at what she was sure he was saying.

"I mean, I'm quitting the force," Joe said softly, as if it would hurt her less that way.

Midnight stared at him for a full minute. All she could think was *No!* over and over again. Her mind was screaming at the thought of losing him. They hadn't actually been partners in years, but she still relied on him as her best friend and confidant. "Joe, wait…" she started to say, shaking her head. He was just being irrational—he'd been through a lot.

"No, Midnight, I can't wait," Joe said firmly. His eyes narrowed as he looked out over the water. "They tried to kill her, Midnight. They were gunning for *her*." He shook his head with certainty. "I can't let that happen. Me, okay, but not Randy. I can't take that chance anymore."

"Joe, we'll catch these guys! I have people on it round the clock—they won't get away with this." Midnight was fighting for her life now; she felt like someone had just hit her in the stomach with a sledgehammer.

Joe's face was calm, and his blue eyes were sad, but very sure. "Midnight," he said, so solemnly it made her catch her breath. "It was like my parents all over again. Someone I loved was dead because of me, because of what I do."

"This had nothing to do with you, Joe," Midnight said, almost desperately. "It was Donovan they were trying to hurt."

"Yeah, well they managed to catch me in the crossfire, didn't they?" Joe countered. "Midnight, you have to understand this. It's my

3

family we're talking about here, not my fellow officers. *My family—* do you understand?"

Midnight nodded, closing her eyes and swallowing convulsively against the huge knot in her throat, not sure what else to say.

"There's something else," Joe said then, looking pensive.

"What?" Midnight asked, almost afraid to know.

"I'm taking them back home." He said it so simply it took Midnight a moment to catch up, to actually repeat his word.

"Home?" she said, feeling stricken as she realized what he was saying.

"To England," Joe supplied, knowing she'd already surmised that by the look on her face. "Midnight, you and I both know quitting law enforcement is like trying to quit a gang. It's not that easy to just leave—the bad guys still remember your name, your face, who your wife is…"

Midnight nodded, turning away from him, trying to control the tears that flowed down her cheeks. Not only was she losing her partner, but she was indeed losing her friend too. She felt him move closer to her. She knew she needed to be strong in this, but at the moment she just couldn't muster the will to do that. As his arms wrapped around her, she lost her composure totally. She leaned back against him, refusing to let him see her crying this time. She'd cried in his arms so many times over the years, but now it felt so much like the last time ever. This was so different. He was leaving; he was going "home." Midnight had always considered his home to be San Diego; England was just a place he came from.

When she'd cried herself out, she rested against him, allowing the breeze to dry the tears on her cheeks. Her copper-blond hair blew

4

out over his shoulders, mingling with his dirty-blond hair in the breeze. It said a lot about their friendship.

Joe knew there was nothing he could say to her at that moment to make things any easier. He knew he'd just dealt her a severe blow, but also that he was right. He couldn't bear the thought of a member of his family being killed over something like his job. It was too much like his parents being murdered because of his gang affiliation. It brought too many things home that he'd managed to forget for a while. This time it was too close for comfort. He'd actually watched his wife die—that was much too close.

After a long time, Midnight moved out of his embrace and stood, still not facing him. Without a backward glance she moved to the steps and started up. Joe waited a few moments, then followed her. He knew his partner well; she was dealing with this her way, and right now that meant shutting down her emotions to get through it.

On the way back to the hospital, *Slang* was still playing in the car, and the song "Blood Runs Cold" came on. Midnight reached over and turned it up, listening to every word, sure that somehow the band had known about this moment in their lives and had written the song just for them.

Midnight knew what was happening; Joe was saving himself while he still could. He'd done enough to make up for what had happened to his parents, and it had almost cost him his wife. His halo of thorns was falling—he was giving it up. It was over.

Midnight was silent on the drive back. She wanted to hit something, she wanted to scream, she wanted to beg him not to go. She knew that wouldn't be fair to him. He'd done his duty; he'd been there for her so many times, taking her in, making her whole again.

He'd been her solid rock when Rick had strayed, he'd been her friend and even her lover. He'd been the lifeboat she'd clung to when one of her members had been viciously killed, when she'd thought she'd had all she could take. He'd been the one to talk her into handing her firearm over—he'd even gone so far as to tell her to shoot him as long as she didn't hurt herself. There'd been so many times, so many tears, but also so many laughs. Joe was her solid support no matter what happened. She always knew that if she needed him, he'd be there for her. He was her best friend, and even that title didn't seem to encompass all that he was to her. And now he was leaving...

At the hospital, she reached blindly for the door handle, getting out and walking away before he could even get out. He caught up to her at her car, his long stride easily bringing him right up behind her. Turning her around, he stared down at her, and Midnight felt her hands ball into fists around two handfuls of his jacket. Joe fully expected her to hit him; he was prepared for that, knew her emotions were in turmoil—he'd been able to sense it all the way back to the hospital. He knew Midnight well enough to know how she dealt with turmoil; she took it out aggressively on whatever was convenient at the time. The hammer of her gun as she emptied her high-capacity magazine into a target at the range, or life-threatening speeds as she pushed her Corvette's engine to its legendary capabilities, or by hitting whatever unlucky sod was caught standing too close to her at the time. He was sure it was about to be him.

She surprised him by letting go of his jacket and turning away from him again, and before he could stop her she was in her car and starting the engine with a roar. He knew he should stop her, but all he could do was jump out of the way as she threw the car into reverse and skidded out of the parking space.

He watched her tear out onto the street, hoping she'd slow down a little bit. Thinking he'd better warn someone, he went inside and called the office. He contacted dispatch and told them to put it out on the air that Chief Chevalier was to be watched and guided safely to the office or home, wherever she went. He was fairly sure she'd go to the office.

Rick got word of Midnight's breakneck speeds and Joe's request to all patrol units that they keep an eye out for her. He was waiting in her office when she got there. Rick stood as she entered and she walked straight into his arms. Using one arm to shove closed her door before moving to sit on the table, he gathered her close. He wasn't sure what was happening, but he knew it had to do with Joe.

The call they'd gotten from Joe late the night before had had her awake and on edge for the rest of the night. She'd left before dawn's early light to go see him. Rick knew she was worried about Joe. They'd talked about it a couple of days before. Midnight had told him that if Randy did die, she didn't know if they'd ever get Joe back. Rick agreed with her, knowing if he lost Midnight he would be a worthless heap for a long time.

After a long while, without releasing his hold on her, he asked softly, "So what is it, babe?"

Midnight was comforted by his tone, and more so by presence. Raising her head, she looked up at her husband. "He's leaving," she said quietly.

"What?" Rick said, shocked.

"He's leaving," Midnight repeated. "He's quitting the force and going back to England." Her voice broke on the last part.

Rick shook his head, as if trying to deny what she was telling him. "Night, he's just upset right now—he doesn't know what he's saying. What it'll mean."

"No," Midnight said dejectedly. "He knows what he's saying, Rick, and he's serious. I know him well enough to know that."

Rick was silent for a long time, not sure what else he could say. He just couldn't believe that Joe would give up his career and everything he'd done in America just to pick up and go back to England.

"What the hell's he gonna do in England?" he asked, more to himself than her.

Midnight shrugged. "Be the rich playboy his parents always wanted, I guess."

Rick didn't answer. He wanted to point out that Joe had never wanted that life, but there really was no point in it. Maybe he'd changed his mind.

"Perhaps when Randy gets better and things have a chance to calm down, he'll change his mind," he said hopefully.

"I don't think he's gonna wait long enough to change his mind," she replied, laying her head on his chest again.

Rick's jaw tightened as he clenched his teeth. Just when Midnight was getting back on track, Joe had to go and derail her again. He couldn't help but be mad.

Rick left her office a little while later, but made a point of checking on her indirectly through their mutual friends.

Spider and Dave Dibbins were the first to wander into her office an hour after Rick left. Spider settled his short, wiry frame into one of the chairs in front of her desk. He leaned his forearms on the desk, interlocking his fingers and gazing at her with a questioning, if casual look. Dave perched on the table just behind Spider, his sky blue eyes watching Midnight carefully.

Midnight looked up from the report she was writing, grinning in spite of her current mood. "What is it, boys?"

"We heard a rumor," Dave began.

"And we wanna hear it from you," Spider finished. Finishing each other's sentences was a habit the pair had fallen into years before when they were partners in FORS. They had long since moved over to narcotics. Spider had become a lieutenant, like Rick, and now ran the unit. Dave had stubbornly remained a sergeant, and dug his heels in every time Midnight even looked in his direction during promotion time. He had, in fact, become one of her most valued training sergeants for new narcotics officers, a far cry from the stoned leader of the Apostles he'd been when he'd come to FORS. They were both very dear friends as well. Midnight knew it was in that capacity that they had come now.

Midnight looked back at them for a long minute, then nodded. "The rumor you heard is true, if it's the one about Joe leaving." Her face was passive as she said it, but both men could see the pain in her eyes. They'd been through a lot with Midnight Chevalier—they knew her well.

"Damn…" Dave said, stunned.

"Shit…" Spider said at about the same time, in about the same tone.

Midnight leaned back in her chair, resting her elbow on the arm, her head on her fist, her index finger at her temple. "That's two more countries heard from."

9

"So you're actually letting him go?" Spider asked incredulously, sounding almost like a petulant child.

Midnight couldn't hold back the grin that came to her lips as she shook her head slightly. She and Joe had always laughed about how FORS' core members had always been like their children. And now "Daddy" was leaving.

With that thought in mind, Midnight said, "It's not like a divorce, Spider. I don't have a choice here."

"Yeah, but…" Dave started, also sounding brooding and anxious, "if you asked him to stay, he would."

"You know that, Midnight," Spider put in, nodding in agreement.

Midnight sat forward, looking at both men, her eyes indicating her appreciation for their efforts, but she shook her head all the same. "I can't do that, guys. He wants to go. He thinks he needs to. What can I say to him to make him stay, huh? 'Stay here even if your wife or kids' lives might be in danger'? 'Take your chances'?"

Both men looked uncomfortable for a moment, but then Spider narrowed his eyes at her. "You mean like the rest of us do every day?" he asked caustically. "Yeah, that's what I think you should say to him."

"Spider…" Midnight began. She wanted to defend Joe, but knew Spider was right too, in a way. "If you wanted to go, I wouldn't try to stop you."

"Midnight." Dave sat forward just a bit in an effort to convey his point. "I know I don't have a lot of room to talk here, 'cause I'm not married, nor do I have kids, but Joe knew the risks. They've never bothered him before."

"His wife never actually died in front of him before either," Midnight shot back. They were silent for a long time, then Midnight blew her breath out in a sigh. "Guys…" she said, allowing her voice to trail off as she shook her head.

"Yeah, yeah, we know, these things happen," Dave said, his tone telling her he knew what she was saying.

"We'll get over it," Spider put in, grinning.

"But will you?" Dave asked pointedly.

Midnight looked from Dave to Spider then back again. She knew this was the whole reason for their visit. She smiled wistfully, enjoying the protectiveness she heard and felt from the two men sitting across from her. It was comforting. "Eventually," she said simply.

"Well, if you need us, you know where we are," Spider said, his voice a mixture of tenderness and strength.

"Just yell," Dave added, his tone the same.

"We'll come runnin'," Spider finished, his face serious.

"I know you will," Midnight replied, her voice equally somber. "Thanks, guys."

The two men stood and left. Midnight stared after them for a long time. She was thinking about all the years she'd been there. All the times she'd shared with those two men, as well as her other dear friends. She'd been with the police department for twenty years. Many of those years had been spent with Joe, Spider, Dave, Tiny, Kana, and Rick. They were her extended family. They were always there when she needed them. But Joe had been the one she'd turned to for so long. Sometimes she even turned to him instead of Rick, which, to Rick's credit, never caused too much of problem nowadays. But now… Midnight realized there was a lot of stuff that was going to fall on Rick's shoulders. She'd always used Joe as her place to vent, but now Rick would probably end up hearing the brunt of her troubles, something he'd gotten out of before. She didn't know whether he'd be too thrilled with this new side of their relationship.

The day continued, and Midnight received a visit from Tiny, accompanied by his wife, Jessica. Jessica looked on Midnight and Joe as her dearest friends too, since meeting Joe in Sacramento and subsequently Midnight when Joe had needed her. Tiny was his usual quiet self; his presence was enough to let Midnight know he was worried about her too. Jessica asked why Joe was leaving and nodded understandingly when Midnight explained. It was refreshing to have one person understand why she couldn't guilt Joe into staying. Tiny had been just as petulant as the other two men, but was quelled by his wife's obvious understanding of Midnight reasons.

Kana had been the next to visit, wandering in and sitting down in the chair Spider and subsequently Jessica had occupied.

Midnight had turned to her, grinning. "Yes?" she'd asked, already feeling the humor of the situation. It reminded her of a time years before when she'd been welcomed back to the office after an extended absence with what she'd coined a "twenty-one-page salute." It had been quite funny then, the procession of "visits" from her core members.

"Joe's not really leavin', is he?" Kana asked, always one to get straight to the point. Her intimidating size was a testament to her way of interacting with people. She did, however, have a very deep respect for the petite blonde Chief of Police.

"Yes, he really is."

"Goin' back to England?"

"Yep," Midnight replied, the idea of it getting a little easier to handle.

"And you're not stoppin' him," Kana said, this time not making it a question.

"Nope."

Kana raised an eyebrow. "You pissed at him?"

Midnight grinned. Her friends definitely covered all the bases. "No, I'm not pissed at him."

"It's because of Randy, huh?"

"Yes, because she almost died last night—did, actually, for a full minute."

Kana nodded, then gave Midnight a sly look. "And you don't want to guilt him into stayin' 'cause all this ain't over yet, right?"

"Right," Midnight said, marveling at the almost telepathic way her people communicated with each other. Unless they'd had a mass meeting somewhere that she didn't know about—they were from different units on different floors—though of course there was the telephone…

Kana looked satisfied with Midnight's answers. Then she gave her a narrowed look, as if searching for something on Midnight's face.

"So you're okay with this?" she asked skeptically.

Midnight hesitated a minute before answering, pursing her lips as she gave Kana a sidelong glance. "I wouldn't say I'm okay with it—

I'm mad as hell that it's happening. But I know that he has to do what he feels is right, right now, and I don't have a right to stop him."

Kana snorted, shaking her head. "You're too damned fair, if you ask me."

"I'm not asking you," Midnight said mildly, a grin playing at her lips.

"Yeah, yeah, I know," Kana said, grinning too. "But you're okay, right?"

"Right," Midnight replied, knowing that was what Kana wanted—needed—to hear.

Rick showed up at her office two hours later. "You interested in lunch?" he asked, his deep blue eyes assessing her mood.

Midnight looked up at him, her smile warm as she nodded. He walked her to his car, his hand at the small of her back. He felt the hard frame of her gun, set there in a holster. In a way it was a comfort. Midnight could take care of herself, and Rick realized that it relieved him to know that, since Joe was basically his backup where Midnight's safety was concerned. Joe leaving was affecting Rick more than by just making him need to comfort Midnight.

Rick looked over at her as he started the car. "You look better now," he observed mildly.

Midnight grinned, nodding and pinning him with a look. "I think I have you to thank for that."

Rick shrugged. "I thought you could use a little member roll call today."

"Yeah," Midnight said, then looked thoughtful. "Guess I have a lot of people I can count on, huh?"

"Yes, you do," Rick said, giving her a long look when they stopped at a red light. "You'll always have me, you know."

"I know."

"What?" Rick asked, sensing that she meant more than the simple answer.

Midnight gave him a measured look. "I was thinking about it today. You know, his leaving is gonna bring a lot more bullshit your way…"

"How's that?" he asked, with no anger or jealousy in his voice.

"Well, I've always used Joe as my sounding board. He's listened to a lot of crap that I need to vent, but which can't be solved." She grinned sardonically. "It's kinda gotten you off the hook, trivial garbage-wise, that is."

Rick laughed, shaking his head. "Yeah, Joe has dealt with a lot of crap, but maybe that's the problem."

"What do you mean?" she asked, realizing he'd been thinking about this stuff too.

"I mean," he began earnestly, "that I've let Joe stand in for me on a lot, and maybe I shouldn't have. Maybe if you didn't depend on him so much, you wouldn't be so destroyed by his leaving." Midnight couldn't detect any anger in his voice, and thinking about what he'd said, she knew he was right.

She nodded. "Yeah, I guess you're right. I mean, I don't think it's your fault—I've always just looked on Joe as my second, and because of that I hang a lot of my worries on him. Maybe I'm not being fair to any of us."

"Night." Rick glanced at her worriedly; he hadn't meant to cause

15

her more grief. "Joe's taken it on, just like you have. I think he likes you relying on him as much as you are used to doing it. I've certainly never heard him complain. But the thing is, it's my job, my responsibility, to listen to your problems and woes." He looked chagrined. "And I've been shirking my responsibilities. I've been there to celebrate your triumphs, but I haven't had to deal with as many of the setbacks or failures. Joe's dealt with those, and *I've let him*." He blew his breath out. "And now, I guess I'm tellin' you that I want you to lean on me more, for everything."

Midnight looked at him for a long moment, understanding what he was saying and relieved that he was willing to take on Joe's role in her life too. "I don't really have a choice, ya know," she said, grinning. "You're the only other person I'd trust with all my woes."

"Good," Rick replied, grinning too. "Then I guess that's settled—I'll start doing my job as your husband from now on. It's a hell of a lot more important than my other job."

"Yes?" she said, her eyes suddenly glittering with tears.

"Oh yes," he said as he stopped the car in front of the restaurant and turned to face her. He touched her face gently, then placed his finger under her chin and guided her lips up to his.

When their lips parted Midnight looked up at him. "You'll never know how much I love you," she said softly.

Rick looked back into her eyes, then canted his head to the side. "Oh, I think I have an idea." It was obvious he meant that it could only be equaled by his feelings for her.

They went and had lunch, talking about other things, even discussing what Midnight thought she might do in terms of finding a new captain for the vice unit. On the drive back to the office, Midnight realized that suddenly it didn't hurt as much that Joe was going. It hurt, certainly; her heart ached at the thought that he wouldn't be just down the hall anymore, or up the street. But it didn't have that ferocious shattering effect it had originally had. She knew too that Rick was responsible for that transition, and she loved him all the more for it.

This new thinking made it a lot easier for her when she went to see Joe at the hospital that afternoon. She was told by the nurse that Randy was actually doing better after her brush with death. The antibiotics they'd been treating her with was actually working. Her prognosis was good; Joe was very relieved. However, when Midnight walked into the room, his face clouded over with worry again. He stood up, looking at her with a guarded expression. Without saying a word, Midnight walked over to him, reached up, and pulled him into an embrace.

"I'm not gonna say I'm happy that you're going," she whispered, "but I understand, and I'll miss the hell out of you."

She immediately heard him expel his pent-up breath and relax in her embrace. She knew he'd probably been worried about her all day.

"You look like hell," she said, stepping back and grinning. "You need about a week's worth of sleep."

"I'll catch up eventually," he said, a slight grin playing at his lips.

They were quiet for a while, each of them lost in their own thoughts.

"Could I interest you in some coffee in the hospital cafeteria?" Midnight asked after a long while.

Joe glanced over at Randy's still form, then nodded. After her crisis the night before, the doctors had thoroughly sedated her. It was their belief that her anxiety over her inability to breathe properly had been partially to blame for her cardiac arrest. They had told Joe that if her progress continued, they would stop administering the sedative that afternoon and go from there.

They walked down to the cafeteria, oblivious to the looks they received from many people on the way. There was something about the pair that frequently caused a stir among "outsiders." Midnight's petite appearance combined with the strength that seemed to emanate from her was a powerful attraction alone. But add to that Joseph Sinclair, six foot two inches of powerfully built, dirty-blond-haired, light-blue-eyed Englishman with a fairly formidable presence of his own… As always, he walked two steps behind and to Midnight's left, his eyes ever watchful even in a fairly safe environment like the hospital. They made an engaging pair, and everyone they passed noticed them.

Once seated in the cafeteria, Joe looked over at his long-time partner. "So give it to me straight. How are you, really?"

Midnight looked contemplative for a moment, then nodded. "I'm okay—really. Rick has been his usual incredibly supportive self, and it's helping me adjust."

Joe nodded, knowing she was downplaying her real feelings but also sure she wouldn't lie outright.

"So how's the case going?" he asked, realizing he had no real idea what had been happening since Randy's accident almost a week before.

"It's going okay. We've got some good leads. Donovan's running down everything he gets his hands on, like a bloodhound. These guys sure underestimated our family," she said, shaking her head ruefully.

Joe nodded. "They were probably sure that would put Donovan off the case for at least a while."

Midnight wanted to point out that they'd partially succeeded, since they'd managed to run Joe off, but she knew it wouldn't be fair. Joe had his reasons for leaving and she had to respect that, even if she hated the thought. Instead she said, "Betcha they didn't count on Blue either."

"Christian? What's he doin' on this?" Joe asked, worried about a non-peace officer, especially a member of his family, getting involved in such a dangerous case.

"Don't worry." Midnight knew exactly what Joe was thinking. "I'm being very careful to keep his involvement and assistance tightly under wraps. No one knows about it but me, Jeanie, and Donovan. And they fully understand what we're up against here."

Joe nodded, satisfied with her answer. He knew her well enough to know she was extremely competent when it came to safety issues. He had another thought then. "Donovan and Jeanie really back together?"

Midnight nodded, grinning. "Yeah, looks like it. She showed up at his place the night of Randy's accident. They've been together ever since."

"Good," he said, sighing. "He and Darrell aren't gonna be real happy with me taking Randy away…"

"Probably not," Midnight agreed. She gave him a quizzical look.

19

"You haven't told them yet, huh?"

Joe looked a little guilty. "No—I was waiting to talk to Randy first."

"You told me," Midnight pointed out.

"Yeah, well, I knew it would take you a lot longer to adjust."

"Gee, thanks."

"Anytime," Joe said, his grin lopsided. "Hell, you didn't take as long as I thought—I must be losing my appeal."

"Cute," Midnight replied drily.

Later, Midnight walked him back to the room and hugged him again. Joe held her for an extra moment, giving her an extra squeeze, which told her he was grateful for her acceptance of his decision. When they parted, Midnight ducked her head to hide the tears that sprang to her eyes. She left a few minutes later, heading back to the office.

Joe walked back into the hospital room feeling better. He knew it was right for them at that point especially. They still hadn't figured out who was dirty at the department, and the thought of his family in danger made him worry all the more. Joe Sinclair had long since accepted the dangers to himself in the career he'd chosen, but when the danger involved the woman he loved, it was too much. He knew he was reacting to actually seeing her die, but it had brought back too many fears and heartaches to continue tempting fate. He knew deep down that he was running away, that the bad guys had won this round. But he wasn't willing to risk the lives of his family to win this time—the price was just too high.

Taking up his place in the chair next to the bed, Joe leaned back, stretching his legs out in front of him.

It was twilight when Randy began to stir. Sitting forward, Joe took her hand in his. "Randy?" he said softly next to her ear. She stirred more at the sound of his voice and the feeling of his hand holding hers. After a long few minutes her eyes fluttered open and focused on his face.

"Hello there," he said, his smile warm, his eyes shining.

Randy's lips tugged in a faint smile, but it was obvious she was still not fully awake. Joe just held her hand, stroking her skin. It was apparent to Randy that he'd been vigilant during her recovery. His face was gaunt, his light blue eyes bloodshot and weary. He'd shaved, but only that day, when he'd felt comfortable enough to leave the room long enough to do so. His clothes were clean, but rumpled from sitting and sleeping in the chair he was in now. To Randy, he was still the most handsome sight she'd ever seen.

"How... long?" she asked, her voice halting.

"You've been here about a week," Joe said, wondering if she even remembered the night before.

"So have you," she said; it was a statement, not a question.

"Where was I supposed to go?" Joe asked softly, watching her eyes. "You're home to me."

Randy blinked, then closed her eyes and drew a deep breath. When she opened her eyes, she looked at him with worry.

"Last night? Was it last night?" she asked, and Joe knew she remembered.

"Yes, love."

Randy nodded, narrowing her eyes in thought. "I remember not

21

being able to breathe, and you touching my cheek," she said, still try-ing to put the pieces together. "You were crying… you were yell-ing…" She trailed off as his face grew grim, and he nodded. "What happened?" she whispered.

Joe looked pained. He reached out, touching her cheek tenderly as he looked into her eyes. "I lost you, babe." His voice held so much anguish that Randy felt tears sting her eyes immediately.

"Joe," she said, her voice reflecting his pain. "I'm sorry."

Joe raised an eyebrow at her. "What are you sorry for?"

"Just that you had to go through that," Randy said softly.

"You came back to me, that's all that matters," he said, his voice deep with sincerity.

Randy remembered his words then—*Don't leave me*. It made her cry to think how horrible it must have been for him.

"Hey!" Joe said, leaning down to press his lips against her tem-ple. "Don't cry, everything's okay now. You're alive, and that's what matters to me."

Randy was quiet for a long while, and Joe just stayed with her, keeping his face close to hers, smoothing her hair back from her face with his hands. The nurse coming in to check on her broke their rev-erie. She was pleased to see that Randy was awake. "After I check you out, I'll get the doctor," she said.

Joe sat back while the nurse did a routine check of Randy's vital signs. When she left, he leaned back down, kissing Randy on the cheek and gently brushing away the remaining tears. "I love you," he said, his voice soft next to her ear. "So much."

"Love *you*," Randy said, turning her head to brush her lips against his cheek. She lay quietly after that, closing her eyes. Joe sat back, still holding her hand. He closed his eyes too, blowing his breath out slowly, the pressure of the last many days beginning to chip away at his strength.

"Joe," Randy said, bringing him back. He opened his eyes, noting the concern on her face.

"What, love?" he asked, smiling tiredly at her.

"You need to go home and get some rest. You look so tired."

"I'm not leavin' here till you do," he said seriously.

Randy knew it was pointless to argue with him. "Okay, how about you go find a comfortable couch somewhere in this hospital and sleep on that."

Joe grinned at her. "How about you lie there and get better, and I look after myself."

"You don't look like you've been doing a very good job of that," she said, raising an eyebrow.

"What? Taking care of myself?" Joe grinned at her returning spirit. "Do I look that bad?" he asked, giving her a questioning look, his grin still in place.

Randy thought about it for a moment, then shook her head. "You look as gorgeous as ever, actually."

"Alright then," Joe said mockingly, his eyes glittering with humor.

Later that evening the doctor came in. He told them the infection was indeed receding and that if Randy's progress continued she'd be out of the hospital by the end of the week. Joe was ecstatic; he called Midnight, Donovan, and Christian to report the news.

When he came back to the room he sat down in his chair, looking serious.

"What's the matter?" Randy asked.

"I need to talk to you about something," he said, sounding chagrined.

"You fell in love with someone else while I was unconscious?" Randy asked, trying to lighten things up a little, still happy with what the doctor had said.

"No…"

"What is it?" Randy asked, worried suddenly; he looked far too serious.

Joe hesitated for a long moment, then took a deep breath. "I'm quitting the department."

He said it so quickly that Randy had to think about it for a moment before she realized what he had said.

"You're what?" she asked, her expression indicating that she was sure she had heard him wrong.

"Quitting the department," Joe repeated, more confidently this time. "*And* I want to move back to England."

"England?" Randy repeated, as if she'd never heard the word before, her brow furrowing in confusion. "Why?"

"Why?" Joe said incredulously. "Randy, whaddya mean, why?" His voice was sharp, but then he closed his eyes, forcing his anger away. When he opened them again he saw her watching him apprehensively. "Randy, that was no accident you had," he said quietly.

"They were trying to kill you, and they almost did." He shook his head. "I can't give them another chance."

Randy was silent for a long time, her mind whirling. She didn't remember much about the accident, just that a white van had cut her off—after that there was nothing. She knew who "they" were—the same people that had shot Donovan. It had been her that had asked Joe what he'd do if they tried to kill one of the kids. That thought amplified in her head suddenly.

"Where are the children?" she asked, alarmed.

"They're fine, Randy. They're safe," Joe assured her. "But I just feel like we're tempting fate if we stay... you know?"

Randy looked back at him for a long minute. She wasn't sure how to feel about what he was saying. She knew that her "death" had been very hard on him and that it probably made on him want to lock them all up so they'd be safe. Then another thought occurred to her. "You're thinking about your parents too, aren't you?" she asked, knowing she was right.

Joe nodded. "I had no control then. I feel like I have none now, and it scares the hell out of me." His eyes searched hers, begging her to understand. She did.

After a long pause, she nodded slowly. "We'll do whatever you think is right," she said finally. It was the least she could do to offset his memory of his parents and now his worry over her and their children.

Joe released his breath in a relieved sigh. He'd been worried about her fighting him on this decision. After all, she'd be leaving behind the only real family she had, in Donovan and Darrell. He wasn't sure she'd thought that far until she asked if he'd told them.

Joe shook his head.

"I wanted to know where you'd stand first," he said, trailing off as he winced just slightly, thinking about the fact that he'd told Midnight. Randy realized it immediately.

"You already told Midnight, didn't you?" she asked.

Joe nodded. "I needed to get her reaction…" he said, trailing off again as he realized how that sounded. "I mean, I didn't know if I was just overreacting or—" he began to explain, but her hand on his stopped him.

"Joe, you don't have to explain," she said, looking at him tenderly. "I know you were probably worried about how she'd take it, right?" Joe nodded, contrite. "How *did* she take it?" Randy asked, knowing how important that would be to him.

Joe shrugged. "She was pissed at first, but she came to see me earlier this afternoon and we talked, and she's okay with it now. Not happy, but okay."

"And you're okay with leaving the department?"

Joe shrugged again, pinning her with a look. "You're more important to me than the department, Randy."

Randy nodded. She knew it wasn't really that simple, but that pointing that out would only make things harder for him.

Donovan was asleep when Joe called with the good news about Randy. Jeanie was sitting in his living room, studying for her tests the following day. Walking into his bedroom, phone in hand, she studied him. She couldn't believe how good-looking she found him again. It was like she'd never been with him before. Since they'd been back "together" they'd done no more than kiss, and that had been the night before they'd heard about Randy's near death. She wasn't sure when or if things would progress any further. In truth, she wasn't sure what Donovan was feeling or thinking. But looking at him lying on his stomach, his strong arms curled around the pillows under his head, his sandy-brown hair still slightly damp from his shower earlier that evening… His back was made up of sinewy muscles that flexed as he stirred at the sound of her voice saying his name softly.

She held the phone out to him as he turned over and sat up. "It's Joe."

Donovan nodded, taking the phone and running an unconscious hand through his hair as he tried to wake up. He moved to sit with his back against his headboard, watching Jeanie as she sat down on the bed next to him. He noted the worried look in her eyes. Joe had sounded cheerful to Jeanie when she'd answered the phone, so she wasn't worried about Randy's health. What she was worried about was that Randy was getting better, and while that was good for the family, it could signal the end of her time with Donovan. She didn't know if he'd still need her when Randy was better.

He nodded, breaking into a wide smile that took her breath away. "That's great, man," he said, his eyes trailing over and looking into hers. "Great. Well, tell her I'll be down to see her tomorrow. And kiss her for me."

His voice was so full of joy that Jeanie felt tears sting the back of her eyelids. A moment later he hung up, breathing a huge sigh of relief. "Joe says that Randy's out of the woods. If she keeps it up, she'll be out of the hospital by the end of the week."

"That's great, Donovan. I'm glad," she said, but her eyes told a different story. Donovan could see sadness and he wondered at it.

He narrowed his eyes contemplatively at her. "We need to talk, don't we?"

Jeanie looked surprised for a moment, then nodded, blowing out her breath. "I need to know where we stand, Donovan, because I just don't know right now."

It was Donovan's turn to nod. He knew what she meant; they'd quietly and carefully sidestepped any real discussion about their relationship.

"Okay," he said, settling himself more comfortably against the headboard. "Why'd you break it off originally?"

Jeanie looked back at him for a few seconds, surprised again by his directness, but she knew it was what they needed to be at that point.

"I was scared, Donovan, plain and simple."

"Of what?"

"Of how serious things were getting with us." She shrugged and looked away from him. "I guess I wasn't expecting things to get so serious so fast, and I didn't really understand it."

Donovan nodded, as if accepting what she was saying. "And now?"

"Now," she said, looking at him critically, "now I know what I was giving up when I gave you up. I see that things with you were special and that not everyone can make me feel the way you do…" She trailed off, looking chagrined. "Donovan, I never meant for you to hear about Blue or Perkins. I wasn't trying to hurt you… I was just—"

"Testing the water," Donovan put in, his look wry.

"I guess," Jeanie said, rolling her eyes. "But no one had ever gotten so close to me so fast, like you did, and I guess I wondered if it had to do with, you know…"

"Sex," Donovan said simply, and Jeanie couldn't hold back the grin that spread across her face. He sounded so businesslike.

"Will you stop that," she said, still grinning.

"Just trying to help," he replied, smiling too.

"I'm just fine, thanks." Jeanie poked him in the ribs, making him laugh. Then she grew serious again. "So what about you?"

"What about me?" Donovan asked, raising an eyebrow.

"I mean Serena, brat," she said, giving him a narrowed look.

"I know," he replied with a straight face, then grinned again, shaking his head. "She seemed like a logical rebound, and I guess she was for a while."

"But?" Jeanie put in, hearing the unspoken word in his tone.

"But," he said, looking at her pointedly, "she wasn't you. She didn't understand or even like my work. She didn't know about the case I'm working on, and I couldn't really explain even if she'd been interested, which she wasn't."

Jeanie nodded, knowing what he meant. Donovan moved his hand to her waist, looking into her eyes. She caught her breath as his hand slid up her side, then up to touch her face. "So what happens now?" he asked, his voice almost a caress.

"Now, I don't want to lose you again," she said, staring back into his eyes.

"You didn't lose me the first time, Jay," he said, his voice softly chiding. "You let me go."

"Then I won't let you go again." She moved a few inches closer to him, reaching out to touch his chest.

"Then don't," Donovan said simply as he drew her to him.

She had time to shake her head in answer before his lips claimed hers; after that she couldn't think straight. There was the feeling of his hands sliding up her back to pull her ever closer, the jolt of excitement as his lips left hers and traveled down her throat, making her gasp. In turn she slid her hands up his chest, allowing her nails to graze his skin, eliciting a shudder and a low moan. His response spurred Jeanie to reached down and unbutton her shirt. Donovan bent his head to kiss the exposed skin as he gently removed the garment and laid it aside.

Before long his hands and lips had her at a feverish pitch. Her upper body was pressed flush against his, the closeness of their skin causing even more heat between them. After what seemed like forever, Jeanie couldn't wait anymore. Rising up on her knees, she slid off her light cotton pants, gasping again as he grasped her hips, his lips traveling sensuously over her belly. He was taking his time, and Jeanie knew he was getting back a little of his own. At that point she didn't care—she wanted him, and she wasn't waiting any more.

Donovan drew in a sharp breath as she moved to straddle his body, literally sliding down over him. The contact and intense heat and pressure that followed were almost painful in the pleasure they gave. Donovan held her steady for a full minute, grasping her waist as he fought to bring his body back under control. Jeanie grinned slyly as she sensed his struggle.

"Hate when that happens," she said softly, leaning close to his ear.

"Brat," he muttered, even as he grinned.

Jeanie laughed as he narrowed his eyes at her. She leaned down and kissed him, making him forget feeling perturbed. After a long moment they were moving together. They took their time, reveling in being so close and trying to elicit more from each other.

After their passion was spent, Jeanie relaxed against him, resting her head on his chest. Donovan still leaned against the headboard, half sitting up. He stroked her hair and back.

"I feel like I'm back where I belong," she said wistfully.

"That's because you are," Donovan replied, his voice still showing the effects of their lovemaking.

Jeanie nodded. Then she lifted her head to look at him. "You're better than I remembered."

"That's because you finally have some basis for comparison," he replied, grinning. Jeanie laughed lightly, noting the self-satisfied look in his eyes. He knew she was saying he was the better of the three, and he was acknowledging that in his usual non-egomaniacal way. Yet another difference between Donovan Curtis and most other men.

CHAPTER 2

Rhiannon O'Neil-Templeton appeared at the chief's office on time for her appointment. Her deep mahogany hair was swept up and held off her face with a black clip. Her black silk suit was impeccable, even if she did feel uncomfortable in it. The rich emerald green velvet camisole she wore under her jacket was the exact shade of her eyes. She was a striking woman, and at five foot nine inches, she was a little taller than average, but not obviously so.

Midnight stood as Rhiannon was escorted into the office. She extended her hand to the younger woman, noting the look of caution and residual sadness in her eyes.

"Sergeant Templeton, it's nice to see you again. I understand you have some interesting information for me."

"Yes, ma'am," Rhiannon replied, her eyes cast nervously downward.

"Two members of my team will be joining us in just a few minutes," Midnight said, gesturing to the small conference table. "Have a seat, and please call me Midnight. 'Ma'am' makes me sound too old."

Rhiannon nodded, smiling at the face Midnight made. She looked around her as she sat. Midnight's office was a bit more sophisticated than the one she'd had when she'd run FORS and vice. Even she herself realized her position as chief warranted some modicum of decorum. The walls were a soft pearlized blue. All of her furniture—the desk, conference table, credenza, and bookcase—were antique mahogany, and all gifts from Rick for her promotion. The soft leather of her chair, as well as the chairs at the table and small couch, was a deeper shade of blue. On the walls were the more important plaques from her sixteen years with the department, and on her desk was her favorite die-cast model of a classic Corvette that matched the one she drove. Her bookcase was lined with law books and leatherbound penal and vehicle codes, as well as binders of all departmental manuals and other law-enforcement-related periodicals.

It was an impressive office and it reflected perfectly the woman who occupied it. After a long look around, Rhiannon turned back to Midnight and noted that the chief was watching her. "You have a beautiful office," Rhiannon said, thinking immediately that she sounded like a suck-up; that's what her younger sister, Stevie, would have called her.

Midnight raised an eyebrow at her, as if thinking the same thing, then waved away the compliment with the comment "Furniture."

Midnight sat down across from Rhiannon, her face serious, her eyes watching the younger woman. "How are you?" she asked, sounding so concerned that Rhiannon felt a lump in her throat. She shrugged, not trusting her voice to speak; it was still too hard.

"Jason was a good cop," Midnight continued, searching Rhiannon's eyes. "It was a big loss for the department when he died. But I know it was devastating for you. You're still overwhelmed, aren't you?"

The question was simple enough, but the fact that Midnight Chevalier—Chief Chevalier—was able to look at her and see that made Rhiannon realize just how far she was from recovering.

Rhiannon had lost her husband, Jason Templeton, in a high-speed pursuit accident almost two years before. She'd been injured in the same accident; they were partners in the narcotics unit. Jason had been her one true love from the day she'd been assigned to him when she joined patrol. They were married eight months after they met, and they'd been together for seven of those months. They were married for almost ten years before he was killed. Rhiannon had worked in an administrative job since then. She retained her peace officer status, but had no desire to return to the street. Stevie, her younger sister, currently a patrol officer with the department, thought she was nuts. Of course, that was because Stevie wanted into the narcotics unit so bad she could taste it.

Midnight Chevalier-Debenshire had been the chief for three months when the tragedy happened. She'd been one of the first people on the scene. Rhiannon remembered hearing Midnight telling the officer there that these were "her people" and that if he didn't want to be driving a desk for a long time he'd better let her through to them. It had been Midnight that made sure the accident scene was properly recorded and that the investigators working it got everything right.

In the end it was proven that Jason Templeton had no fault in the incident. It was further determined that not only he had died in the line of duty, but a hero as well. The accident had occurred when, while chasing a suspect, he swerved to avoid a child running out into the street. His car clipped the bumper of the vehicle they were pursuing, causing both to skid. Jason controlled his slide as well as possible, but the car ended up on its roof against a building. Both Jason and Rhiannon were trapped inside. They said Jason died on impact.

All Rhiannon knew was that he was gone and there was a hole where her heart had been. Almost two years later she still thought of him daily. She'd moved in with her mother after the accident, but that had been too difficult. Six months later she moved in with Stevie. It didn't seem to make any difference anymore.

Now, staring back at Midnight, Rhiannon knew the chief was sympathetic to her pain. After all, Midnight had sustained losses in her life too. Her husband worked closely with her at the department and everyone knew about their legendary love affair. Midnight knew what *devastated* meant.

"I'm still working at getting back on track," Rhiannon said finally. She knew she didn't have to lie to Midnight and say that she was "fine." She wasn't fine; she knew that.

Midnight nodded. "If you need anything, if I can help at all, please tell me," she said, and Rhiannon could tell by the sincerity in her voice that Midnight very much meant it.

"Got any powers of resurrection or reincarnation?" Rhiannon asked lightly, a shadow of her old humor surfacing.

"I'll check on that and get back to you," Midnight replied, grinning.

There was a light knock on the door, and Midnight called for the person to come in. Donovan walked into the room, followed closely by Jeanie. Midnight saw the glow on both of their faces immediately, and she knew they were well and truly back together now.

"Hi, guys," she said, smiling lopsidedly at the two, her eyes sparkling with a knowing look.

Jeanie looked a little abashed, while Donovan just grinned openly, happy to have his girlfriend back.

"Donovan, do you know Rhiannon Templeton?" Midnight asked. The accident had occurred before his time at narcotics.

"No, I don't." He walked over and extended his hand to Rhiannon, his teal eyes warm, his smile subdued. "I've heard of your work, and now I hear your investigative skills may help us out," he said as he shook hands with her, a great deal of respect in his voice. He didn't mention Jason, although he knew all about it—everyone did. It wasn't his place to bring it up. He suspected correctly that Midnight and she had been discussing it before he and Jeanie had come in; there was no point in causing more hurt now.

Rhiannon nodded, appreciating his acknowledgment of her past work without linking it to a statement about Jason. She sensed easily that Donovan was that kind of man. She knew he was Randy Curtis-Sinclair's brother, and she'd heard about his skills as a narcotics officer.

"I've heard some good things about you as well," Rhiannon said warmly. Donovan modestly nodded his thanks.

"And this," Midnight said, gesturing to Jeanie, "is Jeanie Franco. She's in the academy right now, but she's also working with us on this case."

Rhiannon nodded as she shook hands with Jeanie. "Didn't you work for Joe Sinclair before?" she asked. She knew about a lot of things; she was observant like that.

Jeanie nodded. "Yes, for about a year and a half." She didn't know who Rhiannon was, but she seemed nice enough.

"Let's get started, okay?" Midnight said. A few minutes later they were seated and Rhiannon told them about her discovery.

She'd been working on some backlogged invoices from vendors

and had been keeping a list of equipment that had no departmental decals on them; she thought it would be a problem to inventory items without them. When she'd gone further into the invoices, she found vehicle purchases that listed no inventory decal numbers either. Trying to verify that the vehicles really did have ID numbers through Sergeant Devereaux had been a dead end, since he was on a two-week vacation, so she'd gone looking in the logs at the warehouse referencing the purchase order numbers on the invoices.

"That's when things got suspicious," Rhiannon said, noting Donovan's eyes shining with subdued excitement; the same expression was reflected in Midnight's and Jeanie's eyes. "We don't have those vehicles, at least not anymore." She shrugged. "And as near as I can tell, we don't have the guns or computers I've listed either."

She handed her list over to Midnight and sat back. Midnight scanned it, narrowing her eyes at the total amount of "missing" property. It was dangerously close to the $3.5 million deficit the discrepancies in Devereaux's reports reflected, all totaled. She handed Donovan the list and saw him track down to the bottom as well.

"Son of a bitch…" he breathed, glancing back over to Midnight. Devereaux was definitely involved. He had control of equipment invoices, property logs, and tagging the property.

Donovan gave the list to Jeanie as Midnight shrugged. "He probably didn't expect those invoices to be caught up for years," he said. "By then he could 'lose' them after they'd been paid."

Rhiannon knew she'd found something important. She didn't know just how important it was, but she could see that Midnight was extremely pleased.

"Rhiannon, thanks for the good work on this," Midnight said, then gave her a sidelong glance. "Ever think about working in property?"

Rhiannon pursed her lips, aware it was an oblique way of telling her a little about what was going on without saying too much. She shook her head. "No, but I do seem to be between assignments at the moment."

"Oh, I think something might be opening up soon… I'll let you know." Midnight's grin was wry; Donovan tried valiantly to hide his, as did Jeanie.

Rhiannon stood, nodding. She knew not to ask any direct questions. She did have a definite sense that someone's head was about to roll. In a way she was glad she could help Midnight out in this case.

After Rhiannon left, Donovan looked at Midnight; it was easy to see the fire banked in the teal depths of his eyes. Frank Devereaux had been involved in Randy's near death as well as Donovan's own almost fatal shooting, and Donovan wanted to get his hands on him in the worst way.

Midnight nodded. "I know what's going through your head right now, Donovan, but try to pull back a little." Her voice was soothing, but she could see Donovan's rancor rising all the same. Jeanie reached over and put her hand on his arm. Donovan looked across at her. There was a long, tense moment; Midnight heard Donovan blow his breath out, and then he turned back to her, nodding.

"Okay, so what are we gonna do?"

"Remember that technique you learned in narc school? It's called *surveillance*…" Midnight trailed off and Donovan started to grin.

"Yes, Chief, I do remember something about that."

"Good," Midnight said, grinning. "'Cause we're gonna surveil Mr. Devereaux and see if he'll lead us to his friends."

"And if he doesn't?"

"I'll nail his ass to the wall anyway," Midnight said, her voice deceptively mild even as her gold-green eyes blazed and her mind turned over all possibilities. "Who's he been hanging around with lately?"

"All the usual suspects," Donovan said, narrowing his eyes as he thought about it.

"Anybody connected?"

"Don't think so, but we can run it down," he said, nodding to Jeanie.

Midnight nodded. "Any new leads on Randy's accident?"

"I'm still waiting on a couple of eyewitness accounts, but Blue's program is making it easier to run down plates."

"What're we down to?" Midnight asked.

Donovan looked at Jeanie. "At last check," Jeanie said, "we are at about ninety-eight possibles, but we still want to cross-check some names with CLETS."

"I want to get started on this surveillance," Midnight said. "I may pull in a few of my guys for that. We gotta be careful—I don't want to scare him off. I want him and all his friends."

Donovan and Jeanie nodded as they stood up. "Let me know what shift you want me to take on surveillance," Donovan said.

Midnight glanced at Jeanie. "Want some training time for that?" she asked. "I could credit it as some extra ride-along time."

Jeanie looked surprised, but nodded anyway, glancing at Donovan.

Midnight gave them a pointed look, then grinned. "I'm glad you two got it figured out," she said. Her tone was businesslike, but her expression told them she meant it.

"Us too," Donovan replied, smiling.

He and Jeanie left then, and Midnight called Rick. He picked up on the third ring, sounding distracted. "Debenshire."

"Lieutenant," Midnight said authoritatively.

"Yes?" She could hear the smile in his voice.

"I need you," she said, her voice soft and low.

"I'll be right there," he replied just as softly, even though he had three former gang members standing in his office at that moment. He hung up the phone, standing as he did. "Gotta go," he said, looking smug. "Boss *needs* me." Then he was out the door and headed toward the elevators, leaving the two older members to explain to the third about "the LT and the chief."

Rick was in her office three minutes later. He kicked the door closed with a booted foot. "Sorry I'm late, elevator was slow," he said with a wry grin, walking around her desk and perching on the edge. "What's up?"

Midnight looked back at him for a long moment, then said, "Devereaux's definitely involved." She leaned back in her chair, putting her feet up on the desk next to him.

Rick looked surprised. "How?"

"Remember Rhiannon Templeton?"

Rick nodded. "Jason Templeton's wife, narcotics officer, good from what I've heard—yeah."

Midnight smiled at his assessment, proud that he hadn't only referred to her as someone's wife. "Well, she found some interesting stuff." She handed him the list.

Rick looked it over and then glanced back at her. "This the discrepancies you've been seein'?"

Midnight nodded, beginning to tap her pen in agitation. "That bastard's been stealin' from me," she said, her tone dangerous.

"So what're you going to do?"

"Surveillance," Midnight said, still sounding a little frustrated.

"Thorough…"

"Time-consuming," Midnight countered.

"But the best way to catch 'em all."

Midnight gave him a sour look. "I know," she said sullenly. "I had to rein Donovan in a little bit too."

"I'll bet—the kid does have a temper." Rick canted his head. "You want me on this?" he asked, knowing how she thought.

Midnight grinned, giving him an ingenue look. "You want some overtime?"

"Overtime?" He gave her a pointedly blank look. "What's that?" he asked, then shook his head. "You gotta understand somethin' here. My wife is a very influential person in this department—I. Don't. Get. Overtime." His expression was haughty, even as his eyes sparkled humorously.

Midnight put her foot against his hip, shoving him away from her and laughing. "Shut up! You get overtime. Okay, maybe not, but you don't put it down on your timesheet. What am I supposed to do, write it in for you before I sign it?"

"Isn't that what wives are for?" Rick asked blandly.

"Not if you'd like to maintain your current living arrangements," Midnight countered mildly.

"Yeah, there she goes." Rick nodded with a knowing look. "Take away my life's blood first thing…" He raised an eyebrow at her. "Isn't that sexual harassment?"

"Debenshire," Midnight said, her tone all chief, "sexual harassment is the promise of sex, not the threat of denial."

"Oh," Rick said simply, grinning as his deep blue eyes twinkled. "Guess I better watch it then."

"Guess you better." Midnight steepled her fingers, narrowing her eyes. "I think I'm gonna pull Dibbins, Spider, and Jess in on this too. What do you think?"

Rick nodded. "Spider's got a lot goin' on right now though. What about Tiny?"

"Tiny's not exactly unassuming."

"No, but neither is Jess, with all that red hair."

"Good point." Midnight nodded. "I don't want to overload Spider—you're definitely right there. Maybe I could connect with the Bureau of Investigation… They'd have the latest in surveillance equipment."

"Think your old friend Griffin could help out with an intro?"

"I'll bet he could." Midnight nodded, then looked at her husband for a long moment, and a warm smile spread across her face.

"What?" Rick asked, furrowing his brow.

Midnight shook her head, still smiling as she stood up. "I like doin' this with you," she said, putting her arms around his waist.

"Told you I could handle it," Rick said, his voice a warm murmur.

"Yes, you did," she replied, reaching up to kiss him softly.

Rick responded by pulling her closer to him, his lips increasing the pressure on hers. Midnight felt her body tingle at the unexpected sensuality of the moment. She was ever astounded by his effect on her; no one else had ever come close, not even Joe when they'd been together years before. Rick was it for her.

"Love you," she whispered when their lips parted.

"Just remember that," Rick said, hugging her close. "So when do we start?" he asked after a few minutes.

"Soonest," Midnight replied, smiling against his chest. Like Joe's, Rick's mind worked all the time, even when they were close. He knew this case was important to her. These were the people that were running Joe off, and she wanted them bad.

Midnight had contacted Phil Griffin, who was now the chief of the State Bureau of Narcotic Enforcement. He'd put her in touch with the Special Agent in Charge of the San Diego regional office of the Bureau of Investigation, Don Ryan. Ryan, like many other members of the law enforcement community, had heard about Midnight Chevalier-Debenshire and was all too happy to lend her any assistance. Ryan was given the green light by his chief to do just that. A meeting was set up for that afternoon. Ryan brought over all his "toys" to show Midnight, who brought Rick, Dave Dibbins, Tiny, Jessica, and Donovan. Jeanie had gone back to the academy.

The PD officers asked questions and Ryan was all too happy to answer all of them. He showed them a mini camera that attached to the back of a rearview mirror with a handheld eight-inch LCD monitor and dials to zoom in on subjects and record important data on the video recorder in the monitor housing.

"This way," Ryan said, grinning proudly, "we don't look so damn obvious with binoculars. You hold the monitor on your lap, and with the touch of a couple of buttons you got your close-up, and the bad guy's got no idea."

During the discussion, Rick edged up behind Midnight. "Nice connection, boss," he whispered against her hair.

Midnight glanced back at him and smiled.

At the end of the question and answer session, Ryan allowed everyone to try out the equipment. While the officers did just that he walked over to Midnight.

"I hear you have two cops assaulted so far," he said, sounding disgusted at the very thought.

Midnight nodded, knowing she could trust him. Phil wouldn't have put her in touch with someone he didn't trust, and she had implicit faith in Phil Griffin. "Yeah, I gotta take these guys down."

"Internal, right?" Ryan asked, having surmised it from what Griffin had told him as well as the fact that everyone in the meeting seemed very close to the chief herself, but they weren't IA or strictly narcotics. Midnight Chevalier was playing it close, and that meant internal problems.

Midnight nodded.

Ryan nodded too. "My stuff's good for long range, so it'll be harder to notice people they know."

A pained look crossed Midnight's face. "It pisses me off that I have people I gotta watch this way."

"Yeah, but they're hittin' cops," Ryan said. "So you gotta hit back."

"You got it."

Later that afternoon, Rick went over to the hospital, leaving Midnight poring over surveillance schedules.

Joe looked better than he had days before; Randy was scheduled to get out in three days.

"Hey," Rick said, walking in.

Joe grinned. "You here to kill me?" he asked, only half joking. He hadn't seen Rick since he'd told Midnight he was leaving, and he knew his best friend well enough to know he was pissed at him about it.

"Maybe," Rick said, his expression stern. Then he walked over to Randy. Bending down, he kissed her on the cheek. "Glad you're okay," he said, his smile warm.

Randy smiled up at him, then looked over at Joe. "You two need to talk—I can see that. Should I leave?"

"Funny," Joe said, standing up and leaning down to kiss her gently. He looked over at Rick. "Let's go," he said, nodding toward the door. He glanced back at Randy. "Take a good look now—I may not look the same when I get back."

Randy laughed, wagging a finger at both of them. "Play nice, boys."

Outside, Joe lit up a cigarette, catching Rick's expression. "So shoot me," he said, shrugging. "I've been a little edgy lately."

Rick nodded, understanding what he meant.

"So let's have it," Joe said when Rick didn't say anything.

Rick shrugged, shaking his head. "I ain't gonna ream ya, though I wanted to that first day. You know damn good and well that you shouldn't'a told her that way."

"I know." Joe sighed, bending his knee to rest his foot against the wall he was leaning on and looking up at the trees in the quad. Then he turned to Rick, his eyes narrowing slightly. "Tell me this— is she really okay with it?"

Rick shrugged. "Who knows with her?" Then he gave Joe a pointed look. "You know her well enough to know that no one knows how Midnight feels unless she wants 'em to."

"Yeah, but you're good at knowing when she's fakin' it. Is she?"

Rick thought about it, his mind touching on their conversation that afternoon. "I don't think so."

"Good." Joe sounded relieved. "Randy's tellin' Donovan and Darrell tonight when they come by. I'm not looking forward to their reactions."

"Donovan's bound to be in a bad mood anyway," Rick began.

"Why?" Joe asked, sensing something important had happened.

"Devereaux's in on it—we have proof now," Rick said briskly. He knew Joe hated being out of the information loop.

"When did that happen?" Joe asked, indeed sounding halfway between disgruntled and angry. "Never mind," he added. "When's Midnight arresting him?"

"She's not yet," Rick said, bracing himself for Joe's anger. He received it full force.

"Why the fuck not!" Joe yelled, coming off the wall and tensing in his fury.

"Now hold on." Rick held his hands up in a halting gesture. "There's other cops involved, and she wants 'em all."

Joe looked ready to rebel at the thought of leaving Devereaux free to cause more trouble, but then he nodded, dragging deeply on his cigarette in an effort to calm down. "So what's happening?" he asked, hungry for information, suddenly feeling left out.

Rick told him about the meeting with Rhiannon, then about the BI's assistance and the surveillance on Devereaux. Joe nodded, lighting two more cigarettes during the narrative. It was an hour before he returned to Randy's room.

He opened the door to find Donovan standing next to Randy. Donovan turned and looked at him, his teal eyes blazing with barely contained anger. Joe leaned against the door jamb, his face deceptively passive. Donovan noted the determined look on his brother-in-law's face, but his anger wouldn't allow him to back down either.

Randy sat watching them. She could see that both of them were adamant and that there was going to be no easy end to this. Donovan was extremely irritated about the idea of Joe dragging her "halfway across the world." She'd tried to reason with him, but to no avail.

"So?" Joe said finally, with an exaggeratedly casual tone.

"So," Donovan repeated heatedly, "thanks for dragging my sister off. Guess Darrell and I won't be needing her anymore."

Joe's expression didn't change. "Guess I need her more," he said, staring back into Donovan's eyes.

Donovan had no response for that. He simply shook his head and walked past Joe. Joe watched him go, a drawn look on his face, then turned back to Randy.

"You okay?" he asked.

Randy nodded, staring down for a moment, then back up at him. "You?" she asked, raising an eyebrow at him, referring to his talk with Rick.

"Yeah." Joe walked over to the bed. "Donovan tell you about Devereaux?"

Randy nodded again. "He's really wound tight right now," she said, in an oblique effort to explain his anger at Joe minutes before.

"No, he's really pissed at me too." Joe didn't sound the least bit repentant, because he wasn't.

Randy said nothing, just put her hand in his and drew him down to sit on the bed next to her. "You're doing what's best for us right now. He'll get used to the idea."

"He won't have a choice, Randy. I'm not asking their permission to protect my family," Joe said, his blue eyes blazing even as his voice remained even.

"I know."

Joe looked at her for a long moment to see if he could detect any sarcasm in her expression; he couldn't. He pulled her gently into his embrace, stroking her hair and pressing his lips against her forehead. Randy relaxed against him, knowing she was doing the right thing, allowing him the power to make these important decisions regarding their safety.

Three days later Randy was released from the hospital without incident. Joe had already put plans into motion for their move to England. He wanted his family out of the line of fire as quickly as possible. He talked to Robert Debenshire, his lawyer, about Christian's "probationary" status, and how Joe leaving would affect that. Robert indicated that it was not an official probation and that since Christian Jeremy Sinclair had dropped the charges, his son was a free man.

Joe told Christian all of this on the same day he brought Randy home from the hospital. They were sitting in the kitchen, with the mid-morning sun coming in the bay windows of the breakfast alcove. Christian said nothing as Joe rattled off his statement, only nodding at appropriate times and chewing incessantly on a piece of gum. Joe suddenly realized that his young cousin, sitting across from him in faded jeans, black cotton shirt, and black boots, looking for all intents and purposes totally unaffected, was a lot more like himself than he'd thought.

Except for the obvious differences in coloring, Christian had the same bored, nonplussed appearance Joe himself had cultivated as a youth. Of course, by the time he was Christian's age, Joe had been through a horrible tragedy, losing his parents and almost his own life, but before that he'd been the rich gang leader and to everyone's knowledge, by design, highly immovable.

For that reason, Joe knew better than to take Christian's calm response at face value. As it was, he felt like he was deserting the cousin he was just getting to know.

"Christian," he said, "what's goin' through your head? I need to know you're gonna be alright here."

In response, Christian lifted his chin slightly, looking like he was considering the thought for a moment. Then he nodded slowly, giving Joe an indolent, smug look, as if saying, "What do I need you for?"

Joe read the look easily, knowing it well. He'd used it; a number of the gang members he'd dealt with did too. He knew it was a defense mechanism, designed to keep everyone at arm's length. Christian's purpose was no different. But after a long, purposeful pause, Joe nodded, shrugging. "Okay…" he said, not sure what else to say without sounding like an egotistical jerk.

He told Christian that he was more than welcome to stay in the house. Joe fully intended to leave an account set up to keep the house maintained and the pantry stocked. Christian would have full run of the place at no cost; Joe was making sure of that. Money for Christian wouldn't be an issue, since Midnight had made no bones about the fact that she'd be requiring his expertise for a long time to come. She'd already paid him handsomely for his work on the inventory program. Joe came away from the conversation with Christian feeling like he'd abandoned the younger man, but he didn't know what he could do to fix that.

Susan found Christian in his room two hours later. He answered the door with a bottle of Jack Daniels in his hand and a fairly nasty scowl on his face. He left the door open and walked back over to the bed, sitting down and leaning against the headboard, regarding her remotely.

"So what do you want?" he asked tersely.

Susan said nothing for a long few moments, searching his face as she sat down next to him. "You are upset about Joe leaving, aren't you?"

Christian looked back at her, his light blue eyes narrowing darkly. "What makes you think that?"

Susan canted her head to the side, giving him a caustic look. "I'd say getting tanked at…" She looked at her watch, then back at him. "Twelve o'clock in the afternoon is some indication of upset."

"Yeah, well what about you?" Christian came back, his tone jeering. "From the sounds of it, you don't have a job no more."

"That's not true," Susan said, drawing herself up unconsciously in her defensiveness. "Joe said I could stay on with them and go back home."

Christian gave her an "oh really?" look, then grinned evilly. "Bet you're goin' for that, huh?" he said derisively.

"What are you talking about?" Susan asked, aware he was baiting her but not sure what he was getting at.

Before answering, Christian pointedly stretched his long legs out in front of him, crossing them at the ankles. "Well, you get to stay around Joe—that ought to make you happy."

"Why should I care?" Susan replied, too quickly.

Christian grinned, his eyes sparkling with triumph. "Oh, you care," he said chidingly.

"For your information," Susan said, her voice tight and irritated, "I'm not going with them."

"So what're you gonna do?" Christian asked, though he didn't sound like he really cared one way or the other.

Susan suddenly looked hesitant. "I'm not sure exactly…"

Christian caught the hesitation and narrowed his eyes at her. Then he started to laugh, shaking his head. "You don't think for a

51

minute that you're stayin' here with me," he said, his tone indicating that she'd better not be.

Susan stared back at him for a long moment, and he could read the hurt in her eyes but chose to ignore it. She shook her head and gave him a sour look. "What makes you think I want to live with you?"

Christian shook his head, as if he couldn't imagine. Then without warning he slid his hand around her waist and drew her to him. His lips came down on hers and he kissed her hungrily. Susan put her hands against his chest with the thought of pushing away from him, but her body ignored what her mind told her to do. Within moments, her hands slid up his chest, and up and around his neck. After a long few minutes, he pulled back, looking down at her knowingly.

"That's what makes me think you want to live with me," he said heatedly.

Susan looked back at him for a long moment, trying to regain her senses as she shook her head. It took her a long moment to find her voice. "I don't want to live with you," she said finally.

"No?" Christian replied, his tone indicating he didn't believe her.

"Warren has asked me to move in with him," Susan said haughtily as she disengaged herself from his arms.

"So what's the problem?" Christian said, his voice still husky.

"There is no problem," Susan replied, trying to gather her composure.

"I think there is." Christian slid his finger from her shoulder down her front. Susan couldn't stop the shudder that ran through her as his fingertip traced over her breast. Christian smiled smugly, knowing that he was getting to her. "Do you want to live with him?"

Susan didn't answer for a long moment, sure he didn't want to hear that she didn't but feeling weak for him again at that moment. Finally she shook her head slowly. He slid his hand around her waist again, drawing her to him, bringing her face within an inch of his. "Do you want to stay with me?" he whispered huskily.

"Yes," she answered, abandoning all efforts to be unaffected by him.

His lips came down on hers again, and she could no longer wonder what this meant, if he actually cared about her or if he would just use her. She didn't really care right then either. They made love most of that afternoon and slept into the evening. They didn't, however, talk. Susan was afraid to ask too many questions; she simply decided that she would not move in with Warren and would stay on at the house instead. That night Christian lay awake, wondering what had possessed him to give her the option of staying with him. He knew he was being stupid, but he couldn't seem to be cruel and mean to her. He wanted to be—he wanted to distance her again—but having her so close made it very hard to think straight. His body didn't listen to what his mind said; his body wanted her, and it worked on its own volition, and his mouth and vocal cords seemed to be in cahoots. Damn them.

Joe was thrown a going away party the day before he and Randy left California. It was organized by Rick and Midnight and took place at their favorite hangout, The Pit, which was still run by retired officer Tom Ryan, Midnight's original mentor. Ryan had closed The Pit to accommodate the party, all too happy to do so for Joe.

Tom looked on Joe as a son he'd never had; married twice, he'd never had children. He'd taken Midnight under his wing when her brother was killed almost eighteen years before. It had been Ryan who'd gotten Midnight to go to college, and his example had gotten her into law enforcement. Ryan liked Joe because he knew Joe was always there for Midnight, and Midnight was definitely the daughter he'd never had. He also respected Joe's cop instincts and abilities.

"Can't believe you're actually gettin' out," Ryan said, shaking his head.

"It's just somethin' I gotta do right now," Joe said, looking chagrined.

Tom nodded. "I hear ya, I hear ya." Midnight had explained about Randy and why Joe was leaving.

There were a lot of people at the party. All the original FORS members were in attendance, and just about every available narcotics officer as well as cops from other vice units. Even the off-duty patrol officers were there. Randy had also gone, even though she was still supposed to be resting. She had insisted on coming, knowing the day was going to be important as well as hard on him, and she was determined to be there for him.

When it came time for speeches, Spider got up to speak on behalf of narcotics and the original members of FORS. He made jokes about Joe's accent, and the fact that every time things went bad financially Joe always tried to buy himself a police department. "God knows he can afford it!" he said, laughing. Tiny made a few comments about Joe's fighting abilities, indicating he was "still surprised that Sinclair had lived as long as he had." Everyone who'd seen Joe fight laughed at that; Joe was one of the best when it came down to good old-fashioned street fighting.

The current rangemaster spoke next, talking about Joe's perfect marksmanship and presenting him with a framed target that had his name and score on it. It was the target from his last qualification; as usual it indicated a perfect score. Joe laughed uproariously as he read the engraved plate on the bottom: *Captain Joseph Sinclair, San Diego Police Department's TOP GUN*. Then, in smaller letters: *Caution: this man is a licensed lethal weapon and could hit a gnat at 1,000 yards.* The rest of the party got a good laugh at that as well.

The last person to speak was Rick. Everyone had noticed that Midnight was keeping fairly silent. Everyone who knew her well knew that she wouldn't make a speech, that saying goodbye to Joe publicly would be far too difficult.

Instead she had Rick give Joe a Letter of Appreciation and his badge in a custom-made shadow box. Rick read the letter out loud, outlining Joe's achievements and his unwavering loyalty to Midnight herself and every member of the department. It also indicated that for purely sentimental reasons—which as the chief she could get away with—she was retiring his badge number, 355, and presenting it to him. The last paragraph of the letter referred to friendship in its purest form and how knowing someone could change one's perspective on life forever. By the time Rick finished, there wasn't an unaffected person in the room. Rick's own voice was constricted with emotion. Joe himself was choked up as he accepted the letter and badge. He shook hands with Rick, then hugged him tightly.

Then he turned to Midnight, who had stood off to the side during the speeches. Taking two steps toward her, he reached out and gently took her hand, pulling her into a fierce embrace. There were whoops and hollers, whistles and catcalls that only escalated when he pulled back and kissed her softly on the lips. It wasn't a passionate kiss; it was almost apologetic, quick but gentle enough to relate his deep feelings for her as his best friend, partner, confidant, and whatever else he needed at the time.

"I'm always a phone call away," he whispered as he held her tightly again.

"I know," Midnight said, fighting back the wave of sadness that kept threatening to spill over.

"Do you?" Joe asked, his voice so deep and concerned that the tears she'd managed to keep at bay now came unheeded.

"Yes," she said as she buried her face against his chest. She didn't want everyone to see her crying like a baby. Rick watched the two, his expression pained and sympathetic at the same time. He knew what Midnight was going through. He remembered the day years before when Joe left England after his parents were killed. Rick had been bereft; Joe and he had been friends since they were kids.

After a few long moments, Rick stepped over, his back to the gathering. Midnight lifted her head from Joe's chest, sensing Rick's presence instantly. Without a word, Joe released Midnight, and Rick put a supportive arm around her shoulders, still shielding her from the crowd. At that point everyone knew it was time to mingle, and they all started to talk and laugh.

The core members of FORS made their way to the front, lending their support to Midnight as well as wishing Joe all the best. Joe shook hands with many people, his eyes trailing over to Randy frequently. She was watching him, her eyes showing her concern over his mental state. Joe smiled at her, and she nodded, smiling back. It was their way of confirming that they were okay.

Randy was sitting looking at the letter Midnight had given Joe when Midnight walked over and sat down next to her.

"So how's it going, Curtis?"

"Okay," Randy replied, looking over at her chief. It was odd to realize all that they'd been through. There had been good times and not so good times, but always Midnight had come through. She'd been the strength that had inspired Randy to become a police officer, in spite of Joe's wishes. It had also been Midnight's example that had spurred Randy into wanting to continue her education. "How are you?" Randy asked, knowing that Midnight was far more affected by Joe's leaving than she was letting anyone really know.

Midnight shrugged, shaking her head slowly. "I hate like hell to lose him, but I know he's doing what he thinks he has to."

Randy looked at Midnight for a long moment, narrowing her eyes slightly. Midnight had spoken as if Joe were just another officer, like losing him would just mean having to find a new captain of vice. "Okay, now that you've given me the canned answer, how are you really?" Randy asked, her tone direct, not unlike Midnight's usual way of speaking.

Midnight narrowed her eyes back at Randy, a grin starting on her lips. "I'm not too bad off. Things are just gonna be real quiet around here without him."

Randy nodded. "Yeah, it's going to be weird not being here either. I haven't really gotten used to the idea yet."

"That makes two of us," Midnight said, biting her lip.

"You know," Randy began, her tone low, "if you need him

57

here—if you really don't want him to leave—all you have to do is say the word and I'll tell him we can't go." Her voice was serious, her expression equally sincere.

Midnight grinned, looking like she was considering the thought, then shook her head. "I couldn't do that to him. If something happened, it would be my fault."

Randy didn't say anything. She knew how both Midnight and Joe thought; they usually blamed themselves for things going wrong. She knew Midnight was thinking of Joe and his family, and she couldn't help but respect her for that.

"You'll be okay?" Randy asked skeptically.

"I survived before he came along," Midnight replied caustically.

Randy grinned. "Yes, I know."

The next day, Joe, Randy, Kat, and JT left for the airport. Midnight, Rick, Donovan, and Jeanie showed up to see them off. There were a few long, sad silences and a lot of nervous laughter. Eventually boarding for their flight was called and they hugged their goodbyes. Rick and Joe shook hands, and Joe gave Rick a serious look. "Take care of her, huh?"

"You know I will," Rick replied, his tone circumspect.

Joe nodded, turning to Midnight. She looked up at him, her gold-green eyes somber.

"Quit that," Joe said, sounding choked.

"I'll miss you," Midnight replied, not even able to smile at his attempt at levity.

"You know I'll miss you too, Night," he said softly. He took her into his arms, hugging her tight. The lump in his throat tightened further as he felt her arms close around his waist. He knew she was fighting back tears; he also knew that if he saw her crying, combined with the fact that he'd caused it, it would be too much. He held her an extra amount of time, giving them both a chance to regain their composure. When he stepped back, holding her at arm's length, he saw the glossy look to her eyes and shook his head.

Donovan stepped up then, extending his hand to Joe. He was still very unhappy about the move, but he'd realized that Joe needed to do what was right for his family. Like it or not, Randy was Joe's wife, and he came first in her life. Randy had put it just that way the night before when Donovan had come to see her. After a moment's hesitation Joe took Donovan's proffered hand, shaking it as he stared into the younger man's eyes.

"We'll get you and Darrell over for a visit as soon as you can come," Joe told his brother-in-law.

"Yeah," Donovan said, nodding, his face still serious.

Joe gave Jeanie a quick hug, and then Randy, he, and the children headed for the gangway. Midnight leaned back against Rick as they waited for the plane to leave the terminal. "You okay?" he whispered next to her ear.

Midnight nodded, not trusting herself to speak. She was fighting the definite desire to run down the gangway after Joe and tell him he couldn't go. She still couldn't believe he was actually leaving. The thought kept going around in her head, driving her crazy. It didn't get better once she got back to the office that morning.

Everyone was walking on eggshells around her. The core members of FORS continually dropped in to check on her. Midnight spent the day trying to read and re-read a report, but her mind wouldn't stay focused. Finally, at two o'clock that afternoon, Rick stuck his head in the door.

Midnight looked up, report in hand. She was reclining on the couch, her legs extended in front of her. Rick looked down at her, canting his head to the side in an assessing gesture, then nodded back toward her door. "Come on," he said.

"Where're we goin?" Midnight asked cautiously.

"Just come on," Rick said, grinning at her. He took her hand and pulled her to her feet. He gently took the report from her hand and laid it on her desk. He turned and led her from the room and out to his car, where he opened the passenger door for her before getting in.

Midnight gave him a narrowed look. "What's going on, Richard?" she asked, her tone not matching her suspicious, angry expression.

"We're playing hooky," he said simply. An hour later Midnight found herself at the Hard Rock Cafe in La Jolla, assailed by the music and the sounds of people enjoying themselves and having lunch. Afterward he drove her over to Mission Beach and took her on the roller coaster, bought her cotton candy, and held her hand while they walked along the boardwalk, looking for all intents and purposes like two young kids on a date.

By five o'clock that afternoon, Midnight couldn't help but grin up at her husband. They were lying on the grass alongside the boardwalk, watching skaters sail past and looking out at Mission Bay. Midnight lay flat on the ground with Rick on his side facing her, propped up on one elbow.

"Thank you for this," she said warmly.

"No problem," Rick said, his grin lopsided. "That's part of my new duties as assigned, you know. As part of my new 'better husband' plan, it's my responsibility to make sure you're as happy as possible at all times."

Midnight smiled. "Well, you've succeeded admirably, sir."

"Thank you so much," Rick replied, inclining his head then lowering it further still to kiss her. Midnight wound her arms around his neck to pull him down to her. Many people in the area looked on smiling as they kissed; one man skating by said, "Alright!" It was a sweet moment, and everyone that saw it thought the same thing—if only they had a love like that one...

****

Christian was working down in Devereaux's offices that day, compiling the information for the inventory; he'd been there for the last few days. He'd kept his mouth shut and remained unfriendly to everyone, giving off a very definite vibe of insolence.

"Must be rough, your cousin leavin' an' all..." Devereaux said.

Christian glanced back at the man, then shrugged. "S'alright, gives me more room to breathe, ya know?" His expression was practically a sneer.

"Yeah, but don't he run the money in the family?" Devereaux sat back in his chair, eyeing Christian warily.

"Well, looks like he's jus' runnin' now, don't it?" Christian said irreverently.

"So you two weren't close?" Devereaux asked, his tone still

guarded.

Christian considered the question for a long moment, then shrugged again. "He put up with me, but that's about all. His father basically made it so he had to—he didn't have a lot of choice."

Devereaux looked confused. "I thought his father was dead?"

"Oh, he is, but he told my mother that if she ever needed anything, to contact him. Well, when I got into trouble she contacted Joe through his lawyer. I guess Joe felt like he was obligated to help me out."

Devereaux nodded. "So what's your beef with Debenshire?" he asked, remembering the day Rick had punched Christian in the mouth.

Christian grinned lewdly then, his eyes twinkling with delight. "I fucked his niece—he didn't like that too much."

"So I guess he don't consider you family, huh?" Frank said derogatorily, indicating what he thought of the Debenshires.

"Shit, she's engaged to big money, and I don't have none—what's that tell ya?"

"Tells me Debenshire's a fucking hypocrite. He married Chevalier—she didn't have shit."

"Double standard, I guess," Christian said, his lips curled in disgust. "You know the old golden rule. Their gold, their rules."

Devereaux shook his head disdainfully. "But you're working on that inventory system for Chevalier, aren't you?"

"Yeah, she's got me doin' all the fuckin' grunt work while she and her friends sit up in the ivory tower, clean and proper. Guess that tells me my place in the food chain, huh?"

Devereaux made a clicking sound with his tongue, shaking his head. "So's Sinclair kickin' ya outta his place or what?"

"I can stay there till it sells, he said. Guess that way he has a live-in guard for the place too," Christian said, his tone indicating disgust, then shrugged. "But guess it's better than livin' on the street."

"You can't go back to England?"

"Not yet, my father's still a little pissed 'bout me tryin' to kill him and all."

"I heard somethin' about that," Devereaux said, then gave Christian a pointed look. "So what're you doin' for spending money?"

Christian shrugged. "I make some money doin' this, but it ain't enough. I don't know what I'm gonna do yet." He looked a bit cha-grined then. "I probably shouldn't tell ya this, you bein' a cop and all, but you're pretty cool... I got this little habit to support—I was cool about it when Joe was here, but now that I'm free to do as I please, I plan to."

Devereaux nodded, looking like he understood perfectly. "I might be able to help you out."

"Yeah?" Christian said, looking doubtful. "I ain't into bussin' tables and shit, if that's what you got in mind."

"Nah, nothin' like that. Let me talk to a couple of my friends and I'll get back to ya."

"Cool," Christian said, nodding.

CHAPTER 3

The first night after Joe left, Christian made a point of staying out of the house. He didn't want Susan to think they were going to play house now. He made his way to the bar in Pacific Beach and spent the night at the club, waiting for Tara to get off. He followed her to her apartment then, closing the front door quietly so as not to wake up her daughter. Tara sent her babysitter home, but not before the girl eyed Christian with interest as he leaned indolently against the doorway to her kitchen.

"You stayin' for breakfast this time?" Tara asked, as she did almost every time he ended up at her apartment.

Christian grinned. "Maybe…"

"What's goin' on now?" she said, knowing a little about what he was going through with Susan and all that. Christian had talked to Tara as well as Jeanie about the situation. Tara's opinion had been similar to Jeanie's—that Christian was falling for Susan and that was what was bothering him. Unlike Jeanie, however, Tara understood the problem perfectly; she'd made the mistake of falling in love and she'd sworn she'd never do it again. She understood Christian's desire to stay away from the emotion.

"You gonna ask questions all night?" Christian asked, moving toward her purposefully.

"Maybe…"

"Not," Christian finished for her as he put his arms around her, pulling her to him and kissing her on the lips. Tara sighed, giving in to his kisses easily. Eventually he picked her up and carried her to her bedroom. He made love to her there, taking her with more aggression than usual, as if trying to drive thoughts of Susan from his head. Afterward, he lay on his side, trying to catch his breath, his eyes closed.

"Okay..." Tara said, her tone indicating she was waiting for him to talk.

Christian said nothing for a long minute, then opened his eyes and shook his head. "I don' wanna talk about it, okay?"

Tara nodded, frowning at him as if trying to read something in his eyes. "What's eating you, London?"

"I said—"

"I know what you said," Tara cut in, her tone rising slightly. "But I want you to tell me what's goin' on. It's not just Susan, is it?"

Christian shook his head slowly, rolling onto his back and blowing his breath out in a frustrated sigh. Tara moved to look down at him, propping her head up on her elbow. "Talk, London."

Christian glanced at her, seeing the determined look on her face. He closed his eyes for a moment, then looked at her again. "One of the guys that tried to kill my cousin's wife approached me today."

"So what does that mean?"

"That means I think they're going to ask me to join them, and I'm not sure what I should do."

"Tell the cops," Tara said, matter-of-fact.

Christian guffawed, shaking his head at her. "They are the cops, Tara."

"I meant the good ones, the ones you work with."

"Yeah..." Christian said. "Thing is, there's nothin' to really go on yet. I figure I should wait till I can actually give them something."

"Isn't that a little dangerous?"

Christian shrugged. "No more than the shit I was doin' in England. I figure this way I can help them catch these guys. They certainly ain't gonna approach no one else that's associated with Joe, Midnight, and the rest. Maybe I can keep 'em from hurting anyone else. Or at least warn 'em if somethin's comin'."

Tara nodded. "Yeah... but London, you're not even a cop or anything. You could get yourself killed."

Christian shrugged again. "Better me than them."

Tara stared at him, stunned, then shook her head. She didn't understand him, though she knew he was very loyal to his newly acquired family—but dying for them?

Christian managed to stay away from the house for the following three nights. He spent time with Tara, and one night even went home with a woman he met at the bar. When he finally made it back to Joe's house on the fifth night after the Sinclairs' departure, the place was quiet. Susan wasn't there and Christian found himself wandering around feeling a little bereft. After a couple of hours he gave up trying to get comfortable in the too big, too lonely house and went to bed. Even then he had trouble getting to sleep.

He was just dropping off when he heard the door to his room open. He turned over and saw Susan coming in.

"You are here," she said softly.

"Yep," Christian replied drily.

"I was worried…" she began, but seeing him raise a cynical brow, she trailed off.

"Don't be," he said evenly. "I'm a big boy—I can take care of myself." With that he turned over on his side, putting his back to her as if dismissing her.

Oh really? Susan thought. She was in the perfect mood to teach one Christian Joseph Collins a lesson about being cool to her.

Christian knew she hadn't left; he could still sense her in the room, could still smell her perfume. He figured she was trying to think of something to say. He was wrong. Christian's breath caught in his throat as she slid into bed behind him wearing nothing at all. His stony resolve to stay away from her crumbled instantly as she pressed against him, her hand sliding over his waist and up his chest suggestively.

"God…" was all he uttered as his body responded to the feeling of her body against his. He didn't turn to face her, but reveled in the sensation of her hands on his skin. Closing his eyes, he knew there was no way he could resist her. This new, more aggressive side of her only served to strengthen his reaction to her. It jabbed at him then that Warren might be responsible for bringing this out in her. It was that thought that made him turn over to look at her. But Susan wasn't done with her foray into explicitness; before he could say anything, she lowered her head, kissing his chest. Christian's breath came faster as his hands buried themselves in her hair.

"Zan…" he said, his voice a thick whisper.

Susan continued her exploration of his chest. Then she moved to kiss his neck, nipping at his skin with her teeth and drawing a few excited gasps from him. Even as her lips traveled up his body, her hands traveled down, touching him with a confidence she'd never displayed before. Within minutes he was groaning and pulling her against him, but Susan kept him from dragging her body over his, her hands set squarely on his chest. She lifted her hand, looking down at him. She could see the desire burning in his light blue eyes, and it excited her no end.

"What do you want, Christian?" she whispered, searching his eyes.

Christian closed his eyes slowly, a grin playing at his lips at her words, which sounded so much like his. Then he opened his eyes and looked directly into hers. "Make love to me, Zan," he said, his voice husky and deep. Susan couldn't hide the shiver that ran through her.

Slowly, she moved her body over his and, with confidence born of numerous unions with this man, slid herself down over him. Christian grasped her hips as he held her fast against him. He was once again fighting for control of his body, the heat of hers making him almost lose his usually iron-clad control.

"What?" Susan asked softly, noticing that his eyes were tightly closed and he wasn't allowing her to do what he'd told her he wanted her to.

Christian shook his head slightly, tensing as he felt her shift her body to look down at him. "Don't…" he said, his voice a strangled whisper. "Just stay right there," he added, his breathing heavy.

Susan watched his face and understanding finally dawned. She knew he was close to losing the battle and she wanted to push him over the edge if she could. Once again she lowered her head to kiss his chest, keeping him inside her the whole time. But he'd regained enough of his control to keep that from being effective. Susan decided she needed to try something else. Remembering something one of her racier girlfriends in England had told her, she concentrated on tightening a particular group of muscles. Conveniently those muscles happened to be surrounding a particularly sensitive part of his body at that moment.

"Jesus!" he exclaimed almost harshly as he tried to pull himself away from her.

"What?" she asked again, her expression pointedly innocent.

"Don't do that," Christian said through clenched teeth.

"Do what?" Susan asked then, her deep blue eyes twinkling as they widened mischievously.

"You know what, don't you?" Christian said, his tone halfway between accusing and amused.

This time Susan gave him a guileless smile.

"You little..." Christian said, grinning in spite of himself. Then, putting his hand at the back of her head, he pulled her to him to kiss her deeply. She slid down over him again and they made love for a while. Once again she fought for the upper hand, but he was onto her this time, using his hands to caress and fondle her, making her gasp in pleasure. His mouth on hers kept the heat between them mutual. In the end they climaxed together and lay panting as they tried to regain their strength.

After a long few minutes Christian touched her under the chin, bringing her eyes up to his. "Where did you come from?" he asked, his tone amazed.

Susan gave him a jaunty shrug and said, "Don't stay away so

long next time and I won't have to teach you another lesson." Her voice was haughty, but her grin lightened her words.

Christian pursed his lips; if any other woman had said that to him, she'd be on her backside on the floor right now. But he had no desire to shove her away from him. Finally he grinned and inclined his head in a touché gesture. "Yes, ma'am."

He was rewarded with a brilliant smile and a warm, sensuous kiss that set his nerves tingling all over again. God, she was a bad habit!

****

Things between Donovan and Jeanie were progressing smoothly. She'd returned to her old routine of leaving his house around 11:00 p.m., staying later on weekends. It was two weeks after Joe and Randy left, and they'd spent the morning walking through the antique stores in the business district of downtown San Diego. They'd had lunch at a fish restaurant on the shore in La Jolla and spent the rest of the day looking in the shops in the small coastal town. It had been a long, pleasant day, culminating in a quiet evening at his house. She sat in his kitchen as he cooked, drinking wine and talking with him about the academy, and about his experiences with the department. They'd laughed about a lot of things, and everything seemed to be getting back on track. That was why Donovan was feeling so comfortable that night.

They'd made love and were lying in his bed talking. It was a warm, relaxed conversation about nothing at all. They were discussing one of her brothers; she was telling him about how he had scared off her date for the prom.

"So how'd you get him back?" Donovan asked, grinning.

"Well, that's the thing," Jeanie said. "I made Mario go and get him back." She laughed then. "I heard he actually had to pay for the limo to get him to come back."

"That was an expensive lesson."

"Serves him right. Men can be so dumb sometimes," Jeanie said, rolling her eyes.

"Excuse me, I happen to be a man."

Jeanie gave him a pointed look "Yeah, and?"

"I see... and you're saying?"

"Well, you know..."

"Stop it," he said, grinning wider now. "I've warned you about comparing me to other men." He shrugged, looking very put upon. "I guess I'll just have to teach you a lesson."

"And what would that be?" she asked, already smiling widely.

He leaned over, bending his head to kiss her shoulder, then moved his lips to her neck.

"Oh... I see..." she said, her breath coming faster.

"Do you?" he asked, his voice already husky.

"Mmhmm..." she practically purred.

An hour later they lay together, he on his stomach and she on her back, his arm thrown over her waist, his lips still pressed against her temple. "Jay?" he said, his voice still warm and slightly breathless.

"Hmm?" she said, still a little out of breath herself.

71

"I love you." He said it in a gentle whisper, but he felt her tense instantly. He knew he'd just made a mistake.

Jeanie sat up, looking down at him with an expression of concern. "Donovan…"

"Forget it, I didn't say that," he said, his voice showing his hurt even as his eyes narrowed slightly.

Jeanie stared at him for a long moment, searching his face. "You did say it, Donovan—but did you mean it?"

Donovan couldn't help but roll his eyes, giving a short, almost disgusted laugh. "No, Jay, I didn't mean it. I always say things like that to women I sleep with. It goes right along with sending them flowers."

Jeanie shook her head. "I'm not trying to hurt you, I just… I can't say how I feel right now. I don't want you to think… I mean…" She trailed off as she shook her head helplessly.

"Don't want me to think what, Jay? Think that because I said it you have to? Think that because we sleep together and spend almost every day together it gives me a right to expect something from you?" His eyes showed the hurt he felt at her rejection. "What is it you want from me, Jay? Huh? I'm supposed to just be with you, make love to you, but not want anything from you? I'm supposed to just wait around till you decide to leave again, and not tell you how I feel? Is that what you want?"

Jeanie had remained silent during his tirade, watching him with sad eyes. She could sense the tight wire she was walking, and she already knew what it was like to be on the other side of him. "Donovan, I care about you a lot, so much… but I just don't know about love yet. It's a big deal to me—it's everything to me. I don't just say it to

72

anyone." She knew then she'd said the wrong thing.

Donovan closed his eyes, shaking his head with a sarcastic grin. "So I guess that puts me in the class of guys that do, huh? Hell yeah, tell 'em you love 'em—it works every time? And what would I be going for, Jay? Your virginity? I already got that, if you'll recall. So what's my angle here, huh?"

"Donovan, that's not what I meant."

"Then what did you mean?" he countered, sitting up, his eyes searching hers.

"I just meant I need some time," she began. "*Not* away from you," she added quickly when she saw the look on his face. "But I just want to be sure before I say those words."

Donovan said nothing for a long moment, then nodded, blowing his breath out slowly. "Guess I don't get a choice here, do I?"

Jeanie didn't answer. Instead, she leaned forward to kiss him, wrapping her arms around him and sliding her hands up his back. She was telling him with her lips that she hadn't been trying to hurt him. After a long moment she felt him relax in her embrace. She didn't know if he'd accepted what she'd said, or if he was just giving in for the moment.

She found over the next few days that things were indeed tense between them, and she worried that it would serve to erode their already precarious relationship. Donovan didn't mention the conversation again, and he certainly didn't tell her he loved her again.

****

73

As usual, Christian and Susan were on again, off again. Christian worked late many evenings, trying to get as much into the inventory system as possible. Devereaux had re-approached him two weeks after their first discussion and asked him to "miss" a few things on the inventory, so that "Chevalier" wouldn't know what she didn't have. He also discussed with Christian the possibility of bigger things pertaining to altering the departmental case designation system, allowing assignment of certain narcotics cases to the "right" officer. Christian indicated he was always happy to make more money. Devereaux had been pleased with the young Englishman's response. At that point Christian was trying to get as much legitimate work done on the system as he could, "just in case." It made for many late nights, which he explained to Susan, but he knew she didn't quite believe him. Some nights he'd go to the bar after work and drink a fair amount, then go home and drink some more to make himself pass out.

One night he was too buzzed to drive; Tara wisely took his keys and called him a cab. Christian arrived home and noted immediately that Warren's car was in the driveway. The guy drove a white Mercedes 680 SL.

"Pretentious asshole," Christian muttered as he let himself into the house. He made a point of walking with heavy footsteps; he could already hear them in Susan's bedroom. When he passed by the room, however, they were only talking on her bed. Warren sat with his back to the door; Susan saw Christian and instantly looked worried. Warren noticed her expression and craned his neck around. He raised a condescending eyebrow at Christian.

"I assume this is acceptable to you?" he asked, gesturing to the distance between himself and Susan, his voice dripping with sarcasm.

Christian looked nonplussed. "For now," he replied, everything about his expression and tone indicating a veiled threat. He turned and walked down the hall, closing his door behind him.

He was fully asleep two hours later when he heard a crash. He jumped up from his bed and ran out into the hall. He heard Susan's voice, then Warren's, raised in anger. He strode down the hall, wearing only the black jeans he'd had on before.

Christian made it to Susan's open door and surveyed the scene before him. Susan was sitting on the floor with her back to him, wearing very little. Warren was standing over her, breathing heavily, his clothes in disarray. It was all Christian needed to see. He stepped into the room, his very body language a threat.

"You touch her again and you're a dead man," he told the other man, his light blue eyes fixed on Warren.

Warren looked up, his eyes blazing, his face contorted in anger. "Yeah? So besides fucking her, you're gonna be her protector too?"

If Christian was taken aback by the fact that Warren knew about him and Susan, he didn't show it. He stood with his hands at his side, waiting for Warren's move. He said nothing, simply raised his chin a little higher, saying without words, "Just try me."

This incensed Warren, who moved around Susan and started toward Christian. Susan jumped up, putting herself between the two men, facing Warren.

"Warren, don't," she said, holding up her hands. "This is between you and me."

Warren stopped and looked down at her, his lips twisting in disgust. "Oh, it's between the three of us, I'd say—wouldn't you?"

"Warren…" Susan began.

"Shut the hell up, Susan!" Warren yelled, reaching out to shove her aside.

Christian was faster. His arm encircled Susan's waist, pulling her back against him and out of Warren's reach.

"I warned you about touching her again," Christian said, raising a jet black eyebrow. "I'll consider that you're not very bright and that you didn't hear me the first time." His expression darkened. "Now get out."

Warren hesitated, and Susan felt Christian tense. She knew she had to stop them; Christian could easily kill Warren, or at least injure him severely. She didn't want him in trouble because of her. What she didn't realize was that Christian hadn't seen the already darkening bruise on her cheek or the cut on her lip. When she turned to reason with him, his eyes went directly to the injuries. In one fluid motion, he pulled her aside with his left arm and shoved her behind him as he took one long stride forward, punching Warren square in the face with his right fist. Warren never had a chance; he sank to the floor, unconscious. Christian stood over him, almost wanting him to get up so he could knock him down again.

Susan stepped up behind Christian, grabbing his left arm, trying to distract him. "Christian."

He turned to her, his light blue eyes searching her face again. He looked pained as he surveyed her bruises. He reached up, lightly touching her cheek, brushing her hair back so he could see the extent of the damage. "He didn't do this," Susan said, touching her cheek. "I fell against the dresser…"

"And this?" he said, touching the corner of her cut lip and the red mark around it.

Susan looked chagrined then, and nodded. Warren chose that moment to groan and start to stand. Christian turned, grabbed him up by two handfuls of his shirt, and literally dragged him through the house. At the front door, he heaved the smaller man up so that they were face to face. "Don't ever touch her again. You hear me? Or I swear to God I'll break you in half." With that he shoved Warren backward through the open door. Warren fell to the ground, then got up as quickly as possible and hurried to his car. Christian slammed the door, then walked back to Susan's room. She was sitting on her bed, with tears on her cheeks.

"I'm sorry," she said as he walked into the room.

"Bullshit," Christian said softly. He sat down on the bed, gathering her into his arms. Susan leaned heavily against him, her tears coming again.

After a few long minutes, Christian moved to lean against the headboard, pulling her with him. He held her, her head resting against his chest, her tears mingling with the hairs there. Christian stroked her hair with one hand, his thumb brushing near her temple.

"What happened, Zan?" he asked softly.

Susan was silent for a long moment, then began to tell him, her voice muted because she didn't lift her head from his chest. "At first everything was okay. We were talking about things—school, Joe and Randy, stuff like that. Then after you walked by he started kissing me and trying to touch me. I knew we shouldn't do anything here, but… he was insistent. I didn't want to be difficult, since he and I haven't, well, you know, in a long time…" She trailed off as she gave him a chagrined look. Christian nodded, his eyes twinkling in satisfaction, but he said nothing, wanting her to continue. "Anyway, I guess I wasn't responding the way he thought I should, and he started taunting me, saying I was frigid and all."

Christian laughed at that, shaking his head. "Not hardly, love."

"Well, I don't know, maybe that's just with you…"

"No," Christian said. "He's just not doin' it right."

Susan shrugged, shaking her head. "Either way, he was angry and mean, and it made me angry too. Without thinking I told him that you had never had any complaints about me sexually." She bit her lip then, realizing she was assuming a lot.

"You're right, I haven't and I won't," he assured her. "But I guess that's what set him off, huh?"

"Yes, he slapped me and I fell and hit my cheek."

Christian gave her a long, hard look, then shook his head. "Why would you want to marry a guy like that?"

Susan shrugged, suddenly looking dismayed. "It may not be an issue now anyway, not after what I told him."

"Doesn't give him a reason to lay his hands on you," he said vehemently.

Susan didn't say anything for a few moments, then glanced up at him. "You have to admit, it isn't exactly sporting of me to be engaged to him and sleeping with you."

Christian raised an eyebrow at her. "And I suppose it's bloody sporting of him to knock you around because of his inabilities in bed?"

"No," Susan sighed. "But I'm not being fair to him."

Christian was silent, not willing to argue with her about Warren, because he knew he had no right to tell her to leave the guy. He couldn't understand the kind of commitment she had to Warren, and he didn't care to.

"So you're still plannin' to marry him, huh?" he asked finally, his tone indicating what he thought of the idea.

She nodded. "In three weeks."

"That soon, huh?"

"Yes," she replied, sounding far from enthusiastic. In truth, she was resigned to the fact that marrying Warren was the wisest thing to do at that point. She knew Christian would never love her, and that she was just involved in another hopeless crush that would go nowhere. It was just like when she'd had a crush on Joe; she'd known he was in love with Randy and that she never had a hope in the world of anything happening. And now she had a crush on Christian, a man whose mantra was "I don't believe in love, never have, never will." She'd begun to wonder if it was some fear of commitment on her part that kept her wanting men she couldn't ever have. It was one of the subjects she'd studied in psychology. It was as if actually being in love with and committed to the same man was too hard for her to handle. Instead she picked impossible relationships that would never go anywhere. She thought she'd solved it with Warren, and she had, until Christian Joseph Collins had turned her head with his movie-star looks and his exciting ways. Now she was lost once again in hopeless desire, and she knew she had to stop. Marrying Warren was how she planned to do that.

Christian didn't question her any further, not really sure if he really didn't care or if he just didn't want to hear her reasons. He knew that he cared about her far more than he was comfortable with. The feeling of sheer rage that had welled up in him when he saw Warren standing over her that evening, and then again when he saw the bruises on her face, had been almost blinding. He'd wanted to kill the man. He'd controlled himself because he was still mindful of his precarious position in America. He was well aware that his feelings of protectiveness over Susan came directly from the closeness they'd shared in bed. He wanted to think it had everything to do with the sex and nothing to do with the discussions they'd had or the things he'd shared with her that he'd shared with precious few others.

He continued to hold her late into the night, eventually lying down and pulling her back into his arms. He knew she was feeling guilty about their relationship. He wondered if she'd stop seeing him as a result. Christian half hoped that would be the case. If she refused to sleep with him, or avoided him all together, it would make things much simpler for him. He could get her out of his system once and for all.

He had no idea that the decision would be more or less taken out of both their hands. Two days after the night Warren hit Susan, Christian was working in Devereaux's office when he was blind-sided by a furious, light-brown-haired Englishman. Rick charged him, knocking him to the floor with one well-placed powerful punch. Christian glared up at the older man, wanting to tell him that it was very un-lieutenant-like of him, but Rick was not a cop at that moment. Christian saw in Richard Debenshire the gang member he had been years before, in his stance, in the set of his jaw, in his very being. Christian wasn't sure what he'd done to warrant the attack, but he was very aware that it would go a long way to further convince Devereaux of his ongoing estrangement from Joe's friends. As it was,

Devereaux jumped to Christian's defense.

"Whoa, Debenshire!" he yelled, standing up from his desk.

"Stay outta this, Devereaux," Rick said.

"Like hell I will. You just assaulted a citizen in my presence, Lieutenant. I don't fucking care who your wife is—that's a firing offense." Devereaux's eyes glittered with barely contained hate and glee.

Rick narrowed his eyes at Devereaux as Christian got to his feet, wiping the blood from his lip with the back of his hand.

"You okay, kid?" Devereaux asked solicitously. Christian nodded, narrowing his eyes at Rick as if he wanted to hit him back. In truth he did, but he knew playing the wronged individual was the way to go right now.

Rick's glance jumped between the two men, then settled on Christian. Christian knew Rick had made a connection there, and he was worried that he would say something to blow the whole thing. To distract him from his thought, Christian sat on the edge of his desk and shot him a condescending look. "You still hit pretty hard for an old guy," he said.

"Yeah?" Rick retorted, his voice harsh with barely contained rage, his deep blue eyes flashing dangerously. "You ever hit my niece again, and I'll fucking show you how hard I can hit, Joe's cousin or not."

So that was it, Christian thought. Knowing he needed to use this turn of events to his advantage, he sneered at Rick. "If she knew her place, there wouldn't be a problem, but she keeps crawlin' into my bed—what can I say?"

81

"You son of a—" Rick snarled, stepping forward and raising his arm. Devereaux jumped in, attempting to push Rick back, his mouth going a mile a minute.

"Get outta here, Debenshire, or I'll write the fucking report myself and personally make sure you get canned as well as being brought up on charges. And even Chevalier won't be able to help you on this one!"

Rick's stare shifted to Devereaux, even as he easily swept aside the other cop's hands. "Don't touch me unless you wanna end up on that floor," he said, his face a mask of antipathy. He looked back at Christian and said, "You an' me, we're gonna tangle, and I guarantee you, you won't win." With that he turned and walked out the door.

Devereaux turned to Christian, his expression incredulous. "What'd you do to piss him off?"

Christian shrugged. "His bitch of a niece was raggin' at me, mouthin' off. I slapped her—big deal."

Devereaux nodded understandingly. "Damned women, can't ever manage to keep their traps shut and their legs open." He laughed at his little joke, and Christian laughed with him, all the while wanting to bust the guy in the mouth.

They went back to work after that, but Christian noticed that Devereaux started talking more freely about his "side business." That was the day he found out about the IA guy, McCaffery, being in on the whole thing. Christian knew that bit of information was important, and he felt if he could just find out who their connection was he could go to Midnight with it. He wasn't sure how this whole thing with Susan was going to affect things, but he knew one thing for sure. He definitely needed to stay away from Susan now. He decided that he'd go home that evening and get some stuff. He figured he'd stay with Tara if nothing else.

He found out later that Rick had gone to take Susan to lunch. That was when he'd seen the bruises. When Susan had been slow to tell him who had inflicted them, Rick had assumed it was Christian. Rick hadn't understood why Susan had insisted on staying at Joe's with Christian when Warren had offered to let her move in with him. It was inconceivable to Rick that clean-cut, all-American Warren could have hit his niece. He'd left in a rage and gone straight down to confront Christian.

Christian didn't see Susan again after that. He knew she'd ask too many questions about things he couldn't talk about yet. So he got his things together and moved in with Tara. Tara was happy for the company, and it had long since been established that Tara's daughter, Tabitha, adored Christian, much as Kat had.

Christian suddenly felt cut off from everything and everyone. Tara was the only one he was able to be honest with anymore, and she was the one to get him through the hellish two weeks that followed. He had to distance himself from everyone, including Jeanie. He didn't want to take a chance that Devereaux would figure out that he was being played. Christian was very aware of the fact that he was playing a dangerous game, but he knew the outcome was important. If he could help catch the men that had threatened the lives of two family members then he felt he would be vindicated of his attempt to kill his own father. In a way it had become a mission to make things right and pay Joe back for his generosity. Christian fully intended to make full restitution to his cousin and his family, and then some.

After about two weeks, Jeanie couldn't take the tension between her and Donovan anymore. He'd been quiet and reserved, and they had spent a lot less time together. He'd been going on more night raids with his narcotics unit, and he claimed to be "tired" on the weekends, *all weekend*. Jeanie knew she had to say or do something.

One morning he was driving her to the academy; her car was in the shop for maintenance. She waited for him to say something, and when he didn't she finally spoke up.

"Are we ever going to get back to normal?" she asked plaintively.

Donovan didn't reply, just looked over at her like he wasn't sure why she was asking.

"Donovan," she continued, "I wasn't trying to hurt you. Why can't you understand that?"

He'd turned back to the road by this time, and he didn't look at her as his eyes narrowed. "I don't know, Jay—maybe constant rejection by my girlfriend is too hard for me to comprehend."

"I wasn't rejecting you!" she said, exasperated now. "I told you I care a lot about you, I'm just not ready to say those words yet. I want to be sure…"

"Uh-huh," Donovan said, nodding. He reached over and turned the radio up, effectively ending the conversation. He had a Van Halen album on, and one song ended and another began—"Why Can't This Be Love?" Donovan shook his head as he sang with relish, glancing over at her a number of times.

When the song ended Donovan saw that Jeanie was watching

him with a raised eyebrow.

"What?" he asked, not able to suppress the grin that came to his lips.

"Convenient timing on that, huh?" she said, her tone lightly accusing even as she smiled.

He shrugged. "Hey, it's on the tape. I didn't make it up."

"Mmhmm…" she said, nodding. Her eyes softened as she reached over to touch his hand on the gear shift. "I just want to be sure, Donovan," she said gently.

"What's it gonna take, Jay?" he asked softly as he pulled up to the academy.

She shook her head. "I don't know, maybe just time."

Donovan nodded, not saying anything for a long minute. Then he turned his hand over, taking hold of hers. "Don't worry, I'm not going anywhere," he said, looking right into her eyes. "And I'm not letting you go anywhere without a fight."

She smiled. "No, huh?"

"No, huh," he said, and leaned over to kiss her softly on the lips.

Later that morning, Donovan was in a briefing when to his surprise Jeanie's academy class filed into the room. He acknowledged her presence by raising an eyebrow at her and giving her a half-grin, then turned his attention quickly back to Rick, who was leading the raid being discussed.

Jeanie's class had been doing a sight tour of the department and the various units. When the training sergeant had heard there was a raid briefing in progress, he'd asked Midnight for permission to attend. She'd given it, knowing Rick wouldn't state anything confidential in the presence of any uncleared persons.

Midnight had been working almost constantly after Joe left, and Rick knew she was anxious to put away the criminals that had run her partner off. He understood it, but he didn't have to like it. He had been leading numerous raids with a team Midnight had put together. Donovan was on that team with her other highly trusted officers—Tiny, Spider, Dave Dibbins, Jessica, Kana—and Midnight had added three SWAT members that she also trusted: Clancy, Simmons, and Manning. They were hitting a number of houses with the intention of smoking out their shooters and the driver of the van. They'd long since established the man driving the van was not one of those who had shot Donovan; they'd received eyewitness accounts of the van driver, and he was described as Mexican. Now they were looking for clues to his whereabouts, through his old affiliations.

As Rick talked about the layout of the house, Donovan continued to take notes. He, like the rest of the team, was dressed casually, and that feeling prevailed in the briefing room. Most of the team had been together for years and knew each other very well.

Jeanie watched in fascination, having never seen Donovan actually on the job as an officer before. They'd worked together on "the case," but he'd never done the actual enforcement part of it. He was sitting sideways in his chair, one jean-clad leg stretched out, his foot resting on another chair. His sandy-brown hair fell across his forehead as he wrote notes on his pad. He looked very intense, clearly concentrating on Rick's plan.

"Donovan," Rick said at one point.

"Yeah?"

"You up to full strength yet?"

"Yeah." Donovan nodded.

"Been cleared at the range?" Rick narrowed his eyes slightly, his mind working through his plan.

"Qualified day before yesterday," Donovan said, sitting back in his chair. "Five points under a perfect score."

"Show off," Spider muttered next to him.

"Jealous," Donovan replied with a grin, garnering laughs from the rest of the team.

Rick looked at Spider, his lips twisted in mock disgust. "What'd you expect, he's Sinclair's brother-in-law." Joe was legendary for his perfect scores at the range.

"Got any other sisters?" Dave Dibbins piped up, looking hopeful.

"Sorry," Donovan said. "But I do have a brother that's still single if Jess is interested."

"She's not," Tiny put in menacingly, even as his eyes glittered with humor.

"Hold on a minute here," Jessica said, holding up her hand and grinning mischievously. "Does your brother look anything like you, Donovan?"

Donovan started to laugh, as did the rest of the team, while Tiny started to nod, giving his wife a sour look. "I see how it is…"

Rick laughed too, but quickly got the meeting back on track. "As I was sayin', I want Donovan on the entry team."

"Front or back?" Donovan asked, all business again.

"Back, with Clancy and Simmons. I want the front entry team to have really good backup on this one."

"So what does that make us?" Spider muttered, then looked pointedly innocent when Rick's gaze fell on him.

"Old," Rick said, his eyes narrowed, his face stern, but then he started to grin at the openmouthed reaction he received from Spider and Dave Dibbins. "I know you guys know your stuff on this, I just remember distinctly how often we get fucked—er, sorry, messed up—on these with a bunch of shooters and no decent backup."

"Tell me about it," Spider said, poking Dave in the ribs.

"I'm never livin' that down, am I?" Dave said, shaking his head ruefully. It was well known among the members of FORS that during the service of a search warrant almost ten years before, Dave had been Spider's backup and Spider had been shot.

"Not likely," Rick put in.

When the briefing broke up half an hour later, Donovan made his way over to Jeanie, who was talking with the rest of her class. "Fancy meeting you here," he said, bending his head to talk right next to her ear.

Jeanie turned around, looking up at him and grinning, mindful of the people watching. She knew that many members of her class were jealous of her connections with the department, and she knew they thought that was how she'd gotten in. They were wrong; her connections had helped her while in the academy, but she'd had to pass the same tests the rest of the recruits had. She was currently in the top five percent of the class, and that was grounds for a lot of envy as well. This time it *was* thanks to her connections. Donovan and she had had many discussions about ethics and procedures; he'd also told her what his training sergeant had told him about allowing suspects to keep their dignity, thus avoiding a lot of fights. That particular piece of advice had proven very helpful during her ride-alongs, garnering her great assessments by her training sergeants. Her test scores were higher than many of her classmates' as well, but that had a lot to do with being a member of a law enforcement family. She knew the penal code pretty well without studying; with studying she'd mastered it easily.

Now, looking up at Donovan, she couldn't help but grin. Things between them seemed better already, and they'd only talked that morning. She was glad—she hated having tension between them.

"What're you doing for lunch?" Donovan asked warmly.

"Looks like we'll be here," she said, looking at her watch; it was 11:30 a.m.

"Think you could stand to have lunch with me?"

Jeanie smiled. "Oh, I might be able to handle it." She had to resist the urge to reach up and kiss him; he looked so good, and he seemed so much more compelling to her at that moment.

"I'll pick you up out front," he said, once again leaning down close to whisper in her ear.

Half an hour later they were on their way. In the car, Jeanie looked over at him. "You're different at work," she said simply

Donovan glanced over, his brow furrowing. "You've seen me at work."

"Yeah, but not as a real-life cop getting ready for a raid."

"Oh... sorry."

"Don't be sorry, it was interesting—you're just different, that's all. I'd actually love to see you in action."

"You would, huh?" he asked pensively. "What're you doing around two o'clock? Didn't you say you were off this afternoon?"

"Yes, the training sergeants have some meeting to attend. Why?"

"Wanna come on the raid?"

"Can I?" she asked, her eyes showing her excitement.

"I can ask Rick, and you'd have to stay way back…"

"I know, I know, but it would be cool to see how these things go down." She saw him smile and shake his head. "What?"

"I just like the way you talk," he said.

"Yeah? And how would that be?"

Donovan grinned. "Like a cop."

They talked about the raid plan while they were at the restaurant. That was when Jeanie remembered something that had been said in the briefing.

"So why didn't I know you were back to full strength?" she asked, sounding slightly offended.

Donovan looked at her for a long moment, then shrugged and gave her a lopsided grin. "I'm not totally, but I was able to qualify, and that's what counts."

"Five points under perfect?" she asked, sounding disgusted. "You call that 'able to qualify'?"

Donovan laughed, then gave her a pointed look. "Jealous?"

"Hell yes!" she replied, grinning. "Okay, next question—how come Jess was interested in Darrell and not you?"

"She wasn't interested in either of us."

"I know that, but how come you said Darrell was still single, and not yourself."

"Because I'm not single," he said, taking a bite of his salad.

"Well, you are, I mean literally speaking…" She held up her left hand and wiggled her ring finger.

"I know," he said, giving her a look she didn't understand. "To them I'm taken, though."

"Why?"

"Because they like who I'm taken by—they think you're right for me."

"Versus…"

"Versus Serena," he finished for her. "Or any of the other girls I've dated."

"Oh… and they've met the other girls you've dated?"

"Yeah," he said matter-of-factly. "Jay, I've known most of those people since I was about seventeen. I've spent a lot of time with them, at work and otherwise. They've seen 'em come, and they've seen 'em go."

"And they didn't like Serena, huh?" Jeanie asked, her eyes twinkling happily.

"Nope."

"Either time?"

"Nope."

"Why?"

"Because she wasn't a cop-type girlfriend."

"But you weren't a cop the first time," Jeanie pointed out.

"No," Donovan said, grinning at her quick deductions. "But she competed with me all the time, and in the end she wanted me to be something I'm not."

"A chef."

"Right."

"So what's different this time?"

"You."

"What makes me different?"

"You're a cop—you understand cops. That makes the difference."

"What if Serena suddenly developed an understanding of the cop mentality?"

"They still wouldn't like her."

"Why not?"

"Because she isn't you," Donovan said, looking directly into her eyes.

"Ah," Jeanie said, then grinned rakishly. "So I've ruined ya, huh?"

"Yep," Donovan said, grinning back.

They talked about other things for a while, and then the conversation turned to Christian.

"So what do you think about this stuff with Blue?" Donovan asked.

"I think he has bad judgment in friends."

"You're his friend."

"Some of his friends."

Donovan nodded. "Uh-huh."

"Just because he's friends with Devereaux doesn't mean he's dirty too, Donovan."

He shook his head. "I don't know…"

"Midnight trusts him."

"She did," Donovan said. "And even she's not infallible."

"He's not involved," Jeanie replied firmly.

"Have you talked to him lately?"

"No—why?"

"How long's it been?" Donovan asked.

"About two weeks."

"About the amount of time we know he's been buddying around with Devereaux. It actually looks like it started around the time Joe left."

"So?" Jeanie said, her tone a little more defensive now. Christian was her friend, even if Donovan didn't understand it.

"So," Donovan repeated, his voice softening a little, "he may be involved, Jay. I don't want you caught in the crossfire." He wasn't trying to make her mad, just aware that Christian might not be what he appeared.

"Blue's been down in Devereaux's office since right after Randy got out of the hospital. Isn't it possible that Blue's just being friendly?"

"Friendly? Blue?" Donovan's expression and voice indicated he didn't think the two words belonged in the same sentence.

"Yes," Jeanie said sourly. "Is it possible he's doing some UC work for Midnight on the case?"

"If he was involved, I'd know about it," Donovan said confidently. "You just may have to face the fact that Blue has a criminal background and that now that Joe's not around to keep an eye on him, it may be resurfacing."

Jeanie shook her head, unconvinced. Christian was her friend and she wouldn't believe he was capable of working with the men who had tried to have both Donovan and Randy killed. It wasn't him.

After lunch, they went back to the office. Donovan got permission for Jeanie to attend the ride-along. Rick gave her a very stern look. "But you stay well back from the whole thing, you understand?"

"Yes," she said, nodding seriously.

An hour later they were outside a house in South San Diego. Jeanie stood with the rest of the team as they put on vests, checked ammunition, and loaded new clips. Donovan walked over; he wore a bulletproof vest under a navy blue windbreaker with *POLICE* written on it in large yellow letters. He was carrying his gun, having just slid the clip into place. Reaching up, he holstered the weapon. "You know where to stand, right?" he asked, his tone all business. She nodded, understanding that this was serious business. "Okay," he said, giving her a stern look. "You stay there till one of us signals you that it's okay to come in. Alright?"

She nodded again. "Okay."

Clancy joined them, nodding politely to Jeanie; he'd met her a few minutes before and was aware that she was a cadet at the academy as well as Donovan's girlfriend. "You ready, Curtis?"

"Yeah," Donovan said, doing another quick check of his ammunition clips.

"Mount up!" Rick called, and everyone headed toward their spots.

Jeanie watched from the vacant lot in back of the house. Donovan held up a hand to the two men behind him. She could see that he was listening for the knock and notice to be given, as well as Rick's radio signal to hit the door. A moment later he dropped his left foot back, then brought it forward and kicked the door open with one powerful strike. With guns in hand, he and the SWAT members moved inside. There was a lot of yelling and orders being shouted. Jeanie could hear calls like "Let me see your hands!" and "Down on the floor, now!", and others in the team yelling "Clear!" as the room they were checking was secured.

She saw a young man come running out the back door Donovan and his team had gone through. He wore only faded jeans, and he had a plethora of tattoos all over his upper body. He turned and leapt down the back stairs, then took off in the direction of the vacant lot Jeanie was standing in. Just as she was wondering if she should pull her weapon and order the man to lie down, Donovan came charging through the same door. He vaulted the railing, hitting the ground running. Donovan's long strides enabled him to catch up to the fleeing man easily. He threw himself forward, tackling the young man and taking him to the ground. The man struggled, but he was no match for Donovan's strength; Donovan simply increased his pressure on the man's wrist until his struggles subsided. Keeping one knee placed squarely in his back, Donovan reached for his handcuffs and slapped them on the man's wrists.

Finally, Donovan stood and hauled the kid up off the ground.

"Where were you goin'?" he asked.

"Out for a smoke," he replied arrogantly.

"Yeah?" Donovan countered. "Well, tell you what, if you can manage it, you can smoke on your way to jail."

"Fuck you!" the young man spat.

"No thanks," Donovan said evenly. "I'm into women." His eyes trailed over to where Jeanie stood about three yards away. "One in particular." With that he turned and led the kid back to the house.

Jeanie didn't see him again for another half hour, when she was cleared to enter the house. He was standing with Dave Dibbins when she walked in. She noticed that he was moving his left shoulder around gingerly.

"You okay?" she asked as she walked up to him.

He looked down at her with a grin. "Yeah, just overdid it a little bit."

Rick joined them, nodding to Jeanie then turning to Donovan. "How does it look?"

"Pretty good," Donovan replied. "We got three parole violations, four of the guys on the warrant list, some serious hardware, not to mention a couple thousand in cash, and two pounds of meth."

"Good haul," Rick said with a nod. "Garcia on that list?"

Donovan nodded even as he double-checked the list in his hand. "He was my runner," he said, gesturing toward the young man now sitting in the corner.

Rick smiled. "Good catch." He turned and walked toward Garcia.

It took another hour to clear up the details of the warrant, and then Jeanie and Donovan headed back to his house. Once home, Donovan went to take a shower. Jeanie sat on his bed and waited for him to get done. When he came out of the bathroom twenty minutes later, he wore only a pair of gray sweatpants. Jeanie's eyes were drawn to his chest and arms. "How's your shoulder?" she asked, remembering he'd said he'd overdone it.

"Hurts," he said simply as he lay down on his stomach on the bed, his head right next to her legs.

"A lot?"

"Not too bad."

She turned so she was facing his side. She smoothed her hand over the muscles on his back, her nails grazing his skin.

"Mmm…" Donovan practically purred, "That's very nice…"

"Yeah?" she said, sliding her hand down from his shoulders to his waist and up again.

"Keep that up and you'll find out…" he said, his voice muffled by his arms.

"Is that a threat, Sergeant?"

"It's a promise, Cadet."

"Yeah, yeah, promises, promises," she chimed.

Donovan surprised her by turning over and pulling her down to him. His teal eyes stared up into hers.

"I've missed *being* with you," he said.

"I've missed *you*," she said, her expression serious.

"I'm sorry, I guess I've been sulking."

Jeanie didn't reply. Instead, she leaned down and kissed him gently on the lips. "My fault too," she said softly.

"Yes," he said just as softly as he moved to kiss her.

They didn't talk anymore; he really didn't want to, and she wasn't ready to either. They kissed for a long time, as if starting from the beginning again. After a while, Jeanie kissed his neck, his chest, and then moved back up to his lips. Donovan turned onto his side, his hands at the buttons to her shirt. When they were undone, he pulled her body close to his. Jeanie's breath quickened at the feeling of his skin against hers again. When he began to tug on the button to her pants she stood, obligingly removing all of her clothes. Donovan watched her, his eyes on hers, a grin tugging at his lips.

Before Jeanie could rejoin him on the bed, he sat up. He drew her close to him again, pulling her head down so he could kiss her. He slid his hands up her body, caressing. Jeanie's hands moved from his shoulders into his hair, pulling him ever closer to deepen the kiss. After a few minutes, he rested his head against her chest, his lips just above her breast. Her hands urged him on; his lips grazed her skin, leaving a warm trail across and down her breasts. She gasped as his lips touched her erect nipples, driving her half mad with desire.

"Donovan…" she groaned, holding his head against her because she couldn't take any more. Without warning, she pushed him back on the bed, lying over him.

He grinned. "What're you doing?"

"Attacking you," she said simply, then looked at him pointedly. "Got a problem with that?"

"Not really, no," he said, giving her a meaningful look.

She moved down his body, kissing all the way, pausing at the waistband of his sweatpants. Slowly, almost painfully so, she removed them.

"Jay…" he said, his voice a groan.

"Yes?" she replied innocently.

"Babe… I need you," he said, his voice so low, so husky that she couldn't hold back the shiver of excitement that ran through her.

"Yes," she said, nodding as she moved over him, her voice soft but confident. "Yes, you do." With that she moved her body down over his, sliding easily over him, making him groan in pleasure.

They made love, taking the time to enjoy each other again. Eventually he moved to lie over her, taking her to all new heights with his lips and his body. She cried out over and over, almost making him lose control, but he was determined to show her that she needed him too. He proved his point. By the time he allowed himself to reach his climax, she was clinging to him, begging him to stay with her, no matter what.

Donovan felt a great warmth spread over him as he lay next to her that day. He knew he was right about her—he knew she was the one. He was looking at her when she opened her eyes.

"What?" she asked, seeing something she didn't understand in his eyes.

"Nothing," he said, his voice taking on a mysterious tone.

"Donovan."

"Jeanie," he replied easily.

"Tell me what you were just thinking."

"No," he said simply.

"Please."

"No," he said again, grinning.

She gave him a dirty look, but didn't move out from under the leg and arm he'd thrown over her possessively. They were stretched out crossways on the bed, and after a while he shifted them both so they lay properly. As he settled next to her again, leaning over to kiss her shoulder, the phone rang.

"Ugh," he groaned, reaching across to pick up the phone. "Yeah? Oh, hi, Chief. What's up?" He looked down at Jeanie with a grin.

He listened for a minute, nodding, then said, "Okay, what time?" He nodded again. "Okay… I'll see you then." He hung up.

"What was that about?" Jeanie asked.

"Midnight wants to go down to Mexico tonight."

"Tonight?" Jeanie asked, sounding disappointed.

"Yeah, babe, she thinks she has a lead on Randy's hit and run guy."

"Oh," she said, understanding the essence of time. "How long will you be gone?"

"Three or four days," he said, looking into her eyes. "Will you miss me?"

"Maybe…" she said playfully.

"Maybe?" He gave her a long kiss. "I can fix that."

"Yeah, how?"

"Like this…" he said, and kissed her again. After a long while they made love again, as if they weren't able to get enough of each other. They fell asleep for a few hours afterward.

CHAPTER 4

That day at the raid, Rick had received the tip they'd been waiting for from Garcia. He was a gang member who had run with the shooters' old gang. Garcia had told Rick he'd heard that Emilio had headed for Mexico and was hanging out in Mexicali, where he had family. Rick asked Emilio's last name; Garcia wasn't sure, but he thought it was Benitez. Midnight had the name run through everything she could. They found out that Emilio Benitez was part of an IA investigation on Tiny, that he had claimed police brutality. Midnight wasn't sure what that meant—whether or not someone from IA was involved, or if Benitez just had a beef with cops and a smart cop had used it to his advantage. When she told Rick she was going to Mexico herself, he just about fell out of his chair.

"Like hell you are!" he said, his deep blue eyes flashing.

Midnight looked back at him, her face composed. She waited until he calmed down a little bit, then grinned. "And who else should I send?"

"I'll go," he said matter-of-factly.

Midnight laughed. "And how much Spanish do you speak?"

"That's not the point," he replied hotly.

"And how do you talk to Mexicans who don't speak a word of English?"

"Midnight…"

She grinned. "Richard…"

"Take me with you then."

"And who'll watch the bad guys for me while I'm gone?"

"Someone else."

"Rick," she said, giving him her sweetest begging look, "what if I took Donovan with me—you trust him, don't you?"

Rick looked disgusted for a moment, but finally nodded. "Alright, but you damn well better be careful."

"I will."

"When'll you go?"

"Tonight."

"*Tonight?*"

"I wanna get there before the little dirtbag has a chance to know I'm comin'."

He grinned. "Go in under the cover of darkness, huh?"

"That's the idea."

Later that night Rick sat on their bed watching her pack. His deep blue eyes followed her from their bathroom to her bag, to the closet and back, and then to her dresser and back. Midnight looked up, grinning. "Don't you have anything else to do?"

"Nope."

"Swingin' life you got there, Debenshire," she said. She raised an eyebrow at him. "What else do you do for fun—watch paint dry?"

"I do not equate watching my incredibly beautiful, sexy wife to that type of mind-numbing recreation," he said haughtily, his grin still intact.

"Uh-huh." Midnight nodded. "Don't get out much, huh?"

"Funny."

"Thanks!" she replied brightly.

"Hey," he said, his voice softer.

She glanced up from her packing. "What?"

"Come 'ere," he said, his voice lowering an octave.

"Why?" she asked suspiciously.

"Just come here," he said, his words measured, his eyes on hers.

She walked over to the bed, looking down at him. In one fluid move he pulled her down and into his arms, his lips claiming hers instantly.

After a long kiss she pulled back, looking up at him. "I see," she said, grinning. "Long cruise, sailor?" she asked, raising her eyebrow at him again.

"Ten minutes without you is too long, love," he replied seriously. "How long did you say you'd be gone?"

"Three, maybe four days." She made no move to extricate herself from his embrace, having no desire to do so.

Rick rolled his eyes, shaking his head.

"Oh, you'll survive," Midnight said. "If I can get back sooner, I will," she added, seeing his doubtful look.

"You better."

"Yeah, yeah," she said, grinning again.

Rick leaned down to kiss her gently, then nuzzled her neck with his lips. "I love you," he said into her ear.

"I love you too," she whispered back, closing her eyes as his lips traveled down her neck. "Rick…" she said, her voice already filling with longing. She felt his grin against her skin. "Richard…"

"What, love?" he asked innocently, as if he couldn't fathom a problem.

"I gotta meet Pony in an hour—I'm not even packed yet… oh…" she said as his hands slid under her shirt. "God," she gasped, feeling his fingers brush her breasts. "God, don't do this to me," she said, far from stopping him.

After a few more minutes, she sighed, dropping her head against his chest. Moments later he felt her lips on his bare skin; his shirt was open. Minutes later they were making love, and Midnight knew, but didn't care, that she was going to be late. Afterward he lay on his side next to her, one hand propping up his head while he lightly stroked her skin with the other.

"You are such a bad influence," she said, still a little out of breath. Their sexual encounters were always nothing if not earth-shattering. They shared a very physical attraction to each other.

Rick grinned unrepentantly. "I know."

"Does your mother know what a bad boy you are?"

"Only you know how really bad I am," he said languidly.

She smiled. "And I'll never tell."

"Problem solved."

"There was a problem?"

"Not for me."

"I see…"

"Do you, now?" he asked, his eyebrow raised.

"Yes, sir."

"Good girl."

"Woof," she replied, making him laugh.

He looked at her seriously then, his index finger on her chin. "I love you, and I want you to be careful down there."

"I love you, and I will," she said, then saw the concern in his face. "This isn't my first trip into the field, you know."

"I know, but I won't be there to watch out for you."

"I'll have Donovan," she reminded him. "You know, 'Sure-shot' Curtis?" He'd told her about Donovan's range scores.

"Yeah, yeah, I know."

"Okay then."

"Okay then."

After a few more minutes of lounging in bed, Midnight reluctantly got up to take a shower. "Call Donovan for me and tell him I'll be about an hour late."

"Yes, ma'am," Rick said sarcastically.

"Hey, it's your fault I'm late, Sergeant. Just make the call," she said jokingly.

An hour later she pulled up in front of her old house in Pacific Beach, the one Donovan was renting from her. Donovan came out and put his bag in the trunk.

"Sorry I'm late," Midnight said, grinning lasciviously.

"No problem, *Chief*," Donovan said, stressing the fact that he'd have no place to question her.

"It was the lieutenant's fault," she said, pulling back out onto the road. Donovan nodded, amused.

Everyone who knew Rick and Midnight knew they were crazy in love with each other and that the spark in their marriage had certainly not died. Donovan had also heard about short staff meetings because "the lieutenant" had made eye contact with "the chief" one too many times. Joe had told him about that one. Very few people actually knew why those staff meetings were cut short, only the couple's very close friends. It didn't affect the ability of either of them to do their jobs as cops or as ranking officers, so Donovan had nothing but respect for them both. He also had a healthy desire to have what they had some day. He wondered if Jeanie was the one… He thought she was, but her constant caution with her feelings made it impossible to know for sure.

"So how're you and Jeanie now?" Midnight asked, as if reading his thoughts.

"Okay," he said, but Midnight detected the hesitation immediately.

"What happened?" she asked, worried.

"Nothing *happened*. I just made a mistake, that's all."

"What kind of mistake?"

"Telling her I love her," Donovan said, his tone forcibly light.

"Ouch," Midnight said, immediately understanding. "She didn't reciprocate, I take it."

"Nope," Donovan replied, trying to look less morose than he

felt.

"What *did* she say?"

"She said she wasn't sure, that she cares a lot about me but she's not sure about love."

"Sounds familiar," Midnight muttered.

"How so?"

Midnight looked at him for a long moment, as if gauging what she wanted to say. "That's about what I told Rick once."

"Really?" Donovan asked incredulously.

"Yeah, really," Midnight retorted, then smiled. "He was a little too much for me at first, more than I could take."

Donovan considered her words for a moment. "Was that because of Joe?"

"No, it was because I was used to being in control of everything around me all the time. Rick made me feel out of control. My feelings didn't make sense—they were too hot and cold, and I couldn't control them. I didn't like that too much."

Donovan considered that for a long moment, then shook his head. "I don't think that's Jeanie's problem."

"Why not?"

"Because it's not the same... I mean, we're not..." he said, trying to qualify what he was saying but not wanting to be rude. "We're not like you two, I mean."

"Oh, really?" Midnight narrowed her eyes in thought. "How would you classify Jeanie? Dependent or independent?"

"Independent, definitely."

"Okay, is she the emotional type or the think-things-through type?"

"Second one," he answered easily.

"Would you say she likes to be in control?"

"Of the relationship?"

"No, of herself, her emotions."

"Oh yeah."

"That's me," Midnight said seriously. She gave him a measured look. "I'd say you're very intense, very masculine, obscenely good-looking, and hard to resist. Like Rick."

Donovan smiled at her assessment, inclining his head in appreciation, but then gave her a pointed look. "But controlling?"

"Did it drive you crazy to let her go the first time?"

"Yes."

"Did you want to take her and shake some sense into her when she went with Blue?"

"Yes."

"Do you hate it that you can't make her say that she loves you?"

"Yes."

Midnight smiled broadly, shaking her head, then gave him a sidelong glance. "Want to ask me that controlling question again?"

"No," he answered simply, easily seeing her point and realizing again how sharp she was. Her degree in psychology certainly wasn't going to waste. "Okay, so you win—we're a lot like you and Rick, in some ways. Do you think that's what's happening with Jeanie? That she's afraid to lose some sort of control if she commits to me?"

"Maybe, but then again, maybe she really doesn't realize she loves you. It took Rick getting shot and almost dying to get it through my thick head."

"I was shot," Donovan pointed out.

"But that was real early in your relationship. That was probably just too overwhelming for her then."

"She did say it was really a lot to deal with at that point…" he said, thinking back to the conversation.

"See."

"She said she needed time."

"And maybe that's all it will take, but don't give her too much room—your feelings count here too."

"So what if she takes too much time, and how do I know what's too much?" he asked plaintively.

"If she tries to back out on you again, it's too much."

Donovan nodded. "That's true. She didn't really want to totally back out last time, but I was a hard-ass and told her I wouldn't date her."

"I think you were right. You got her back, didn't you?"

"Yeah, after Randy got in a car accident."

"But she was there for you—that's what counts."

"Yeah…" He nodded. "But what about now? What if she's decided she's done her good deed and seen me through?"

"Knock it off, Curtis." Midnight gave him an almost dirty look. "You've got so much more going for you than being a charity case. That's not why she's back with you, believe me. She wants to be with you. You just gotta give her enough time to buck up and admit the truth to herself."

"And if she doesn't?"

"You force her hand, tell her it's all or nothing. That you can't spend your life waiting for her to get her proverbial shit together."

"And if she leaves?"

"If she leaves, Donovan, she's nuts and she doesn't deserve you," Midnight said with so much vehemence he couldn't help but smile."

"Okay," he said simply, shaking his head at her clarity of thought as well as her instant defense of him. "So…" He grinned and looked at her as if for the first time that evening. "How are you, Midnight?"

Midnight laughed. "Couldn't be better."

For a while they talked about things in the office and around the department. Eventually the conversation made its way to Christian's activities.

"You think Blue's working the other side?" Donovan asked, curious about her view on the matter.

"I think he's walking a fine line," she said, nodding. "But I don't think he's really involved."

"Rick does though, doesn't he?"

"Rick still thinks Blue hit Susan," Midnight replied sourly.

"And you're sure he didn't?" Donovan asked skeptically.

"I think Blue's a lot of things, but a woman beater is not one of them. Besides," she said with a shrug, "Susan swears up one side and down the other that it was Warren, and that Blue actually came to her defense."

"So how come Blue didn't defend himself when Rick went after him?"

"Who knows," Midnight said, still seething a little bit about the whole thing. "Maybe he still has some misplaced loyalty to Joe and doesn't want to get into a knock-down drag-out with Joe's best friend."

Donovan nodded, then gave her a pointed look. "Think it could be anything else?"

Midnight looked over at him contemplatively. "You thinking he might be working Devereaux?"

"I didn't think so at first, but Jeanie's staunch defense of him got me to wondering. And now hearing about this thing with Rick, and him not fessing up to his rescue of Susan versus actually attacking her... It makes me wonder if it didn't have something to do with a little show for Devereaux's benefit."

Midnight nodded, thinking it over. "Yeah... makes some sense, doesn't it?"

"In a way..."

"It'd have to be that damned Sinclair blood in his veins," she said, rolling her eyes.

Donovan laughed. "Or we could be totally wrong."

"Do you really think so?"

"Not really, no."

After that, the conversation took a different direction, and the rest of the trip to Mexicali passed quickly. They arrived in two hours and found a hotel and checked in. Agreeing to meet first thing the next morning, they went to their rooms.

The next day was an exercise in frustration. Donovan and Midnight went to the Mexican *policía* headquarters to see what they could find out about Emilio. They didn't have a lot to go on, but they had the police sketch that Rick had had made using the description given by the young man Donovan had caught. Unfortunately, Benitez was a fairly common Spanish surname. It was a slow process even with Midnight's accent-perfect Spanish. The man they were dealing with didn't like women anywhere outside of the home where they apparently belonged. Since Midnight's credentials not only designated her as a peace officer but also as the Chief of Police of one of the largest departments in the United States, that didn't really help matters any. Donovan spoke very little Spanish, and most of that poorly accented, so he wasn't much help.

After two hours of wasted energy, Midnight finally became irritated enough to make a move to go over the man's head. "*Dondé está Moncarro?*"

"*De vacaciones,*" the man said, irritated that she was asking about his superior.

"When will he be back?" Midnight asked in Spanish.

"*Mañana,*" he replied shortly.

Midnight nodded. "We'll be back tomorrow," she said, her tone no-nonsense even in Spanish.

"As you wish," he said in broken English. He was happy to be done dealing with this *juerita* with the cat eyes, but worried about what she'd say to his chief the next day.

"Who's Moncarro?" Donovan asked as they walked out to Midnight's Corvette.

"Chief of Mexican police," Midnight said, shrugging. "I met him a few years back. He's easier to deal with. Less hang-ups about women belonging beneath him, literally." Her eyes glittered dangerously. Donovan knew the man they'd been dealing with for the last two hours had sorely tested her patience.

"If it makes you feel any better," he said, grinning, "I respect you."

"Yes, but will you in the morning?" Midnight asked, laughing. Donovan laughed too.

Later that day they were having lunch in a local cantina. The conversation eventually turned to Rick.

"Is everything between you two okay now? I mean..." Donovan trailed off as he realized he may be overstepping his bounds, asking such a personal question.

Midnight waved away his apparent chagrin. "Pony, you and me, we don't just work together—we're family too. You can ask me anything. You should know that by now. But what specific crisis were you referring to?" she said the last with a self-conscious grin.

Donovan laughed. "Well, I meant since the baby, you know..." He trailed off again, but this time Midnight knew it was because he didn't want to say "abortion." She appreciated his tact.

"Things were pretty rocky for a while there, but they're okay now. It was mostly my fault it was so hard on both of us."

"How so?" Donovan asked, picking up his Corona.

"I was being a bitch," Midnight said simply.

"You? Never," he said, his tone serious but his eyes glittering with humor.

"Watch it, Curtis," Midnight said, mockingly dangerous. Then she grinned. "No, I really was just going through it alone and blaming him for making me do it in the first place."

"I didn't think anyone could make you do anything," Donovan said, shaking his head. "But I guess Rick's different, huh?"

"He does have an effect on me, yes. But in this case he got Mikeyla involved, and when she begged me not to have the baby for fear I'd die in the process, what could I say?"

Donovan nodded, understanding her point. He could also tell she wasn't really comfortable talking about the whole thing, so he turned the conversation in a different direction. "So how are you since Joe left?"

"I miss him like hell," Midnight replied. "But I'm doin' okay. How are things for you? You miss Randy?"

"Yeah," Donovan said, looking melancholy.

"You still pissed at Joe?"

"I want to be, but how can I be mad at someone who's thousands of miles away?" His voice told Midnight he really did want to still be mad at Joe.

"Pony... You know he was just doing what he thought he needed to to protect them," she said, her voice softening. "He loves her, and he sees it as his job to take care of her."

"I know," Donovan said, but he didn't sound totally convinced.

Midnight looked over at him, her lips pursed in thought, but she said nothing. She glanced to her right, noticing a small boy watching her closely. He looked about five years old, with big brown eyes and long, thick lashes.

"*Hola*," she said softly.

"*Hola*," the boy replied quietly.

"*Dónde está tu mama?*" she asked, wanting to know where the boy's mother was.

"*El baño*," he said, looking surprised that a lady who was obviously American spoke Spanish so well.

Midnight nodded. "*Ah, sí.*"

Donovan watched the exchange, only recognizing some of the words. He could see that the little boy was awed by Midnight. He understood that easily enough. He'd known Midnight for nine years now and was still amazed by her combination of beauty, strength, and intelligence. Donovan had always admired her abilities with people. Midnight Chevalier could make anyone comfortable. She could get on anyone's level; whether they were a United States senator, a professor of law, a street cop, or a five-year-old boy, she could get there and make them comfortable. Now, watching her talk to the boy, he saw her the way many before him had—as a people person with a lot of guts, but nice as hell too.

A few minutes later a young woman returned to the nearby table, sitting down with the boy. The kid whispered to her, pointing over at Midnight. She looked over at Midnight and smiled.

"My son says he thinks you are very beautiful," she said, her English heavily accented.

Midnight smiled, looking at the little boy. "*El niño es muy guapo*," she said, inclining her head to him, her eyes sparkling. The boy giggled and smiled, his brown eyes shining brightly.

"What did you just say?" Donovan asked.

"I said that he is very handsome."

They were just finishing their meal when a man walked into the cantina. He was short but stocky. He looked around and then stalked over to the young woman with the boy. He had a full mustache and a red bandana around his neck. He was also glowering angrily at the woman. He began speaking to her in rapid Spanish.

It took Midnight a moment to catch up to what he was saying. He was berating the woman for being at the cantina and for bringing their son there. He went on to tell her that she belonged at home in the kitchen. The woman quickly explained that she was there because she knew he'd be there that afternoon and she needed to talk to him about this job of his. She lowered her voice then, and Midnight couldn't make out everything she was saying. She heard a few words, like "*carro*," "*trabajar*," and "*mátalo*," but couldn't really pick up anything else. Realizing she was eavesdropping, she pointedly turned back to Donovan. It was at that moment that the man raised his arm as if to backhand the young woman.

Quicker than lightning, Midnight was out of her chair and striding toward the other table. Donovan followed her, but only as backup.

"Hey!" Midnight yelled to distract the man from his apparent course of action.

His head snapped up. His eyes narrowed, his lips twisting in disgust. "Stay out of this, puta."

Midnight raised an eyebrow at him. "You kiss your mother with that mouth?" she asked in Spanish.

"I kiss a lot of bitches with this mouth," he replied, still speaking in heavily accented English, as he drew himself up to his full height of five foot eight inches.

Midnight nodded cynically. "I'll just bet you do." Her voice dripped sarcasm, even in Spanish.

"You don't want to fuck with me, *juera*," he said, his eyes glittering dangerously, as he realized the entire bar was watching now.

"No, huh?" Midnight replied evenly, her eyebrow raised once again. Her stance was anything but subservient or intimidated.

"*Puta*," the man practically spat. "Your man needs to teach you a lesson—he should put his foot in your ass more often. But I will assist," he said as he strode menacingly toward her.

Midnight didn't back up or even flinch, and when Donovan made a move as if he were going to intervene she shook her head slightly to warn him off. The man reached Midnight, grabbing her arm and pulling her toward him. She waited until their eyes connected, waited for that moment when his expression changed. She'd been around men like him long enough to know there was a very fine line between anger and heated passion—she and Rick walked it often enough. This man did absolutely nothing for her, but she could see it wasn't mutual. The moment he weakened the slightest bit, she brought her knee up, connecting solidly with his crotch. She then brought her left hand up and through to break his hold on her arm, her wedding ring effectively slicing his forearm in the process. She stepped back as the man doubled over, cussing acidly. He said words Midnight had never even heard before.

The man recovered faster than Midnight had expected him to, but she was ready all the same when he launched himself at her from a half-crouch. Again she waited that extra couple of beats until his plunge was irreversible, then jumped out of the way, bringing a booted foot up to catch him in the face. He fell to the floor with a thud.

Not even winded from the exchange, Midnight looked around at the attentive faces surrounding them. She shrugged one delicate shoulder, her face passive.

"*Tengo un problema con la violencia contra las mujeres,*" she said calmly. Then she turned and walked out of the cantina, leaving half of the crowd stunned, the other half laughing. She also left behind one very grateful young woman and a young boy who was sure he was in love.

Donovan looked around for a moment, then shook his head and shrugged as if to say, "What can I say?" He followed Midnight out of the cantina and found her outside, leaning against the hood of her Corvette, waiting patiently for him.

"What did you just say?" he asked, leaning on the fender next to her.

She grinned impishly. "I just said that I have a problem with violence against women."

"I'd say," Donovan said, grinning back. "So what was she saying to him that got him so mad?"

"I don't know for sure. She was saying something about his job being murder and something about a car. Who knows?" She shrugged. "Maybe he's a coyote smuggling aliens across the border. It's not my problem till they cross over."

As Midnight stood up, the young woman walked out of the cantina with her son beside her. She came over to Midnight, her hand extended.

"Thank you," she said in English. She looked back at the cantina. "Julio is very angry sometimes."

Midnight nodded. "I know how that can be." She looked at the little boy again and smiled. He was staring up at her with his big brown eyes.

"*La señora es muy fuerte*," he said.

"*Usted también va a estar fuerte*," Midnight said, saying he'd be strong someday too. The boy grinned, holding up a small arm and flexing it as if to show off his muscle. Midnight laughed, as did Donovan and the boy's mother.

"My name is Marta," the woman said. She indicated the boy. "His name is Ricardo."

"I'm Midnight, and this is Donovan," Midnight said, then looked at the boy again. "My husband's name is Ricardo too," she said in Spanish. Then she turned to Marta. "Well, it's actually Richard—he's English, so I guess it wouldn't translate as directly," she said in English.

"It is nice to meet you both," Marta said, furtively looking up at Donovan. She thought he was very handsome, but had assumed he was Midnight's husband. They did make a nice-looking pair. "Well, we must go. Thank you again for what you did." She took Midnight's hand in hers, her brown eyes, like her son's, looking into Midnight's. "No one else would have stood up for me. I'm certainly not brave enough to stand up for myself."

Midnight nodded. "You're welcome. Just take good care of yourself and this little guy. In fact…" She opened the car door and reached into the glove box, pulling out a card. She handed it to Marta.

"If you ever need anything, or think you'd like to get away from him, call me."

Marta's eyes grew wide as she read Midnight's rank and title as Chief of Police. She looked back at her with renewed respect. "Thank you," she said, sounding a little awed.

Midnight smiled, then reached down to touch Ricardo on the cheek. "*Pórtate bien*," she said, telling him to be good.

The little boy smiled, nodding enthusiastically, then held up his arms to her. Midnight knelt, gathering him in a hug. She felt his little arms around her neck, felt his little hands pat her hair. She didn't know that he would always remember her pretty face and her soft hair, and that she even smelled pretty. It did warm Midnight's heart to have earned such a warm gesture from him. When she stood up, she had to blink back tears as she thought of the child she'd given up.

Later that night, Montavo Marquez heard endlessly about the beautiful American that had come to the rescue. Ricardo talked about Midnight incessantly. He told Montavo, his uncle, that Midnight was married to a man with his name, and that he hoped someday he'd marry someone like her. Montavo smiled and nodded, listening to his nephew and glancing at his sister. He was pleased to hear that this woman had intervened in the fight between Marta and Julio. He knew that his sister had suffered a number of beatings at the hands of her husband. He didn't like Julio, and he knew the man was into things he shouldn't be, but he couldn't convince Marta to leave him.

Marta had gone to school in the States and Ricardo had been born there, by design; Marta wanted to make sure he was an American citizen. She had dreams of sending him to college in the United

States one day. Marta wanted her son to become a very important man and have the life she had never really had. Montavo loved his sister dearly and hoped she could make her dreams come true. But even at eighteen, Montavo knew the way of the world, and people like them never really made it; they were just trash under the rich man's feet. He was very impressed with what Marta had told him about this American woman; he'd never heard of a woman having so much courage, as well as skill in fighting.

That evening, after Ricardo had gone to bed, Marta and Montavo talked over coffee. Marta pulled out the card Midnight had given her, showing it to him proudly. Montavo looked at it for a long moment, and his almost-amber eyes widened as he read the name and rank. He looked up at his sister, his expression grave.

Ricardo lay in his bed listening to his uncle and mother talk. He thought again of the beautiful lady he had met that day. He remembered how soft her voice was, how well she spoke Spanish, as if she weren't an American at all. He hugged the memory to him, sure he would never see her again but happy to have met her. He tried to hear what his mother and uncle were saying, but it was no used; they'd lowered their voices.

Across town in a hotel room, Midnight sat on the bed, phone clutched in her hand. She had dialed her home number and was waiting for Rick to pick up.

He answered after the third ring. "'lo?"

"Hello," she said softly.

"Oh, it's you," Rick said, his voice warm and close.

"What're you doing?"

"Lyin' here tryin' not to think of you."

"And why is that?"

"When are you comin' home?" he asked, ignoring her question.

"A couple of days yet."

"That's why."

"I see." Midnight nodded. "Miss me already, huh?"

"Yes, I do."

"I miss you too, babe," Midnight said, her voice soft, almost a caress.

"Don't talk to me like that," he said, his voice suddenly husky.

She grinned. "Sorry."

"So how's it going?" he asked, smiling as well.

"Okay. Well, actually, not okay. We basically wasted today."

"How?"

Midnight proceeded to tell him about the man at the Mexican police department and his apparent opinion of women.

"You should've kicked his ass," Rick said.

Midnight grinned. "Well, I ended up doing that later to someone else..."

"What?" Rick said, his protective side surfacing instantly.

"No big deal," Midnight said, waving away his concern, even though he couldn't see her. She told him about Ricardo and his mother and about their exchange between the two tables. Then she explained about the man and what had happened between him and the young woman, and the man's subsequent actions.

"And of course you had to get involved, right?" Rick said, knowing her well.

"Duh," Midnight said, then told him about the confrontation, about the mother coming out of the cantina and thanking her, and finally about Ricardo giving her a hug.

"Uh-oh…" Rick said, smiling.

"What?"

"Another young man jaded for life."

"What's that supposed to mean?" Midnight asked, her tone indicating her raised eyebrow.

"Just that you've ruined him for all other women now. He's gonna want to grow up and marry someone like you."

"Not if he had to live with me though."

"Bullshit," Rick said, not willing to let her push aside the compliment. "I know how lucky I am," he said seriously.

"As lucky as me," she said, her tone softening.

"I love you," he said, suddenly feeling bereft.

"Love you too." Midnight knew that if she'd been at home he'd have kissed her at that moment. She found that she missed him desperately. She missed his arms around her, his body next to hers, the scent of his cologne, the feeling of his hair brushing her cheek as he bent his head to kiss her. "Rick…" she said longingly.

"I know, babe, I know," he whispered, lying in their bed over a hundred miles away.

"Pretty pitiful when we can't be away from each other for more than twenty-four hours, huh?" Midnight said, grinning self-consciously.

"It's not pitiful." Rick shook his head. "It's called love—maybe you've heard of it," he said playfully.

"Something about it, I believe," she said, her voice lightening again. He was always able to bring her out of her reverie. "Maybe I can manage to wrap this up tomorrow," she said, her voice becoming normal again.

"If you can, you can—I know you wanna catch this guy, so don't rush on my account. I'll be here when you get back," he said, his grin evident even over the phone.

"Good," she said, smiling. She changed the subject then, moving on to something she'd been thinking about since the cantina that day. "Rick, I've been thinking about something… and I want to get your view on it."

"Okay."

"Well… hugging that little boy today made me start thinking about another baby again—but I know we can't do that," she added hurriedly as she sensed his instant tension. "But I was thinking about… well, about adopting."

Rick closed his eyes, relieved that she was finally thinking about another way of attaining the baby she wanted. "Night, yes—why do you sound so hesitant?"

"I wasn't sure how you'd feel about it. I mean, with your parents and all…"

"Midnight, my parents want me to be happy."

"And would you be if you adopted someone else's child?"

Rick was quiet for a moment. "Would it make you happy?"

"Rick," she said, indicating she knew he was avoiding the question.

"Would it make you happy?" he repeated. "Would it fill this need you have to have another child?"

"I think it would, yes."

"Then yes, it would make me happy."

"Simple as that, huh?" she said, her tone showing her disbelief.

"Night, I want you to be happy. I can't make that happen without endangering your life, and I won't take that chance again. If adopting a child would fill that need, then that's what I want to do."

"But there's more to it than that, Rick."

"Midnight," he said, mildly reproachful. "You think I don't know that? In fact, I know everything that is involved in adopting a child. I spoke to my father about it a few weeks ago. He told me about all the paperwork and red tape and interviews with social workers and shit like that. Hell," he said, grinning now, "I could probably tell you a thing or two about the process, Chief."

"I see," Midnight said, curling her lips in a sardonic grin. "And you did all this and didn't tell me…"

"I wanted to give you time to get over the baby," he said softly.

Midnight nodded, knowing she was probably the luckiest woman in the world at that moment. He knew her so well—he knew when to back off, when to give her time. It was something that she valued greatly about their relationship. They knew each other inside and out; he always understood what she needed, as she did for him. It was knowledge hard won, and they'd fought for every second of happiness they had, but it was worth every tragedy, every heartache.

"You're something, you know that?" she said.

"Mmhmm." He sounded unconvinced, but was enjoying the closeness they were sharing, even if it was over a phone line.

They talked for another hour, finally hanging up when he sensed her getting sleepy on him. She promised she'd call the next night.

Midnight didn't call; instead, Spider and Tiny showed up at the Debenshire home, unannounced. Rick opened the door to them wearing jeans and a blue shirt with no shoes. He held a beer bottle in his hand, and wore a grin. "Don't tell me they both threw you out?" he said when he saw the look on their faces, referring to Tammy and Jessica.

Spider shook his head even as Rick stood back, gesturing for them to come in. Rick preceded them into the living room, glancing back as he did. His brows furrowed as he realized how tense they both were.

"What's goin' on?"

"Rick..." Spider began, his voice trailing off as he shook his head, as if to clear it.

"Spider, what's going on?" Rick asked again, subconsciously tightening his hand on the beer bottle.

"Okay," Spider said, putting his hands out in front of him at waist level, palms down—a gesture Rick knew was the man's way of centering himself. That was what made him apprehensive. "Rick, there was a car bomb. It was in Midnight's car..." He trailed off as all the color drained from Rick's face. Rick nodded numbly, swallowing convulsively and praying he didn't know what he was about to hear.

He stared at Spider, watching him talk, seeing the words he mouthed and feeling them hit him like knives. "Rick, she's dead." It was three simple words, but they managed to drain all of the strength out of Rick's body instantly.

Rick sank to the floor, sitting with his back against the couch. He clenched the bottle tightly in his right hand. He stared straight ahead of him, but it was obvious he wasn't seeing anything at that moment. His knees were up to his chest, his arms draped over them. He looked as if he was having trouble catching his breath. In truth, he couldn't think of anything but one phrase that kept screaming in his head: "She's gone!" The fact that his body knew how to function without conscious thought was a good thing, or he would have died on the spot.

Everything stopped at that moment for Rick. His life ended. He started thinking how unfair it was that they'd just been getting things back together since the baby and now… Rick didn't even flinch when the bottle shattered and cut an inch-long gash in his hand. Spider and Tiny moved quickly to remove the shards and wrap his hand in a cloth. Rick didn't even seem to notice; he was in shock. Every so often he would close his eyes for a long moment and silent tears would slide down his cheeks. Spider and Tiny took up places in the living room, knowing it was going to be the worst night of all of their lives.

Jeanie was at her parents' house, sitting in the living room with her brother when the news break came on the television. She stared at the TV in stunned silence as the dark-haired reporter spoke.

"The law enforcement community has been rocked by the death of one of its own tonight. Details are sketchy at best at this time, but we understand that two officers from the San Diego Police Department were in Mexico on a case. One officer is confirmed dead; the other has been critically wounded. The department is not releasing the names of the officers until their families can be notified."

Jeanie's blood ran cold. *Confirmed dead?* she thought. *The other critically wounded...*

All she knew was that she needed to find out what was happening, but suddenly she couldn't think clearly. She stood up and blindly made her way to her room, thinking she'd go to Mexico to find out for herself who was dead. She knew she couldn't call anyone—how do you ask if your boyfriend was the one that was dead? Who do you ask a question like that?

Either way, the news was awful. The idea of Midnight being dead was unthinkable... yet the thought that it could easily be Donovan... The tears started then. She felt sick to her stomach. When she finally came out of her room, her brother, Juan, was in the hallway waiting for her.

"Where do you think you're going?" he asked quietly.

"I've got to go down there, I have to know..." she said, her voice halting at the thought of saying she needed to know if Donovan was dead. She couldn't even think the words.

"I'll drive you." Juan knew his sister well enough to know she wouldn't be talked out of going.

A half hour later, Jeanie sat in the passenger seat of Juan's Monte Carlo, her mind swirling. She forced herself to face the fact that Donovan could be dead, and that even if he was the one to have survived, he could still die before she got down there to see him.

"What will I do..." she said, thinking out loud.

"It'll be okay, Jeanie," Juan said, putting his hand over hers reassuringly. "He'll be okay."

"He could be dead right now." Jeanie shook her head, as if trying to deny the thought. "God..." She looked up, as if to God himself, feeling awful. "I thought last time... when he was shot... I thought that was the worst I'd ever feel. But that's... this is worse." She looked at her brother again. "What if I've really lost him this time?"

Juan glanced over at her, seeing the devastation in her eyes and knowing what she hadn't yet realized herself. She loved Donovan Curtis, whether she wanted to or not.

Christian was in Devereaux's office that evening, finishing up for the day. He was just standing to leave when Frank's phone rang. Frank picked it up and listened a moment. He nodded a couple of times, then said, "Great." He hung up, a Cheshire cat smile on his face. "Case closed," he said smugly.

"What?" Christian asked, having no clue what the man was talking about.

"Chevalier's dead." Devereaux sounded jubilant. Christian couldn't hide his shock. He hadn't known they'd been planning a hit on Midnight.

"Hell, we might even have gotten Curtis this time," Devereaux continued, oblivious to Christian's shock.

Christian thought to nod, but couldn't begin to form any falsely gloating words. "Gotta go," he muttered, and all but ran out of the office to his car. He peeled out of the parking lot and careened toward the bar in Pacific Beach. Once in the lot, he sat staring into space.

Shit, shit, shit... was all he could think. Midnight was dead. Jesus. Joe's partner... his cousin's best friend... the woman who had trusted him from day one... Jesus...

Throwing open the door, Christian climbed and out and strode inside. He went up to the bar, ordered a double tequila shot, and told Tara to keep them coming.

He got well and truly drunk that night, and got into two fights in the bar. He ended up lying in Tara's car, waiting for her to get off work. She drove him back to his apartment, and he managed to make it to her bed before he passed out cold. He spent the next two days that way, unable to cope with the fact that he'd aligned himself—albeit to smoke them out—with the people who had killed Midnight Chevalier-Debenshire. Jesus...

Joe was fast asleep when the phone rang next to him. He groaned, and Randy turned over, muttering, "Didn't we move away from these late-night calls?"

Joe grinned as he reached over. "You can never move too far away, love." He picked up the phone, ready to ball Midnight out royally for forgetting the time difference again.

Spider said, "Joe?"

"Spider? Hey man, what's up?" he asked, assuming Spider had no clue about the time difference either.

"Joe... it's Midnight."

"What did she manage to do to herself this time?" Joe asked lightly. In his sleepy state he hadn't picked up on Spider's tone.

"Joe, man... she's dead," Spider whispered.

"She's what?" Joe sat up, praying that he'd heard Spider wrong.

"She's dead, man. Killed, murdered, the bastards got her." His voice broke on the last part, tears flowing down his cheeks now.

"Oh, Jesus…"

Randy heard the anguish in his voice and sat up immediately, touching his shoulder.

"Look, Joe, can you come?" Spider asked, his voice almost desperate. "Rick's really hangin' on to the edge here."

"Yeah…" Joe said, thinking as he did that he didn't know how much help he'd be. "I'll be there."

He hung up a few minutes later, looking absolutely blown away.

"What happened?" Randy whispered.

"Randy… God…" Joe shook his head, not sure he could repeat Spider's words. The tears in his eyes glistened in the semi-darkness.

"Is it Midnight?" she asked. Joe nodded. "Is she…" Randy began, her breath catching in her throat.

Again Joe nodded, pulling her to him, clutching her tightly as he gave way to the tears he'd been holding back. Randy cried with him, not believing this was possible.

"I have to go there," Joe said, his voice ragged.

"I know," Randy said.

"Spider says Rick's not doin' too well."

Randy nodded. "You go—we'll be right behind you."

Joe looked pensive for a moment, but Randy gave him a stern look. "I need to be there, Joe—if nothing else, for you."

After a long moment, Joe nodded. He could only imagine how

131

hard it was going to be in San Diego.

Joe left to catch the Concord an hour later. Randy planned to follow him the next morning with the children on a regular flight. She had no idea that Donovan had been involved in the explosion that had killed Midnight. She found out the next day, when Darrell called her. She changed her passage to the Concord and was headed to the States two hours later.

Jeanie was directed to the Mexicali General Hospital. All the Mexican police officers on the scene could tell her was that the Americans had been taken there. They didn't know who was dead. It was still mass confusion at the site, and no one seemed sure of anything.

Jeanie walked into the hospital and up to the main desk. She asked the nurse there about the officers that had been brought in. The nurse asked if she was family; Jeanie said that she was and identified herself as a police officer as well. The nurse nodded and called the doctor over.

The doctor walked up to Jeanie; he was short and stocky, and he had a thin mustache and very kind eyes.

"Sir," Jeanie said, after the doctor introduced himself as Rene Garcia. "I need to know, the officer that was brought in, the one that was alive—is it a man or a woman?" She knew she sounded ridiculous, but she had to know.

The man did look at her like she was crazy, but after a few moments his face softened. "It's a man, and he is doing well."

Jeanie couldn't believe the relief that flooded her body. The stab of guilt, however, was almost as intense. It wasn't Donovan, but, my God, Midnight was dead.

"Can I… Can I see him?" she asked, her voice breaking.

The doctor gave her a gauging look, then nodded. "Come with me."

He led her to a far-off wing of the hospital, explaining they'd put Donovan there to keep the press away. Jeanie nodded, but could barely think straight.

The room he walked into was larger than she'd expected, and nicer. She had no way of knowing that the chief of Mexican police had arranged the room personally, feeling the need to lend comfort to the remaining American officer in his country.

Donovan lay on the bed, his eyes closed. He had many small cuts on his chest and arms; there was a bandage around the lower half of his torso, and another on his forehead.

"He has a number of cuts," the doctor said, looking at his patient. "There's some muscle injury to his back, including some severe bruising to the tissue. He also has a concussion."

"But you said he was doing well," Jeanie said, almost accusingly.

"He is, considering the way he came in." Jeanie gave him a look, prompting him to explain further. "He was thrown through a shop window in the explosion. The shattering glass had cut him in so many places, he was covered with blood when he came in. He was unconscious and not responding to stimuli. At first we thought his back was broken. Yes, I'd say he's doing well."

Jeanie nodded, only able to imagine Donovan covered with his own blood. She shuddered at the image it conjured up. Moving to the side of the bed, she reached out and brushed his hair aside with light fingers. His eyes fluttered open.

"Hi," she said softly.

His expression was serious, his eyes searching her face. "She's dead, isn't she?" he asked softly.

Jeanie swallowed against the lump in her throat as she nodded slowly.

Donovan closed his eyes, his lips tightening in a painful grimace. "Damn it..." he whispered, pressing his head back against the pillows.

"Donovan, there was nothing you could do," Jeanie said, wanting to comfort him.

He opened his eyes and looked at her cynically, but he didn't argue. In truth, he didn't have the strength.

Jeanie stayed at his side for the next two days. Juan showed up the first night, taking her out into the hallway to tell her what he'd learned. Midnight had apparently been killed in the initial blast, and Donovan had been caught by the explosion of the gas tank. It was true that if Donovan had been out there with Midnight at the time of the explosion, he would be dead as well. He had been lucky.

After two days in the hospital, Donovan insisted on going home. Midnight's funeral was scheduled for the next day and he fully intended to be there to pay his respects. The doctor didn't want to release him, but Donovan was adamant. Finally the doctor relented, telling Jeanie that Donovan needed to rest and to check in with his doctor once back in San Diego. Jeanie promised they'd do that.

As Juan Franco drove out of town, Donovan lay in the back seat, his head cradled in Jeanie's lap. He hadn't said much in the past two days; Jeanie knew he was torturing himself for what had happened to Midnight, but she didn't know what to do.

The days after Rick was told about Midnight's death were one long nightmare punctuated by events. The first was the night he was given the terrible news, when Mikeyla returned home from an evening at a friend's house. She knew there was something wrong the minute her friend's mother pulled into the driveway. There were four other cars there besides her father's Mustang.

Mikeyla headed for the living room, seeing all the people gathered there and nodding to them. She could tell by the looks on their faces something was definitely wrong. She found her father where he had sat for the last four hours, on the floor with his back to the couch. She saw the bottle of tequila he held, the blood-soaked cloth around his other hand, and the devastated look on his face.

She dropped to her knees in front of him. "Daddy?" she said, reaching for his injured hand. He shook his head, as if telling her not to worry about it. "What is it?" she asked. His gaze shifted to her face, his own taking on a pained look.

"Daddy?" Mikeyla said, her voice sounding so much like a little girl's again.

"Keyl…" he said, not wanting to tell her what he had to.

"Is it Mom?" she asked.

Rick nodded, closing his eyes for a moment as if trying to gather strength.

"She's okay, right?" Her voice trembled, her eyes begging him to say yes.

Rick could barely breathe as he shook his head. "No, baby, she's…" His voice caught, and he could only shake his head again.

Everyone in the room shuddered at the shriek that tore from the young girl's throat as she threw herself into her father's arms. Tears that had finally dried from hours of crying began again as they all witnessed the anguish of a child losing her mother.

"No, Daddy, no!" Mikeyla cried, shaking her head against her father's chest.

"I know, Keyl. I know..." Rick said, holding her tightly and rocking her.

No one could believe Midnight Chevalier was actually gone. The thought was too unthinkable—after all she'd come through, to have her life cut short so viciously. It was not to be believed.

Joe arrived the morning after her death. He was told that Rick had passed out after drinking most of the night.

"He wouldn't eat, he wouldn't sleep," Jessica said. "He refused to go to bed—he said he couldn't sleep there knowing she'd never be there with him again." There were tears in Jessica's eyes as she said it. She couldn't even fathom that thought; it was too devastating.

Joe nodded, desperately holding back the tears that came to his eyes every time he allowed himself to think about the fact that Midnight was actually dead. He looked over at his lifelong friend. Rick was lying on the couch, his hand still curled around the empty tequila bottle. He shook his head, knowing things were going to get much worse.

Things did get worse. Rick's parents arrived later that afternoon. His mother walked over to her son, who now sat on the couch, still staring into space like a zombie. He'd barely talked to anyone; he'd hugged Joe and had a few words with him, but there wasn't much to say at that point. When Anabelle saw her son, she was aghast. He looked as if he were dead. All his color was gone, his eyes staring absently, his face set in such a grim line it hurt her to see it.

Anabelle sat next to him, touching him under the chin as she had when he was a child. She turned his face to hers, searching his eyes. Rick looked back at her for a long moment, almost as if he didn't recognize her. Then, in slow motion, he leaned toward her. Anabelle's arms went around her son, and she held him, much like Rick had held Mikeyla the night before. That was when the flood gates burst. Rick cried and sobbed, holding on to his mother for dear life.

"They killed her, Mom, they killed her," he said desolately. "She's gone. Oh, Jesus, she's gone..." He trailed off as the tears continued to pour out of him. Anabelle cried right along with him. Many of the people in the room—Jessica, Tammy, Spider, Dave Dibbins, Tiny, and even Joe—had to leave; it was too painful to watch or hear. They knew they were watching Rick fall apart, and there was nothing they could do to stop it.

The following day Joe wandered out onto the beach. Anabelle had asked him to find Rick and keep an eye on him. Rick had been talking about not being able to go on, not wanting to. He'd asked his father the night before about he and Anabelle taking Mikeyla back to England with them, if something should happen to him. Anabelle was terrified that her son was thinking of taking his own life. Joe thought she might be right.

Walking down toward the shore, Joe spotted his friend easily. Rick sat alone on the sand a couple of feet from the water. He wore the same jeans he'd had on two nights before, but the shirt was different. Anabelle had removed the blue one he'd been wearing when she'd arrived, the same one he'd had on the night he'd heard about Midnight—there was still blood on it, and Anabelle had to goad him into putting on a new one. It frightened her to see the utter state of shock her son was in; in many ways he was barely functioning.

When Joe walked up, he saw that Rick held a bottle in his hand, now a permanent fixture. Joe knew he was trying desperately to numb the pain; he also knew it wasn't working.

"Hey," Joe said, sitting down next to Rick.

Rick glanced over, his eyes bleak and bloodshot. "Hey," he replied, his voice gravelly from disuse.

They sat together for a long time, neither of them talking, each thinking his own thoughts.

"We let her down, you know," Rick said eventually. He was looking out at the ocean, his deep blue eyes narrowed, his brown curls blowing in the light breeze. He didn't see the pained look that crossed Joe's face. He'd been thinking along the same lines.

"Yeah," Joe said quietly.

"She counted on us," Rick went on, looking thoughtfully at the beer bottle in his hand, then tossing it angrily out into the ocean. "She counted on us, and we let her down."

Joe didn't answer; he couldn't—the lump in his throat would hardly let him breathe, let alone talk. He'd been thinking about it since the night he'd gotten the call. He was Midnight's backup, always had been. But when things got too hot, he'd run. He'd left her, abandoned her. When she'd needed him most, he wasn't there. Now she was dead. The thoughts kept repeating over and over in his head; he couldn't shut them out. He'd talked to Randy about it the night before. She'd tried to help. In the end she'd held him and cried with him. In a way she felt guilty too; she knew she shouldn't have let Joe take them to England, but she'd done what she thought was right at the time. She knew she'd never forgive herself for playing a part in the guilt that Joe was feeling at that moment. She knew it was her fault too.

Everything was so awful, and Randy knew it was taking a double toll on Joe. He was devastated about Midnight's death, and yet he was trying to be there for Rick too.

"You know," Rick said, his voice softer, "I never thought I'd love a woman so much. So much that losing her would tear my heart out." His voice choked up as he swallowed against his constricting throat. "God, Joe, I don't know if I can do this. I don't know..." He trailed off, shaking his head dismally.

Joe nodded, putting a hand on Rick's shoulder. "I know, man, I know. But we gotta do this, we gotta get through. She'd want us to."

Rick looked over at Joe, searching the other man's eyes. Then he nodded slowly. Joe wasn't sure if he was accepting what he'd told him or if he was just acknowledging Joe's own anguish.

That evening, Rick received a package special delivery. The return address was Mexicalipolice, but Spider, who had had some training with the bomb squad, carefully checked it all the same. Finally he handed it back to Rick to open. When Rick did, Spider began to wish someone else had done it. In the package was a small box and a note of condolence from the Chief of Police in Mexicali. In the box was Midnight's wedding band and engagement ring. Rick stared at them, remembering the significance of the other times he'd held those rings in his hand. After a full minute he slowly closed his fingers over them and walked down the hall to his and Midnight's room. He closed the door quietly behind him, and everyone still standing in the foyer shuddered at the anguished yell he gave as he flung the rings across the room.

Rick stood breathing heavily, his hands braced against the wall. He didn't want the fucking rings back—he wanted his wife.

"Damn it, Midnight," he said, shaking his head miserably. "How can you do this to me?"

Joe found Rick two hours later, lying on the bed, his face buried in Midnight's pillow. The pillow was wet with his tears. Rick heard Joe come in and glanced up at him. Joe handed him a bottle of beer.

"Your mum wants you to eat something," Joe said.

Rick just shook his head, taking the beer gratefully.

Joe glanced around and saw Midnight's emerald-and-diamond engagement ring. He bent down and picked it up. Straightening, he felt the lump rise in his throat again. He'd begun to wonder if he'd ever feel normal again. He remembered thinking the same thing when his parents had been killed. Midnight had filled that void for a long time. Randy had taken over when they'd married. Now he needed something to fill the void Midnight had left.

When Joe looked up he saw that Rick was watching him. He held his hand out, the ring in his palm. Rick looked at it for a long moment, then slowly reached out and took it from Joe's hand. As Joe watched, Rick slid the ring onto his left pinky. Joe nodded and sat down on the bed next to his friend, his own beer in hand. It was another long night.

CHAPTER 5

The morning of the funeral dawned and Rick dragged himself up. He didn't know anymore if the haze he was in was alcohol or trauma related, and he didn't really care. He'd barely eaten in three days, though he'd consumed enormous amounts of alcohol, none of which seemed to dull the pain. Now the day had come when he had to bury his wife. The thought echoed hollowly in his mind as he went to take a shower.

In the end, Anabelle and Robert had made the arrangements, with the help of Carric, Midnight's mother. Rick had refused to do anything, unable to contemplate the very idea of arranging his wife's burial. There was no body to bury; the Mexican police had indicated to Robert that there wasn't much left of it, certainly nothing that the grieving husband needed to see. Carrie had decided that the remains would be cremated and buried in a marble box at the service.

As Rick dressed, he thought of the funeral he'd gone to with Midnight years before. A young man working with FORS had been murdered; Midnight had been devastated. In the end, however, she'd pulled it together, even lending a great deal of comfort to the parents and brother of the slain boy. He'd been so proud to know her that day, and that was before they'd ever exchanged their vows. He remembered then how beautiful she'd been when they got married. He still carried a picture of her in her wedding gown. They'd been through so much together, and the idea of going on without her made him absolutely numb. His mother had been right to worry about him attempting to kill himself. The thought had occurred to him a number of times over the past three days. It seemed a logical end to the agony. Every minute he spent without her was an eternity in hell anyway.

Rick knew that inevitably people would encourage him to "move on." The thought of having to face the loneliness of their house every night, or see her empty office every day, to hear people's condolences...

His tie hanging loosely around his neck, his shirt half buttoned, Rick went straight to the bar in the living room. He grabbed the first bottle he came to. Ironically, it was the Southern Comfort Midnight had always preferred. Shaking his head, he lifted the bottle to his lips, downing half of it in one long swig, feeling it burn through him. Looking around, he saw Joe sitting on the loveseat, a bottle of tequila firmly in hand.

Joe wore a black suit and a hideously bleak expression. "You ready for this?" he asked, his tone dead.

Rick lifted the bottle in a silent toast. "I will be," he said simply, then drank the rest of the bottle down.

Unfortunately, by the time they arrived at the church, Rick wasn't feeling nearly as numb. Walking down the aisle and seeing the flowers, the wreaths, the picture of Midnight in the navy-and-cream suit she'd worn the day she was promoted to chief, and then the marble box, draped with green velvet... *Oh God*, was all he could think.

There were hundreds of officers in dress uniform. All of them wore black bands over their badges, signifying the loss of one of their own. The service was poignant. Many high-ranking officials in the law enforcement community got up and made speeches about Midnight and her accomplishments. The Attorney General, John Davies, spoke.

"Midnight Chevalier-Debenshire was the best damn cop I've ever met, with more fire in her than ten men," he said somberly. "She was a good friend as well, and I can't imagine law enforcement, or San Diego for that matter, without her here." He shook his head sadly, then walked over to where Rick sat with his hands clenched tightly in his lap. Mikeyla sat next to him, holding her father's arm, resting her head against him too. John Davies knelt down in front of Rick, extending his hand. Rick took it somberly. Davies reached out, touching Mikeyla gently on the cheek, his eyes glistening with tears, then looked back at Rick. "If you need anything, if there's anything I can do, I hope you'll let me know," he said, his voice quiet but sincere. Rick nodded, closing his eyes as a tear slipped silently down his cheek.

After the service they drove to the cemetery. Rick sat stoically in the back of the limousine, his parents and Mikeyla with him. He tried to imagine over and over that this wasn't really happening, that it was all a nightmare.

Midnight was being laid to rest next to her brother in the Greenwood cemetery. Robert Debenshire had checked and found that, as if by some divine intervention, the plot next to Thomas was empty. Robert had bought it immediately. It seemed only fitting for Midnight to be buried next to the brother she'd loved so much, whose death had changed the entire course of her life.

Carrie Chevalier was devastated by her daughter's death. She couldn't believe she had now lost both of her children to violence. It didn't seem fair. She was, however, extremely grateful for the time she'd had with Midnight. Their reunion five years before, however strained, had allowed Carrie to get to know her daughter again. It had given her some time to try to make up for the years of animosity they'd held for each other. They'd stayed in touch since, but Midnight had always been so busy. Now… Carrie cried at the thought.

The service was harder on Rick. He stood with his hands clasped in front of him, his head down. Mikeyla stood at his side, silent tears rolling down her cheeks. A missing man flyover was conducted by Army National Guard Counterdrug unit and Bureau of Narcotic Enforcement pilots, a V-shaped formation of four planes but five positions; there was a lead plane, then positions for two left-echelon and two right-echelon planes. The first right-echelon position was left empty, thus signifying the "missing man." It was a poignant reminder of what had been lost.

There was a twenty-one-gun salute conducted by the department's rifle team. As each of the three shots fired from each of the seven rifles rang out, Rick closed his eyes a little tighter, screwing his face up in silent torment. It was as if they were final nails in Midnight's coffin, an end to everything. By the time the bagpipes began to play "Taps," Rick couldn't take any more. He sank to a kneeling position, one knee on the ground. He wore the most pained expression; there was no question as to how he was coping. Joe knelt beside him, clasping his shoulder and talking quietly. All eyes watched them. Rick nodded, closing his eyes as tears streamed down his cheeks.

When the service ended, Joe stood, pulling Rick to his feet. Everyone made their way past the gravesite as Rick stood staring at the small marble box on the pedestal there. He stayed there when everyone else had filed past and moved off. As he turned to go, he caught sight of two men standing off to one side. His blood began to churn as he recognized Frank Devereaux, the man most likely responsible for Midnight's murder. His eyes widened when he realized it was Christian standing with him.

Without hesitating, Rick charged Christian, knocking him to the ground and pummeling him with flying fists. Surprisingly, Christian didn't put up much of a fight, only raising his arms to protect his head. Rick was in too much of a rage to take notice. Joe and Donovan ran over and pulled Rick off Christian. They had to fight to hold him back.

"You sonofabitch!" Rick screamed. "She trusted you! How could you do this to her?" Many people turned to look in their direction. Dibbins, Tiny, and Spider strode over to stand by in case Joe and Donovan needed assistance holding Rick. But Rick wasn't done yet. "You fucking bastard," he spat, narrowing his eyes dangerously. "I'm going to kill you, and I hope you rot in hell!" He strained against the two men holding him. Tiny and Dibbins stepped in; Spider pointedly got between Rick and Christian, glancing back at Christian and shaking his head slowly, a disappointed look on his face. Joe and Donovan managed to turn Rick around and walk him away. Dibbins and Tiny turned to Devereaux.

"Devereaux," Dibbins said, his voice low and threatening, looking much like his former gang leader self. "If you know what's good for you, you better make yourself scarce."

"Why's that?" Frank asked, lifting his chin challengingly.

"Because we just might let Rick come back here and finish up with you."

"That's why," Tiny said, his mere presence ominous.

With that, the three men walked away.

Christian still lay on the ground. He'd raised his head to look at Rick, but when Spider, Tiny, and Dibbins walked away, he dropped back on the ground, coughing in pain.

Later that day Christian sat on the small terrace outside Tara's apartment. He held a bottle of Jack Daniels; he was working his way through his second. Tara had seen him come in after the funeral. She'd touched the bruise already starting on his cheek and dabbed gently at the blood still on his lip.

"What happened to you?" she'd asked softly.

"The widower," Christian replied caustically. He headed for the terrace, feeling the need to get some air. Tara had brought him a damp towel for his lip and a bottle for his nerves.

Christian had told her everything about Devereaux from the beginning. She knew how agonized he was over Midnight's death. She also knew he thought it was his fault, that he hadn't gotten in good enough with Devereaux to keep it from happening. That was why he had pointedly met Devereaux at the funeral. He wanted to get as close as he could now to make sure no one else he cared about died. He knew standing with Devereaux in front of God and everyone was a blatant act of treachery in the eyes of the people he was trying to protect, but he also knew Devereaux would see it that way too. It would make him more sure about Christian; that was the important part right now.

It worried Christian that Joe was back in town and that Randy and the kids were with him. He'd purposely distanced himself from Susan, Jeanie, and Donovan, as well as from Joe's home, to keep anything from happening there. Of course, he thought angrily, it hadn't kept the bastards from killing Midnight and trying to kill Donovan again. Christian had noted that Donovan was seemingly alright, albeit extremely affected by Midnight's death—but alive, at least. He'd also noticed Jeanie firmly at Donovan's side, and he was happy about that.

Christian wasn't sure what he was going to do at that point. With Midnight gone and everyone sure he was in cahoots with Devereaux and his friends, he had the distinct feeling he would go down for this too. The thought dragged at him; even in his inebriated state the words Rick had spat at him came back. *She trusted you! How could you do this to her?* Tears of anger and frustration stung his eyes. "I'm sorry, Midnight," he whispered, forcing the lump in his throat back down.

He knew the "bastard" of Joe's family would go down in infamy for what they thought he'd done. It hurt more to realize that Joe would hate him too. That he'd think his cousin, who he'd taken in, whose mother he'd saved, had turned on him so viciously. That hurt almost worse than the idea of being arrested, of going to prison or to the gas chamber, which he knew was a real possibility. All the people he had come to care about, who had trusted him because Joe trusted him, would hate him now.

Hell, he thought, *they'll probably cheer when they flip the switch on the electric chair.* Murder of a police officer was a capital offense. But Christian knew his death by the justice system would be long in coming. That meant Devereaux's and McCaffery's deaths would be too…

Christian began thinking about taking Devereaux and McCaffery out himself, doing a little street justice for what they'd done to Midnight. If he was going to go down for the murder of a police officer anyway, he could at least make sure Midnight's killers started their time in hell before he did. One police officer, three police officers, what was the difference? How many times could they execute him for it?

He was starting to plan how he would get the two men together and how he wanted to kill them when someone touched his arm. He figured it was just Tara checking on him again, so he was stunned to see Susan sitting on the window box that led out to the terrace.

He didn't know she'd been watching him for the last five minutes. Tears had sprung to her eyes when he whispered his apology to Midnight. Susan was still reeling from the thought of her aunt being dead.

Christian stared at her as if seeing a ghost from the past. Then his face hardened with a guarded expression, as he realized she might be there to attack him just like her uncle had. He wasn't really ready to deal with her hatred right now.

"What're you doing here, Zan?" he asked harshly, but his version of her name overrode the effect.

"Christian," Susan said, reaching out to touch his cheek gently as she shook her head. "Come inside, please." She took his hand and tugged at it to get him to comply.

Christian did as she bid, too surprised by her manner to argue. He felt a fairly good buzz from the whiskey by this time, so he wondered if he was imagining her concern.

Susan led him to Tara's couch. Christian glanced around, looking for Tara, but she was pointedly absent. Susan pushed him down and then knelt in front of him, searching his face and taking in the bruises and cuts. His light blue eyes were fixed on her, his jet black eyebrows furrowed in confusion. She really did look concerned.

"Zan…" he whispered.

"I needed to see you," she said, her voice so strong it surprised him. "I need to see…" She brushed his cheek with her fingers, pushing his hair back as if to get a clearer view of his face. "I know, Christian," she said, searching his eyes. Christian held his breath for what was coming next. "I know that you had nothing to do with my aunt's murder," she said.

Christian could not believe the relief that flooded through him. It was almost painful, as if a huge wave were engulfing him. Without hesitation he pulled her to him, hugging her close, kissing her temple gratefully. He couldn't put into words the feelings he was experiencing; the best he could do was hold her tight against him, practically clinging to her. They stayed that way for a long time.

Susan had needed to see him to really know if she was right about his innocence. His anguish was so apparent, she'd had no doubt the moment she laid eyes on him. Not that there had been much doubt in her mind in the first place. She knew Christian had respected Midnight, something he didn't do for many women.

"How?" Christian asked, needing to hear everything now.

Susan looked up at him, not moving from the circle of his arms. "Christian," she said, looking at him as if she couldn't fathom why he didn't understand. "Whether you like it or not, I *know* you. I know you aren't capable of murder. You're not that kind of man." Her voice was so sure, her deep blue eyes staring right into him, Christian wondered if she could really see his soul.

They were silent for a while. She sat next to him on the couch, turning sideways to face him. "You're trying to stop them, aren't you?" she said. It wasn't really a question. She knew that had to be why he was associating with her aunt's murderers.

Christian nodded. "I've been trying to find out who they're connected with. There's a heavy backing them, I know it," he said, relieved to be able to tell someone else. Tara had been his only confidant, but she wasn't directly involved. "I swear to you, Zan," he said, taking her hand earnestly, "I didn't know anything about the hit on Midnight until it was too late."

"I know that. I know you would have stopped them if you'd known."

"But now…" He shook his head. "No one's gonna believe I didn't know."

"I believe it, Christian, and I don't think everyone is convinced you're involved with them. I know Joe, and if he believed you were in any way responsible for Midnight's death, he would have helped my uncle kill you, legal or not."

Christian looked pensive for a moment, then nodded and shrugged. "Either way, I'm taking Devereaux and his friend down before they do any more damage."

"What do you mean, taking them down?" Susan asked slowly, looking worried now.

He gave her a resigned look. "They're dangerous, and they're not done yet. I can feel it. I'm gonna make sure they meet their maker before they hurt anyone else."

Susan looked terrified now. "They're police officers, albeit bad ones. You'll go to prison, or worse. Killing a police officer is a capital offense here."

"They killed a police officer, Zan," he said, his voice low and determined. "And I'm sentencing them to death."

"But—"

"Zan," he said, calmly cutting off her protest. "They're gonna arrest me either way. At least my way I know Midnight's killers won't get away. Maybe I can plea bargain or something later, who knows."

"And you're willing to take that chance?"

"What choice do I have?" he asked, shaking his head. "I got myself into this—I'm the only one close enough right now to stop them."

"What about asking for help?"

"From who?" Christian shook his head cynically. "At least half the department thinks I helped kill their chief. They'd probably sooner shoot me as look at me."

"What about Donovan?"

"Zan, Donovan was almost killed in the same blast that killed Midnight. I don't think he'd be well disposed toward talking to me either."

"What if I talk to him first?" she asked desperately.

Christian was silent for a minute, narrowing his eyes in thought. Finally he started to nod. "Maybe…"

Susan nodded too. "I can do it, Christian. I can convince him. Donovan's a good police officer, and very smart. If I explain everything to him, he'll see reason."

"We'll see about that," Christian said skeptically.

Susan looked at him beseechingly. "Christian…"

"I'm not saying don't talk to him. I just don't know how willing he's gonna be to believe you."

"It's well worth a try," Susan said, resting her head against his shoulder.

He automatically put his arms around her again. If he'd stopped to think about it, it would have bothered him, but he didn't. He allowed the alcohol he'd consumed to keep the internal alarms at bay. Instead he held her, breathing in the scent of jasmine that he now associated with her. After a few moments he felt her relax against him and heard her sigh.

"I've missed you," she said softly, with no reproach in her voice.

Christian didn't reply. He put his finger to her chin, raising her face to kiss her. It was a soft, gentle kiss that went on and on. He cupped her face for a few moments, then slid his hand back to the base of her neck, caressing her. Susan responded with equal tenderness, touching his chest, then moved her arms around his neck, running her fingers through his hair.

When their lips parted Christian's gaze was heated; her breathing was rather heavy as well, but they both knew this was neither the time nor the place for anything else.

As Susan left the apartment a little while later, Christian's voice stopped her. "Zan," he said softly, and she turned to him. "Be careful." Then, almost as an afterthought, he said, "In fact, after you talk to Donovan, just call me here. Don't come back to this apartment."

"Why?" Susan asked, thinking he was already pushing her away again.

"Because it's not safe," he explained gently. "These guys might be watching me, and I don't want you caught up in this."

"But Christian—"

"No," he said, cutting her off. "I can't take any chances." He touched her cheek, his eyes softening a bit. "Not with you." His words were a soft whisper. Susan felt warmed by them. She nodded in reply, unable to think of anything suitable to say.

An hour later she was standing in Donovan's living room; he was surprised to see her.

"What's going on, Susan?" he asked, realizing she had something on her mind. He sat on the couch next to Jeanie, gesturing for Susan to sit as well. Susan noted that he looked extremely tired, not to mention the sadness in his eyes.

"I needed to talk to you," she said anxiously. "It's about Christian." She saw the quick look Jeanie and Donovan exchanged, but didn't understand it.

"Okay…" Donovan said cautiously as he settled back against the cushions, as if ready to listen to her explanation.

"My uncle is wrong," Susan said determinedly. "I know he thinks Christian had something to do with my aunt's murder, but he's wrong."

"He is hanging out with one of the men we know for a fact is involved," Donovan pointed out calmly.

"Yes, and that's because he's trying to find out who is involved all together," Susan said. Donovan nodded, but didn't look convinced. "Donovan, he knows who Frank Devereaux's partner is at the department." Susan knew that would pique Donovan's interest. It was one of the things she and Christian had discussed before she'd left the apartment.

"Who?" Donovan said, narrowing his eyes slightly, as if telling her that she had better not be lying to him.

"His name is Jerry McCaffery," Susan said, having no idea what that meant.

Donovan was silent for a long time, his mouth hanging open, staring at her as if she were crazy. He looked over at Jeanie and saw the "I told you so" look in her eyes.

"Whoa…" Donovan said, still shocked at the implications of an Internal Affairs officer turning bad. "So how come Christian didn't go to Midnight with this?" he asked after regaining his composure.

"He was planning to when he knew who the third person was, but now…"

Donovan nodded, understanding her reluctance to talk about Midnight. "And you're really convinced he's not bullshitting you?"

Susan gave him a serious look. "I loved my aunt very much. Do you think I would be supporting someone that could be one of her murderers if I wasn't sure he wasn't?"

"I hope not," Donovan said, then nodded. "Okay, tell him to come here tonight at six o'clock. I'll talk to him. But I'm warnin' you," he said very seriously, rubbing at the barely healing cut on his forehead with his forefinger, "if I think he's snowin' me, I'll put a bullet in him myself."

Susan nodded. She understood Donovan's caution, as well as his undying loyalty to Midnight, his chief. She thanked him, then stood to leave.

Donovan stopped her at the front door, and she turned to look up at him. "How come you're doing this for him?" he asked, curious about her relationship with Joe's cousin, especially since she was still set to marry Warren in less than a week; he and Jeanie were planning on going to the wedding.

Susan looked back at him for a long minute, then sighed. "Because I love him," she said simply, shocking him to the point that he only nodded in reply. Susan put her hand on Donovan's arm. "Thank you again, Donovan. Christian was planning to kill those two men himself if that's what it came down to."

"He would have gone to the gas chamber."

Susan nodded. "I pointed that out to him as well. He said he didn't care as long as Midnight's killers went to hell first."

Donovan was taken aback by that, but it did go further to convince him that Susan and Jeanie were right about Christian. Jeanie had been telling him since the funeral that Christian couldn't be involved. "He respected Midnight," she'd said, still upset from the funeral, but angry that her friend was being accused. "He would never have been part of murdering her. And whatever you think, he doesn't hate you enough to want you dead."

After Susan left, he told Jeanie about the conversation he'd had with Midnight on their way to Mexico—how Midnight had been sure Christian wasn't involved with Devereaux.

"Oh, I see," Jeanie said, grinning for the first time that day. "I say he's not involved, you don't believe me—Midnight says it, you do." She nodded cynically.

Donovan grinned too, pulling her close to him on the couch. "Midnight had a lot more experience with this kind of stuff than you do. It was pure wisdom."

"Yeah," Jeanie replied, looking somber again. "Is this ever going

155

to get easier?"

Donovan shook his head. "I don't know, babe," he said softly as he leaned back against the couch. "I do know one thing, though."

"And what would that be?" she asked, glancing back at him and sensing his tension.

"After this is over and we put these guys away, you and I need to have a serious talk."

"About what?"

"About you and me, that's what," he said, leaning down to kiss her gently. Jeanie returned it warmly, putting her arms around his neck. They kissed for a while on the couch, feeling the need to be close after all that had happened. Eventually Jeanie leaned her head against his chest, thinking how glad she was that he hadn't been seriously injured in the explosion that had killed Midnight.

They stayed there for a long time. Donovan made a couple of phone calls, but they spent the rest of the afternoon together. Jeanie was just thinking about getting them something to eat when there was a knock on the door. Donovan got up and went to open it. Christian stood outside looking very uncomfortable.

Donovan looked at him for a long moment, noting the nasty bruise on his cheek from Rick's attack. He stood back, then gestured for Christian to enter. Christian walked in and headed down the hall.

Jeanie stood up from the couch and reached up to hug him. She gently touched his cheek and asked, "Are you okay?"

Christian nodded soberly. "I'll be better when this is done."

Jeanie nodded and then looked over at Donovan, as did Christian.

"So what happens now?" Christian asked, raising an eyebrow. He still wasn't totally convinced that Donovan wouldn't shoot him, or at least arrest him.

"We wait," Donovan said. "I got Spider, Tiny, and Dave comin' over to hear this too."

"Backup?" Christian asked wryly.

"Assistance," Donovan supplied, then shrugged. "I figured we could use the help."

In that statement Donovan conveyed that he was willing to trust Christian, and it made the Englishman relax instantly.

Ten minutes later Spider and Dave arrived, followed shortly by Tiny. They all sat down at Donovan's dining room table.

Christian told them about everything that had happened and what Devereaux was doing. He assured them, as he had Susan, that he had had nothing to do with Midnight's murder. At that point Dave and Spider exchanged a glance, then looked at Tiny. Tiny nodded slowly. Christian wondered mildly if it was acceptance of his story or if they were planning to kill him. He sat patiently, waiting to see. Donovan sat back and glanced at Jeanie, who was pointedly standing behind Christian's chair, as if silently supporting her friend. He gave her a slight grin then turned back to Christian.

"So what are they up to now?" Donovan asked.

"They're cuttin' and runnin'—that's what I think. They've been talking about a big score... Something big go down lately?"

Dibbins nodded. "Yeah, we confiscated fifty pounds of meth and twenty kilos of pharmaceutical-grade cocaine a week or so back."

Christian nodded. "That's probably it then. I think they're planning to take it all, as well as whatever else is in the lockup right now."

"Yeah, but when?" Spider asked, spreading his fingers on the table.

"Day after tomorrow, I think," Christian said.

"Think?" Tiny asked, his look pointed.

Christian shrugged. "They still ain't sure they trust me. They said day after tomorrow, 'cause they're waiting for their connection to call." He narrowed his eyes. "Thing is, it's going down in Mexico."

"The meet?" Dibbins asked, surprised.

"They're runnin', I told you that."

"Shit…" Donovan said, seconded by Dibbins.

"You can't operate down there, right?" Christian said, sounding as if he already knew the answer to the question.

Spider looked at Dave, who looked at Tiny, who in turn looked at Donovan. Without a word, each of the men pulled out their badges and turned them face down on the table.

Christian watched with pursed lips and just a bit more respect. They had just said they intended to catch Midnight's killers, whether as police officers or not.

"Okay…" Christian nodded. "They're supposed to call me tonight and let me know the deal. I'll call Donovan as soon as I know anything."

Spider nodded and stood up, signaling the end of the meeting. They left a little while later. Dibbins and Spider were headed back to Rick's, and Tiny was going home for sleep; they'd all been rotating on being around for Rick. They knew nothing would replace Midnight's presence, but also that he needed people that he trusted around him at that point.

On the way back to the Debenshire home, Spider and Dave talked about what they'd heard.

"You think it's all on the up and up?" Dave asked.

"I think I'll kill him myself if it's not," Spider said, narrowing his eyes, but then he nodded. "Yeah, I think he's okay though. Donovan said Midnight was pretty sure about him."

Dave nodded. "This shit's getting way too dangerous."

"Tell me about it," Spider said. "Tammy's freaked out. She's talking about moving back to Kansas, where her folks are."

"Well, I don't have *that* problem," Dave said, shaking his head.

"No," Spider said, grinning now. "Your problem is too many girlfriends."

"Jealous?" Dave asked, with a raised eyebrow.

"Hell yes!" Spider replied. The two men laughed, glad for a little lightening in the tension. It was a long-standing joke that Dave had never gotten married because he was having far too much fun being single. Spider always said it was because he was commitment phobic, and Dave would tell him it had nothing to do with fear and everything to do with waiting till he found what all his married friends had found—true love. As it was, he had at least three girlfriends at a time.

When they got to Rick's, Spider pulled Joe outside.

Joe lit a cigarette immediately, leaning against the railing of the deck. "What happened?" he asked, having known where the two men were going; Spider had told him before they left.

"He's legit," Spider said. "He's workin' them. But he's asking for help now."

Joe nodded, not surprised that his cousin was apparently doing something so dangerous. Sinclair genes, Midnight would have called it, and she would have been right. It occurred to him once more that he'd never hear that kind of stuff from her again. It was still too unreal.

"So when's it going down?" he asked.

"He's not sure—they're being a little cagey with him right now. Probably because he's your kin." Spider grinned. "Never know, right?"

"Guess not," Joe replied, grinning back.

"Here's the thing though," Spider said more seriously, his look pointed. "It's going down in Mexico."

Joe looked pensive for a moment, then shrugged. "Wherever we go, whatever it takes."

"Think Rick would be up to it?"

"I think wild horses couldn't stop him."

"He's pretty messed up, isn't he?" Spider asked, wanting to know what everyone else wanted to know.

Joe blew his breath out, his expression uncertain. "I don't know if we'll ever get him back."

Spider nodded. "That's about what I was thinking." He shook his head. "I've been trying to put myself in his shoes, like how I'd feel if I lost Tam or little Joe, and man, I just can't do it. I can't fathom losing either of them."

"Tell me about it," Joe said, looking grim. "For all the times I've almost lost Midnight, I can't believe it really happened this time. Almost losing Randy was bad enough…"

"Yeah…" Spider nodded, then narrowed his eyes at Joe. "You're feeling guilty about Midnight, aren't you?"

"Shouldn't I?"

"Why?"

"I deserted her, man," Joe said, giving Spider a pointed look. "And don't fuckin' tell me you all weren't pissed off at me for doin' it either."

Spider looked chagrined. "You caught me, but her dying isn't your fault, man. None of us were there—there was no way to know they were stupid enough to kill a Chief of Police. Nobody could know that."

Joe said nothing, but looked unconvinced.

"Man, she wasn't mad about you going. She understood why you had to do it. We all did after she explained it."

Joe grinned. Midnight had told him that "their children" weren't happy about their "divorce." Joe had laughed at the terms, but knew she was right.

"I guess I should've explained it to the gang, but I suppose I chickened out," Joe said. "I wasn't willing to defend my right to protect my family with anyone at that point."

"What're you going to do now?" Spider asked, aware that everything was still very precarious.

"Don't know," Joe said, shaking his head.

"You stayin?"

"Don't know that either. Things are gonna be pretty hard without Midnight. I don't know if I can deal with it."

"I know what you mean—things are bound to be really strange." Spider looked at Joe for a long moment before adding, "We really need you here, Joe. I mean… Rick will… and, well… to tell you the truth, I think we all will. You're kinda like Midnight's stead, you know."

Joe looked back at Spider, surprised by the other man's frankness, but he knew in a way that it was true. He knew that the core members of FORS had always relied on him whenever Midnight had been out of commission for any reason. He had the general notion that many in the department had started to follow "the gang's" lead on that. Joe wondered how this was going to affect the department as well. Losing Midnight was bound to have an impact on everyone. He didn't respond to Spider's impassioned speech, but he nodded his understanding.

Later that evening, Joe approached Rick, who was once again sitting out on the shore. He'd been silent and withdrawn since the funeral. His anger at Christian had taken a while to dissipate; when it had, he'd grabbed a bottle and left the house, walking along the shore for hours and finally settling on the beach to watch the sunset.

Joe sat down next to his friend, not really sure how to broach the subject of Christian and what was happening.

Rick looked over at him but said nothing; he sensed Joe's hesitation. He knew his friend well, just as he'd known Midnight—he could tell when they were tense about something. "What is it?" he asked after a long minute.

"It's about the guys that did this," Joe said cautiously. "We know who they are, besides Devereaux... and we know what they've been doing..."

Rick nodded, his jaw tightening. "And now you're gonna tell me that your cousin's not really involved, right?"

Joe waited an extra minute to answer, having to push back his anger at Rick's tone. "He's not," he said firmly. "In fact, he's got the inside on them and he's working with Donovan, Spider, Tiny, and Dibbs to take them down the day after tomorrow."

Rick said nothing. His lips twitched as if he wanted to argue with Joe. In truth he just wanted to yell, scream, cuss, and hit anything and anyone.

"Thing is," Joe went on, ignoring Rick's obvious cynicism, "I'm goin' down with them, and I thought you'd go too."

Rick looked over at him for a long moment, narrowing his eyes at his friend. "You thought I'd go?" he said disbelievingly. "You know damn good and well I'll go." His voice held a dangerous note.

Joe knew it would probably be a better idea if Rick wasn't present when Midnight's killers were arrested. If Midnight were making the decision she wouldn't allow Rick to be there; he was too personally involved. But, by the same token, Joe didn't have the strength or the real desire to stop him. In the end, it would be pure justice if Rick was able to kill the men that had killed his wife. Joe knew it wasn't the way he should think as a cop, but he and Rick hadn't always been cops. He was fairly sure Rick was thinking more along the lines of their gang member days at this point. Even he couldn't help but want a little street justice for the death of his best friend.

"Christian's gonna call Donovan with the time when he gets the call from Devereaux," Joe said.

Rick nodded, still looking cynical. He turned to Joe, his deep blue eyes narrowed slightly. "And what if it's all a setup to take the rest of us out?"

Joe glanced back at Rick, danger in his eyes as well. "He's my family, Rick. It's not a set up." This time there was threat in his voice. Joe's family loyalty went just as deep, if not deeper, than his friendship with Rick.

Rick just looked back at him, no compunction in his eyes. "You believe what you want," he said. "But if I even think he was involved, I'll kill him."

Joe's expression was even. "You'll have to come through me first."

"If that's what it takes," Rick said, his tone not lightening in the least. Joe knew then that Rick's pain was deep, and that his state of mind was not getting any better. It was something that needed to be addressed before he confronted his wife's murderers with a gun in his hand.

"Rick," he began, his tone softening, searching his friend's face. "You're going to have to go on sometime, you know."

Rick features closed up, and it was obvious to Joe that he didn't want to talk about this particular subject. *Too bad.*

"Rick, you can't live like this forever. It's not going to bring her back, and it's not healthy for you or Keyla."

"You don't know shit, okay?"

"I know what it's doing," Joe shot back. "I see you trying to drown your sorrows, and I see your daughter becoming a wreck. She needs you, man, and it's your job to be there for her."

"Don't fucking tell me what my job is!" Rick snapped, standing up and glaring down at Joe, his eyes blazing.

Joe got up too. "Yeah, I know you don't want to hear it, because that way you can stay in the bottle you've climbed inside, but it's true. Your daughter needs you, and you're too busy feeling sorry for yourself to be there. You think that's what Midnight would want? You think she'd want you thinking of killing yourself, of abandoning your daughter? Well, let me tell you a thing or two about what it's like to lose your parents, Rick. It's a living hell—it makes you feel rootless and that no one in this world really knows you or loves you like they did. It makes you afraid to love anyone that much ever again for fear you'll lose them too. It tears you up inside so bad that all you want to do is hide and keep the world away. Is that what you want for Keyl? Is that what you think Midnight would have wanted?"

Rick tensed, and Joe was sure he was going to hit him, but then Rick closed his eyes and lowered his head. After a long moment he blew his breath out in a sigh, shaking his head. He looked up at the night sky. "I'm sorry," he whispered. Joe wasn't sure if he was apologizing to him or to Midnight, but he did know he'd gotten through.

That night Rick went into his daughter's room. He and Mikeyla talked for a long time, and she cried in his arms for a long time too. When she'd fallen asleep he laid her down, tucking her into bed and kissing her on the forehead. Then he went out to the living room.

Spider, Dibbs, Joe, Randy, Anabelle, and Robert were sitting around talking. They all looked up when Rick walked in. Joe had to admit he looked worlds better; he was glad he'd taken the chance at making him furious to get through to him. Rick looked around at everyone, his face grim but his eyes showing a lot less anguish. It showed the beginnings of healing. After a long moment, he said,

165

"Let's get these guys so we can get on with our lives, huh?" His voice was serious, but a slight grin tugged at his lips as he looked at Joe. He walked over, extending his hand to his best friend. Joe took it readily. "Thanks, man," Rick whispered, then turned to his mother and father. "How long will you stay?"

"As long as you need us," Robert said.

Rick nodded. "I think we'll both need you for a while."

Anabelle nodded, as did Robert. Anabelle stood, taking her son into her arms and hugging him close. Rick relaxed in her embrace, closing his eyes and feeling the beginnings of his soul mending.

That night he actually ate a meal, albeit a small one, and slept deeply. He dreamed of Midnight, but it was happy dreams, memories and good times and the love they'd shared. The next morning he woke feeling rested and calmer.

The calm didn't last long. That morning they found out that Susan was missing. Joe and Randy had gone back to the house late the night before and hadn't known that she wasn't in her room. They found out when she didn't come out the next day. Joe had immediately gotten in touch with Warren, and when he realized she wasn't there he'd called Christian, hoping she was with him. She wasn't, and Christian became almost frantic with worry. He told Joe that he'd talked to her the day before when she'd called him to tell him about the meet with Donovan, but he hadn't talked to her since. He was absolutely sure Devereaux had her.

"Damn it!" Christian snapped. "I knew her coming here was not a good thing. Shit, Joe... if they hurt her..." He trailed off as he thought about what he'd do to them.

"We gotta wait and see—maybe she just went somewhere to

think," Joe said, knowing in his heart that wasn't the case. He knew Christian was right, that they'd grabbed Susan as insurance for his loyalty. Things were getting more dangerous, fast.

Christian waited for the call from Devereaux with his stomach in a knot. When it finally came he had to keep himself from asking about Susan and make his voice sound as normal as possible.

"So what's the drill?" he asked.

"The drill is this," Devereaux said smoothly. "Meet in the Hotel Cosmos Don Carlos, in Mexicali, tomorrow night at seven. We pullin' the stuff out of lockup tonight and taking a van down. We'll be movin' on to greener pastures the next morning." His voice was calm and even... too even. Christian wanted to climb through the phone line and wring his neck.

"I'll be there," he said. He hung up and waited an agonizing hour before leaving the apartment and going down the street to a local coffee house. There, he made the call to Donovan, careful to make sure he wasn't being observed.

"You think they have Susan?" Donovan asked.

"I know they do. They're planning on using her against me, but I'll get her out somehow," Christian said, more calmly than he felt.

"Okay..." Donovan said. "Meet me at my place at about six o'clock tonight. I'll get the guys over here and we'll map this out as best we can."

"Alright," Christian said, feeling sick to his stomach. He knew there was no way to know what Devereaux and his friends were planning. He still didn't know who the connection was, and he didn't know for sure that he wasn't leading Donovan and the rest of the crew into a trap.

That night at Donovan's, Christian was surprised when Joe and Rick showed up a half hour into the meeting. Rick stared at Christian for a long moment. Christian had stood when he and Joe walked in; eventually Rick extended his hand to the younger Englishman. Christian took it, his expression wary, but shook it all the same. After that they got down to business. With the connections he still had, Joe had been able to get hold of the Chief of Police in Mexicali. After the condolences were relayed again, Joe managed to get a drawing of the layout of the Hotel Cosmos Don Carlos faxed to him at Rick's house. They pored over it, not sure where the meet would actually take place. Christian was tense, feeling the pressure. He knew now that things were much more serious because Susan was involved. It also made things precarious in terms of how they would have to handle the bust. If Susan hadn't been caught up in it they could have hit Devereaux and his friends as soon as they showed up at the hotel and they were sure everyone involved was there. Christian had to get her out before the team could move in; that left a lot of holes in the plan.

"You have a weapon?" Joe asked, looking at his cousin.

Christian nodded. "My Sig."

"Forty-five, right?" Joe said. Christian nodded again.

"You know how to use it?" Tiny asked.

"Duh!" Dibbs said, grinning.

"Sinclair genes, remember?" Spider put in, laughing. Tiny nodded, hitting his forehead with the palm of his hand and laughing too.

"Okay," Joe said, grinning. "So you can do what you have to do to get Susan out of danger, and then we'll move in from here, and here." He pointed to the entrances on the drawing. "Make sure that you're clear when you give the signal—things could get hairy and I don't want Susan in the crossfire."

Christian nodded seriously. They talked for a little while longer, trying to anticipate everything but aware it was impossible to predict what would happen. Devereaux was playing it close to the table, and the team knew that he was doing it because he didn't trust Christian. Joe had actually begun to worry about Devereaux killing Christian and Susan just as a final kick in the head to him and the rest of the department. It nagged at him constantly that night. He hoped Christian wasn't walking into a trap. Christian had voiced his concern that the trap might actually be for the team, if they'd figured him out, but Donovan had waved it aside. "Doesn't matter—we're taking them down one way or the other."

That statement was seconded by the rest of the men. When the meeting broke up, Rick caught up to Christian at the black Jaguar he still drove. Christian turned to the other man, still wary of him.

Rick looked chagrined at his continued caution. "Look," he said placatingly. "I want to thank you for helping out in this. I know you weren't involved in Midnight's murder." He nodded toward the bruise still on Christian's cheek. "I'm sorry about that, but you gotta know how it looked… and I wasn't really thinking clearly…"

"No problem," Christian said evenly. "I know how it looked—I wanted it to look that way."

Rick nodded. "I'm counting on you to get Susan out of there," he said soberly. "I can't have another member of my family killed over all this shit. I know this isn't really your fight—"

"It is my fight," Christian said. "They made it my fight when they took Susan." Rick looked surprised at that, but nodded all the same. "It's my fault she's involved, and I'll get her out of it," Christian

169

explained.

Rick clapped him on the shoulder and walked over to where Joe leaned against his car. Christian stared after him, thinking again that he wished he'd been able to save Midnight. Rick looked like hell. Everyone looked haunted.

That night Donovan told Jeanie about the meeting as they lay in bed. She'd been at home with her parents all evening; they'd become more nervous about her being with Donovan since Midnight's murder, though she'd tried to reassure them that everything was fine. She'd arrived to find Donovan still poring over his copy of the hotel layout and finally coaxed him to bed two hours later.

Now, lying there in his arms, she glanced up at him. "Donovan?" she said, not sure whether he was asleep; his eyes were closed, but with him that wasn't a clear sign. He hadn't been sleeping well at all. Randy had been after him about it since she'd arrived back in California; she'd made Jeanie promise to try and get him to rest more. He wasn't recovered fully from his wounds in the explosion. Jeanie knew he shouldn't be going on this mission the next day, but also that there was no stopping him.

"Hmm?" he answered, bringing his hand up to stroke her shoulder.

"What did you want to talk about—you know, when this was all over?"

"I told you," he said softly. "I want to talk about us, about everything." He glanced down at her and saw that she was waiting for more of an explanation. He sighed, rolling his eyes up to the ceiling. "Can't say that kind of thing to a woman, can you?"

"What?"

"I want to talk about something with you, but not right now."

Jeanie grinned. "It tends to make a person crazy, yes."

"Crazy? Jay, what is it you think I'm going to say?"

"I don't know…" She shrugged. "I guess I'm worried that you want out now."

"Me?" Donovan gave her a dumbfounded look. "Jay," he said, touching her face gently and drawing her up to him. "I love you—that hasn't changed." He made a frustrated sound in his throat. "I just… I guess I want to—need to know how you really feel about me, about us."

"Donovan, I—" Jeanie began, shaking her head.

"No, wait," Donovan said, cutting her off, his voice stronger now. "Before you say anything, let me finish. What I'm saying is that I have to have some kind of commitment from you, something to tell me I'm not spinning my wheels here. This whole thing with Midnight has just polarized the fragility of life for me, and I have to know where we stand." He sounded so serious, his eyes searching her face so earnestly that Jeanie couldn't help but laugh.

"Donovan," she said, putting her finger to his lips. "If you'd shut up for a minute it would make it a hell of a lot easier for me to tell you that I love you."

Donovan said nothing for a moment, staring at her as if he didn't understand what she had just said. In truth, she'd said it so matter-of-factly that it took him a few moments to catch up. "You what?" he said, the beginnings of a grin on his lips. "Can I hear that again for the record, Ms. Franco?"

Jeanie moved to lean down over him, her face an inch from his, her eyes staring into his. "Donovan Jacob Curtis. I. Love. You," she said, measuring out her words as if testifying in court.

"Duly noted, Officer," he replied, then smiled. "And let it be noted that not only do I love you, but I said it first."

"Oh, it's a contest now?" Jeanie said, grinning madly, feeling so incredibly good at that moment that she couldn't think straight.

"Yes, and I win." He pulled her close and kissed her. "I get you," he said seriously. "I love you," he repeated, then kissed her deeply. She caressed his chest as she kissed him back. A little while later they made love for the first time since the trip down to Mexico. It was a poignant reunion for them, but so necessary for Donovan's state of mind.

He felt a little strange about returning to Mexico, like he was tempting fate one more time. He knew in his heart he needed to be there, needed to avenge Midnight's death, but it didn't help to have this feeling of foreboding that nagged at him. That night he held Jeanie extra close after they'd made love.

"When this is all done," he said softly, "I want to go away somewhere with you."

Jeanie glanced up at him sharply, but nodded all the same. "Okay."

"Good," he said. He felt like he was setting things in his mind, moving ahead, moving on. It was a healthy direction, even as his brain nagged at him about the trip the following day down to Mexico. "Love you," was the last thing he said that night before he fell asleep, before hearing her say that she loved him too.

Christian's stomach was in a knot as he drove down to Mexicali, his head swirling with possibilities. He'd lain awake all night trying to push aside the thoughts of Susan and what Devereaux would do to her. He remembered Devereaux's philosophy about women, keeping their mouths shut and their legs open—the idea of Devereaux "trying Susan out" had forced him to his feet. He'd paced for hours, thinking dangerous, murderous thoughts. Eventually he'd given up sleeping and started drinking again. He was fairly far gone when Tara got back to her apartment at three o'clock. She'd forced him to lie down and had even made him take a couple of sleeping pills, then lay next to him, stroking his hair and talking softly until he fell into a deep sleep. He'd woken late that morning feeling rested and more at ease. But now, driving toward his destination, he felt extremely tense again.

He got into the city and proceeded toward the hotel. He noted, much to his comfort, a familiar group of cars parked intermittently in the general vicinity. He saw Joe's Porsche Boxster, Donovan's Mustang, Tiny's Ford Explorer, and Dave Dibbins' classic Dodge Charger. He knew he was covered—now all he had to do was get Susan out of that hotel and he was home free.

"Yeah, that's all," he muttered. Steeling himself with the resolve that had gotten him through any number of difficult times in his life, he got out of the car and headed in to the front desk. After she'd untied her tongue, the young woman there directed him to a third-floor room. Inside the elevator, Christian flipped on the pager he wore on his belt. In reality it was a transmitter that would allow the team to hear everything that went on at the meeting.

He got to the room and knocked. He gritted his teeth for a moment, making himself relax. By the time the door was opened he looked calm and cool. Devereaux smiled widely. "Blue, how's it going?"

"It's goin'," Christian said smoothly. "We all set?" he asked, walking into the room. He glanced around and forced himself not to tense when he saw Susan on the bed. Instead he raised an eyebrow at Devereaux. "Party favor?"

Devereaux laughed, shaking his head. "Now, Blue, is that any way to talk about a lady?"

Christian grinned obscenely. "Don't see no ladies here."

"I thought English women were ladies," McCaffery put in from across the room.

"Not all of 'em," Christian said, giving Susan a disgusted look as he walked over to the bar and poured himself a Jack Daniels. He drank it down with his back to Devereaux, closing his eyes for a moment as he tried to draw on every ounce of strength he had. He'd seen a bruise on Susan's mouth, and it was obvious that she was terrified. The thought of one of these men laying their hands on her made him sick. He needed to get her out of there now. Turning around, he looked from Devereaux to Susan and then back.

"So what're we doin' with her anyway?" he asked irritably.

"Well," Devereaux said, his voice confidential. "She's kind of an insurance policy."

"For who?" Christian said, laughing. "We're in Mexico, you dumb shit. Her family's in San Diego—who's gonna care here?"

"Well, that's the question, isn't it?" McCaffery said, his tone all IA and superior.

"See," Devereaux said, leaning against the table in the corner of the room. "It's you we're not sure of, Blue. Ya know, being a cop's cousin an' all."

"You're a fucking cop," Christian said, shaking his head like the guy was losing his mind. "And I'm trustin' you."

"Yeah, well, I'm also a smart cop, and I know better than to trust someone blindly. She's my insurance that you won't do anything stupid."

"What makes you think I give a shit what you do with her?" Christian leaned casually against the bar with a bored expression.

"You fucked her, didn't you?" Devereaux said with a sneer.

Christian rolled his eyes. "I fuck a lot of women. She wasn't even that good. I don't care what you do with her—just send her back to her uncle and let's get on with the show."

"Oh, we'll send her back alright." Devereaux nodded. "In a body bag. And you're gonna do her, so you're in it with the rest of us. We go down, you go down."

Christian shrugged. "I'm not into killing, Devereaux. You want her dead, you do it."

"Oh no, that's not how this game is played, Collins," McCaffery said, smiling almost gleefully. "You see, you shoot her in the head with your gun, then leave the gun behind with your fingerprints on it. That way you're up for murder just like me and Dev are."

"That way we know you're really in it with us and not just playin' us," Devereaux put in. "You do have your piece, don't you?"

"Yeah, I got it," Christian said, making himself sound irritated at the inconvenience.

There was a knock at the door, and McCaffery went to answer

it. A short Mexican walked in with an only slightly taller man.

"Blue," Devereaux said, gesturing, "this is our benefactor, Rico Gaston, and this"—he nodded toward the other man—"is our hero of the hour, Midnight Chevalier's favorite mechanic, Julio Martinez." Devereaux grinned evilly, and Christian wanted to rip his face off. He glanced over at Susan and saw the anger and hatred burning in her eyes. He was sure she was about to say something, so he made his way over to shake Gaston's hand to try to distract them.

"It's good to meet you," Christian said, his tone friendly.

"Yes, you too."

"Uh, Blue…" Devereaux said, his tone polite but his look pointed. "I believe we have some unfinished business here." He gestured toward Susan, who looked appropriately afraid.

"Who is this?" Gaston asked, walking over to her and touching her cheek. She shrank away from him, seeing the lust in his eyes. Gaston had a thing for blondes; he used them like they were disposable—of course, to him they were.

"She's some piece our friend here's been doin'," Devereaux said. "And now we want him to do her again, just a bit differently."

Gaston looked surprised. "You want him to off this beautiful piece?" He looked down at Susan again. "Without me having a chance at her? Not exactly sporting of you, Devereaux. You know my penchant for *jueras*." He clicked his tongue at Frank, shaking his head.

"There's no time, Rico," Frank said, rolling his eyes.

"There's always time, Frankie." Rico sat next to Susan, pulling her toward him as he stared at her with open lust.

"Look," Christian said, his tone bored even as he raged inside. "You want me to kill her, let's just get it over with." With that he pulled out his gun and pulled back the slide pointedly.

He walked over to the bed, stopping next to Rico. "Scuse me, Mr. Gaston. I believe I have something to take care of." His voice was no-nonsense, and even Rico Gaston wasn't that hot for a lay. He stood up, moving back. Christian glanced over at Devereaux and noticed that he'd produced a gun. He lifted an eyebrow at the other man.

"Just in case you lose your nerve," Frank said. "And step back, will ya—I'll need a clean shot."

"I'm a good shot from any range." Christian took a step back, then turned to look down at Susan. Her deep blue eyes were fixed on him, but he saw how calm she actually looked. She trusted him—he could see that.

"What're you waitin' for, Collins?" McCaffery asked.

"Just thinkin' I'd like one more kiss…" he said, leering.

"Well, get on with it," Devereaux said.

Christian nodded, taking a step forward again, and leaned down to kiss her. When their lips parted, he whispered one word: "Duck." In that instant he spun around and leveled his gun at Devereaux, firing simultaneously. Devereaux fired too—the bullet slammed into Christian, but he continued to shoot until Devereaux was dead on the floor.

Christian staggered and fell to his knees but kept the gun trained on McCaffery and Gaston. Julio had run out of the room the moment the shooting started. McCaffery had gone for his gun, but thought better of it when Christian pointed his weapon at him. Gaston edged

177

toward the door; Christian pretended not to notice and allowed the man to run. "Gaston's on his way out," Christian said, knowing the team would hear him. A wave of dizziness hit him then, and he closed his eyes for a moment. He could feel the sticky warmth trickling down his leg and soaking his shirt.

Susan had screamed when the firing started, louder when Christian was hit. Now she put her hands out to steady him and said his name over and over. McCaffery took that momentary lapse in attention to pull his weapon, but Christian was faster and fired off another round, catching McCaffery in the hand that held the gun. McCaffery dropped his weapon and dashed headlong out of the room. "McCaffery's out too," Christian said, his voice decidedly weak now.

"Christian!" Susan said, pulling him back against her and staring frantically down at the blood at his midsection. "Oh God!" she said, crying now. "You'll be okay, you'll be okay," she chanted, almost as if she could make it so.

"Damn, that hurts…" Christian said, breathing heavily but trying to grin. "I'm okay, Zan… I'm okay." He was feeling very lightheaded and weak.

"Jesus Christ," Joe said from the doorway, holding his gun at the ready. He strode over and knelt by the bed, pulling Christian's shirt up so he could see the wound. He looked tense, and Susan saw that. Pulling out his radio, Joe brought it up to his lips. "Dibbs, get an ambulance here fast. Christian's hit—looks bad."

"Joe?" Christian said, his voice a hoarse whisper.

"Yeah, man?" Joe said, looking up at him.

"We get 'em?" he asked, wincing with the effort.

"Yeah, we got 'em. They're dead. Gaston pulled a gun and

178

McCaffery went for his backup."

"What about Julio?" Christian asked. "He's Midnight's killer."

"He's been arrested—he'll be doin' some serious time in a Mexican prison. Moncarro will see to that."

Christian nodded, lying back against Susan. She held him, her tears dropping onto his chest. At one point he reached up, taking her hand. The ambulance arrived a little while later, and Susan went with him.

Rick sat on the curb outside the hotel. He had his knees up and his arms resting on them, his head down.

"Señor Debenshire?" a man said, sitting down next to him.

Rick glanced over. He didn't recognize him. "Yeah?"

"I am Chief Moncarro." He nodded toward the police cars that had arrived at the scene.

"Thanks for the assistance," Rick said, polite but tired.

"It's been very difficult for you, I know. Your wife's death, I mean."

Rick looked at him for a long moment, then nodded.

"Does this end it?" Moncarro asked. "Did you catch all the men that were involved?"

"Yeah, we *got* them all," Rick said pointedly.

Moncarro nodded. He stood up, looking down at Rick. "Come with me, señor. We have a few things to discuss."

"What?" Rick asked, suddenly wary. He didn't know if Moncarro wanted to arrest him or what, but he wasn't in the mood for another fight right now.

"Just come, señor."

They went on a short drive to a nondescript building, then walked up three flights of stairs. "Where the hell are we going?" Rick asked, irritated now.

"We're going to meet a man," Moncarro said evenly. They went to a door toward the end of the corridor, and Moncarro knocked.

A young man answered, his expression cautious. Moncarro stepped back, gesturing at Rick. "This is Ricardo Debenshire," he said politely. "Rick, this is Montavo Juarez."

Rick nodded, extending his hand and wondering what the hell he was doing here. Montavo shook his hand and then stepped back, indicating for Rick to come inside as he and Moncarro exchanged a look.

Rick stepped into the room. It was very dim. As his eyes adjusted to the light he saw how small the place was, and how poor. He was drawn to the only window letting any light in, and then down below that window. He stopped breathing then. On the bed lay Midnight. She had just turned over and was sitting up. In three quick strides Rick was at the bed, grabbing her up in a fierce hugging, crying and laughing at the same time.

"My God, my God…" he whispered over and over again.

"Rick?" Midnight said groggily, but she held on to him with apparent strength.

"Midnight, we lost you… we lost you…" Rick breathed, unable to think past the euphoric joy pumping through his veins.

"What?" Midnight whispered.

Rick sat back, not releasing her for fear she'd slip away from him again. "We lost you, babe, you were dead—we thought you were dead." His deep blue eyes searched her face, his tears still wet on his cheeks.

"But…" Midnight shook her head, looking over at Montavo.

"We allowed them to think you were dead, señora," Montavo said. "We had to. It was the only way to make sure you were safe."

"I am sorry, Señor Debenshire," Moncarro said, looking at Rick. "But I was sure you'd rather have your wife back safely than risk losing her again while those men were still out there."

"But how?" Rick shook his head, holding Midnight close to him. "I mean, who… died?"

"My sister," Montavo said somberly. "She pushed your wife out of the way before the bomb went off."

"My God… I'm sorry," Rick said. "How did she know about the bomb?"

"It was her husband, Julio, who set it. I knew because I overheard Julio making the deal with the American police officer. He said something about a female police chief and a red Corvette—I told my sister and she was determined to stop it from happening. In the end she couldn't, so she gave her life to save your wife's."

Rick shook his head, unable to fathom such unselfishness for someone you didn't know. "She was the woman you told me about, wasn't she?" he asked Midnight.

"Yes," Midnight said, her eyes sad.

"I think your wife is well enough to travel," Moncarro said.

"When Mr. Juarez called me, I came right away and brought my personal physician. I knew we couldn't check her into a hospital without causing a scene and most likely alerting the men who had tried to kill her. We decided to make the most out of the fact that a woman had indeed died. We put Midnight's rings in the wreckage next to the body to help convince the killers that they'd succeeded in their goal."

Rick nodded, closing his eyes for a moment. Then he lifted his hand, pulling Midnight's engagement ring and wedding band off his pinky and pointedly placing them back on her left ring finger. He stood, easily picking Midnight up in his arms, still amazed that she was there, alive and seemingly fairly well. He walked over to Montavo, nodding gravely to the younger man. "Thank you for everything you did. I am very sorry about your sister, but rest assured I am eternally grateful to her. If you or your family ever need anything, I want your promise you'll contact me."

Montavo nodded, looking at Midnight, whose head rested against her husband's shoulder. She nodded as well, something Rick didn't understand, but he didn't care at that moment. He had his wife back, something he could have only dreamed of an hour before. He felt so incredible he was sure he could fly. He carried her down the stairs, holding her tight against him. Moncarro followed and drove them back to the hotel. Everyone at the scene all but dropped dead when Midnight climbed out of the car, assisted by Rick. Joe had his back to the car and was talking to Dibbins when the man's jaw dropped open; he looked like he was seeing a ghost. Joe turned around and just about collapsed. "Midnight?" he breathed, praying he wasn't seeing things.

She grinned at the look on his face. "In the flesh."

Joe ran to her and grabbed her up in a hug. "You're alive—

you're alive!" he yelled, his voice ragged. "Jesus, Night. Jesus!"

Midnight laughed, feeling happy and sad all at the same time. She knew now what her friends and her husband had gone through in the last few days.. If she'd had any idea she would have crawled back to San Diego on her hands and knees. But now she was back with them, and everything was going to be okay.

CHAPTER 6

Christian was in the hospital for three days. His wound, although painful, was not life-threatening. He was kept an extra day because of a fever he'd developed after surgery. Midnight visited him while he was there. Christian was sure he was hallucinating when he saw her, but she walked over to him and took his hand.

"I knew you wouldn't let me down, Sinclair," she said, her grin wide.

"How… I mean… you… you're… dead… I thought…"

"Yeah, yeah, I know." Midnight smiled. "I've been hearing that a lot lately." She looked chagrined then. "I guess I was missed…"

"And how," Christian said seriously. "I'm glad you're okay, Chief."

"I'm glad you got my bad guys for me. I owe you one, Christian, and I don't forget my debts—believe it."

"I'll trust you on that one," Christian said, grinning. His mother walked in then, and Christian was happy to introduce the two women.

"So you are the famous police chief," Josephine said. "The one that rises from the dead, I understand."

"Yes, well…" Midnight rolled her eyes. "And you are the woman that raised this wonderful young man," she said, gesturing to Christian. "You did a pretty good job. Although I must say, those Sinclair genes certainly have kicked in well." Her grin was wry, and Josephine smiled.

"I tried to tell him all his life that he was a Sinclair, but he wouldn't listen. I think he realizes it now."

"Can't get away from genetics," Midnight said, shaking her head.

"Yeah, yeah…" Christian said, then looked at his mother. "Are you settling in alright at Joe's?" She'd arrived only that morning. Joe had arranged the flight for her, knowing she'd want to be near her son when he was recovering.

"Yes, just fine, Christian. Don't worry about me. You just lie there and get better." Josephine moved to her son's side and brushed his hair back with her fingers. Christian looked up at her, smiling warmly. Midnight knew she was seeing something not many people had. Christian was indeed very different with his mother around. Midnight left a little while later, heading home. She'd promised Mikeyla the day.

Mikeyla had been absolutely hysterical with happiness when her mother came home. Midnight had spent the entire night holding her and reassuring her that she was indeed fine. She explained the whole thing to both her and Rick that evening, as it had been explained to her by Montavo.

She'd told them that the bomb that had been set in her car had been triggered to the door handle, with a fifteen-second delay. She'd gone out to the car an hour and a half after she and Donovan arrived back at the cantina. Midnight remembered opening the door, but

185

that was all. Montavo had told her that he and Marta had tried all day to find her and Donovan. They'd gone to the police department but were afraid to ask too many questions or tell anyone too much for fear that they were crooked too. Mexican police were notorious for taking bribes easily. They had finally found out where Midnight and Donovan were staying and that they were with Chief Moncarro at that moment. Marta had left a note with the front desk telling Midnight that her life was in danger and she should stay away from her car. It had also included the number to Montavo's apartment. They'd left then and waited for Midnight to call. Midnight and Donovan had spent the day with Chief Moncarro, trying to get information on Emilio Benitez. She and Donovan hadn't gone back to the hotel, opting to go to the cantina first to have dinner and talk about what they'd found.

Marta and Montavo had gone back to the hotel to try and see if Midnight had at least gotten the message. Finally, late that afternoon, they decided to try the cantina again. Midnight had parked around the corner and down the street from the cantina so they hadn't seen the car right off. Montavo had been parking his car when Marta leapt out and started running. She'd seen Midnight leave the cantina and head for her car. Montavo jumped out to follow his sister, but he wasn't fast enough. Marta caught up to Midnight just as she opened the door, threw herself at the smaller woman and pushed her to the ground. Marta was caught by the blast. Montavo's scream and the explosion brought crowds of people out of the cantina, including Donovan, who had come at a dead run. Before he reached the car he was caught by the explosion of the gas tank.

He didn't see Montavo pull Midnight out of the way, nor did he see the young Hispanic man pull Midnight's wedding rings off and toss them into the wreckage. Montavo had taken the chief back to his apartment and contacted Moncarro himself, telling him what had happened and that Midnight had not been killed. Moncarro had come immediately. They'd talked about what they should do and decided to allow Midnight to be "dead."

In the two days she'd been home, Midnight had seen parts of her own funeral. She'd seen Rick's devastation, she'd seen the moment when he'd dropped to his knees at the gravesite, and she'd heard the words the Attorney General had said about her. She'd seen the looks on everyone's faces, and was very deeply touched that so many people had been affected by her supposed death. It also made her feel incredibly guilty that they'd all been put through such a terrible time.

Her guilt was especially acute that night when Rick woke from a nightmare. He stayed awake for hours, explaining that he'd dreamed she was still dead, that he'd actually seen her being killed, and that he didn't want to close his eyes and take a chance on dreaming it again. They'd lain awake, talking. Midnight had tried to take some of the worry and fear away, but she couldn't reverse what he'd been through. What she hadn't seen on TV she'd heard from Joe and the rest of the gang. Anabelle had even let slip about Rick talking about suicide. She asked him about it that night.

"Rick, you talked about giving up," she said. "Why?"

"Whaddya mean, why?" Rick said, looking at her like she was crazy. "Babe, you were gone, dead—I couldn't even imagine living without you." He shook his head miserably. "I didn't even want to try."

"But Rick—Keyla…" she said, pointing out what Joe had said so succinctly the night before they found her.

"I know, but I wasn't thinking clearly for a little while there."

"And drinking everything in sight, I hear," she said, grinning.

"Drowning my sorrows, love, drowning my sorrows." Rick looked at her with a silly grin on his face. He couldn't get over the happiness of having her back.

"It's gonna take me a year to dry you out."

"So long as you're here to do it, that's all I care about," he said, and kissed her tenderly.

"Rick," Midnight said softly, looking up into his eyes. "I saw the funeral, I saw your face." She shook her head as tears came to her eyes at the memory. "God, babe, I don't ever want to see you look like that again. It made me feel so awful. You know how you hear people talk about wanting to be a fly on the wall at their own funeral. Well, I wish I hadn't been. Rick, that was the most incredibly sad thing I've ever witnessed."

"Yeah, but you can't have any doubt about how everyone feels about you now, can you?" Rick said, his tone forcibly light.

"Especially not you," she whispered.

"No." He pulled her close again. "I love you with every breath I take, with every beat of my heart. You are the air in my lungs and the blood in my veins." He grinned to lighten the moment. "And if you ever manage to get yourself killed again, I'll meet you in heaven and kick your ass."

Midnight laughed, even though his words had put tears in her eyes. "I love you too, so much," she said, but felt as if the words were inadequate somehow. To make up for that, she kissed him. They kissed for a long time, and she pulled him closer, her hands at his waist and in his hair. She made love to him that night, showing him in every way that she was his and that she intended to love him for a long time to come. She fell asleep lying half over him, her hair fanned out on his chest, his hand entwined in it as he caressed her back. She was home and with the man she loved. All was right with the world.

The morning after the operation in Mexico, Jeanie woke to Donovan's voice. He was in the other room, and she was sure he was on the phone with some rental agency. He walked into the bedroom a few minutes later. Jeanie watched him as he came over to the bed; he looked incredibly good, wearing his navy blue sweats from his academy days and no shirt. He still had minor cuts on his arms and chest, but even those made him look kind of rakish. She knew being in love made her see him differently. He watched her with his teal-blue eyes, an amused look on his face.

"You caught me," she said, smiling at him. "I was checking you out."

"See anything you'd like to buy, Ms. Franco?" He raised an eyebrow at her as he leaned against the headboard.

"Oh, yes…" she said as she sat up, touching his chest gently.

He leaned down, kissing her, his lips moving over hers in a very sensual way, making her shiver.

"Oh, definitely, yes," she said when they parted.

Donovan laughed lightly. "So, tell me something," he said, fingering the T-shirt she wore, one of his. "How fast can you pack?"

"Why?" she asked, shaking her head at the change in subject.

"Because we have a flight in two hours," he replied casually.

Jeanie sat back. "We have what?"

"A flight, my love—a flight," he said, raising his eyebrow comically. "You know, big airplane goes up in the air, stewardess says 'Please put your tray tables in the upright position'…"

Jeanie narrowed her eyes at him. "Very funny, Sergeant. Where are we going?"

"San Luis Obispo."

"What's there?" she asked, surprised.

He smiled. "A few things. But you have to get up and get ready now, or we'll miss the flight and you'll never know."

Two hours later they were boarding a plane. Jeanie was still in the dark about the trip itself. She found it amazing that Donovan was in such a great mood. He had to be exhausted; he'd only had three hours of sleep the night before. He'd gotten home from Mexicali at three o'clock in the morning and spent the next hour telling her about Midnight being alive and how she'd been rescued by the woman in the cantina. They'd finally gone to sleep about four o'clock, and she knew he'd been up at around seven.

When they arrived in San Luis Obispo, Donovan led her to a rental car company and gave the young woman at the counter his name. Jeanie noted that she eyed Donovan with interest, but her gaze eventually strayed over to Jeanie and then down to their interlocked hands. Donovan didn't even seem to notice. He really had no idea how good-looking he was, nor the effect his killer smile had on women. They picked up a red convertible Chrysler Sebring and headed toward the ocean.

They drove for a little while in comfortable silence. Then Jeanie glanced over at him, smiling. "Hey," she said softly.

Donovan glanced over at her, a half-grin on his face.

"You okay?" she asked, sensing some undercurrent in the air.

"I'm fine," he said. "Hell, better than fine—now that Midnight's alive, her attempted killers either dead or behind bars... now that I'm here, driving a pretty cool car along the coast with the most beautiful girl in the world at my side. What could possibly be wrong?"

Jeanie laughed at his litany, shaking her head. "Nothing, I guess." She glanced at him. "So you never did really tell me what all happened in Mexico. I mean, I know Midnight showed up at the end and all, but what happened with Blue and the bad guys?"

"Actually, Blue did pretty damn good for someone who's not even a cop—I do have to say that. He was cool, calm, and actually managed to get plenty of evidence from them before it all came down."

"Did they say why they'd grabbed Susan? She was with them, right?" Jeanie asked, realizing she didn't even know that.

"Oh yeah, she was with them, and Devereaux wanted Blue to murder her so he'd be as guilty as the rest of them."

"Jesus..."

"Yeah, they were real pillars of society," Donovan said wryly.

"Real bastards is more like it," Jeanie said vehemently.

"Yes, well." Donovan grinned. "Your friend Blue took Devereaux out, taking a bullet in the process."

"But you said he was okay, right?"

"Right," Donovan confirmed. "Anyway, McCaffery and Gaston booked and split up. Me, Spider, and Dibbs were headed up one stairway; Joe, Tiny, and Rick were coming up the other. Dibbs and Spider had split from me, checking a hallway, when out of some broom closet comes McCaffery. He put his hands up immediately when he saw me. I told him to keep them where I could see 'em, and holstered my gun. Well, either he was extremely stupid or he didn't remember that I've been trained by the best when it comes to guns, shooting *and* drawing. He went for his backup weapon—I drew and fired. He was dead before he hit the floor."

"Better him than you," Jeanie said definitively.

Donovan smiled at the protectiveness in her voice and reached over to take her hand. "He never had a chance, babe. Those guys were only dangerous when they could shoot you in the back. They were cowards."

"So what happened to Gaston?" she asked, holding tight to his hand, wanting to keep the connection with him.

"Near as I can figure, he must have come out all guns on the guys, 'cause they stitched him up pretty good."

"Stitched? What does that mean?"

"When you shoot a suspect you go for less lethal parts of the body to start with. The goal is to stop the threat. You start here," he said, pointing to his thigh, "and you work your way up until the threat is neutralized."

"Uh-huh," she said, making a face that said *Yikes!*

"You'll learn about it in the academy," Donovan said, grinning over at her. "They save the exciting stuff till close to the end."

"Exciting?" Jeanie said jokingly.

"Yeah. Getting to shoot people with someone else's ammunition—what more fun could you expect?"

Jeanie looked at him for a long moment, surprised until he started to laugh. "You jerk, you really had me going there for a minute!" she said, punching him on the arm. "I thought you'd managed to hide some psychotic streak from me."

"Oh yeah, I have that too," Donovan said, laughing.

The drive proceeded in the same companionable vein. When they arrived at San Simeon, Jeanie still didn't know where they were going. She didn't understand until she saw the sign for Hearst Castle. As Donovan turned into the parking lot they could see the incredible structure high up on the hill. Donovan parked and got out, coming round to open her door for her. Jeanie still couldn't get used to the fact that he did that. He took her hand to help her out and held on to it as they walked up to the front gates of the State Park. Inside he booked them on two tours of the vast home and walked back over to her, admiring her as he did. She was wearing white shorts and a lavender silk tank top with a brown belt and brown sandals. Her hair was pulled back softly from her face with combs. She looked absolutely beautiful. He couldn't believe he was lucky enough to be with her. He watched as she stood to meet him; she certainly had a body that wouldn't quit. At five foot six inches, she had a slim waist, long legs, and perfectly rounded breasts. Her skin was smooth and tanned, and her brown eyes sparkled at him from behind a frame of long black lashes.

Donovan reached out to touch her lightly under the chin as he looked down at her. "Have I told you recently how incredibly beautiful you are?"

"Stop it," she said, looking embarrassed.

He narrowed his eyes at her. "I will not. You are one of the most beautiful women I have ever seen, and I love you like crazy."

Jeanie grinned. "Yeah?" she said, still embarrassed.

"Yeah," he said, leaning down to kiss her and taking her into his arms. Many of the people around them watched with envy in their eyes. They were a good-looking couple, Donovan with his all-American looks and tall, lean frame, and Jeanie with her smoldering beauty and petite but voluptuous body.

They spent a fun day touring the beautiful home of William Hearst. They walked through the gardens and enjoyed the incredible views. Eventually they returned to the car. Donovan drove up the coast a bit, looking around as he did. Highway 1 had awesome views of the ocean and the contrasts of coastline and mountain ranges. There were panoramic vistas of waves crashing against monolithic rocks. Donovan glanced frequently over his shoulder, as if looking for something. Jeanie noticed the behavior after a little while and watched him with a furrowed brow.

"What are you doing?" she asked.

"Looking for something," he replied simply.

"And what would that be?"

"You'll see," he said with an enigmatic grin.

Ten minutes later he said, "That looks good." He pulled over to the side of the road and got out, then opened Jeanie's door and led her quickly across the highway.

"What's up, Donovan?" she asked, laughing as he walked over to the bluff. The view was fantastic. The sun was just beginning to set, turning the sky a myriad of beautiful colors—fuchsia, red, orange, plum. The mountains behind them were covered with soft green grass that flamed orange in the setting sun. The ocean below crashed against the rocks, and the sound of the waves and the scent of the salt air traveled upward to the bluff. There were ten other people standing there, watching the sun set. It was an extremely beautiful sight to behold.

Jeanie thought she'd never seen anything more incredible in her life. She looked out over the ocean and didn't see Donovan watching her. She was just turning to ask him what he had meant by this "looking good" when he dropped to one knee, taking her hand.

"What are you doing?" she asked, smiling down at him as he looked up at her.

Donovan looked thoughtful for a moment, pursing his lips almost comically. Then he shrugged, staring up into her eyes. "Just asking you to marry me."

"What?" Jeanie replied, dumbfounded, sure she hadn't heard him correctly.

"You heard me, Jay. I want to know if you'll marry me."

Jeanie stared down at him for a long time, too stunned to even realize that everyone on the bluff was now watching them. All she could see was Donovan, his perfect smile, his teal-blue eyes fixed on her.

"Could I have an answer, please?" he asked calmly, still smiling. "Or do you want to think about it?"

"No!" Jeanie replied abruptly.

"Is that my answer?" Donovan asked, canting his head to the side, his expression more serious.

"No, oh God, Donovan, no—that's not the answer. I meant no,

I don't need to think about it. And the answer is yes."

"Well thank God," he said, standing and grabbing her up in a hug. He kissed her deeply. Everyone on the bluff cheered. After a long moment, their lips parted and Donovan said, "Oh, yeah, there is this other thing." He reached into his jacket and pulled out a small velvet box, then handed it to her.

Jeanie stared up at him and then down at the box. Donovan noted that her hand was shaking.

"Open it, Jay," he said, smiling. "This is supposed to be the best part."

Jeanie bit her lower lip nervously as she opened the box. She was sure she forgot to breathe when she saw the ring nestled inside the burgundy velvet. It was the most incredible diamond ring she'd ever seen, glistening magnificently in the setting sun. It had a round-cut solitaire with a graduated set of baguette diamonds swirling out from it. It was delicate and elaborate at the same time.

"Donovan…" she breathed. "Oh my God." She shook her head, unable to fathom how much it had cost him, and not sure that she rated such an incredible offering.

"Do you like it?" he asked, looking a bit nervous himself.

"Jesus, Donovan, are you kidding me?" Jeanie grinned. "It's fantastic!" She stood on tiptoe and kissed him warmly, eliciting another cheer from the onlookers. She and Donovan broke into laughter at the sound.

After a short while on the bluff, they walked back to the car hand in hand. A few miles up the road Donovan pulled off on a side street and headed into the hills.

"Now where are we going?" she asked, still totally flabbergasted by the entire thing. She couldn't get over the fact that Donovan had actually asked her to marry him... She was going to be his wife—my God!

"You'll see," Donovan said, grinning gleefully. He couldn't believe she'd actually said yes! He'd been very nervous about the whole thing. He hadn't been sure she'd say anything, let alone yes. He'd wondered mildly if she'd push him off the bluff for asking such an outrageous question. But she'd said yes, thank God—he'd meant that when he said it earlier.

A little while later they pulled up to a Victorian house high up on a hill overlooking the ocean. Once again he got out of the car and opened her door, then led her up to the house. It was a bed and breakfast. When they were taken to their room, Jeanie couldn't believe how beautiful it was. The walls were decorated in a cream damask covering, and the furnishings were all antique mahogany with rich hunter green damask coverlets and burgundy velvet pillows. There was a fireplace which the innkeeper promptly got going. When he'd left, Jeanie turned to Donovan; again, he was watching her.

"This is too much, Donovan. It's so beautiful," she said, almost breathless. She couldn't believe the extent he had gone to, but knew it had been his intention to romance her, and she loved him more for it.

"This was important," he said softly.

"And it's fantastic." She reached up to hug him. "I love you," she whispered, before kissing him.

"Mmm," he purred. "That's exactly what I want to hear." His voice was a warm murmur. "But before I show you just how much I love you…" He grinned. "Let's change and go have dinner."

They went down to the bed and breakfast's elegant restaurant. It was a cozy dining room with a table in the corner reserved just for them. They ate by candlelight and talked about general things. It was very nice just to sit and talk; finally the cloud that had been hanging over everything, the case, was done, over. Now they could talk about normal life. Jeanie told him more about her childhood and her brothers. He laughed when she told him about the time her brothers had played basketball with her, with her as the ball. She told him about the camping trips she'd gone on with her family, and all the times they'd gone up to the mountains to ride horses or hike the trails.

"It was fun being part of a family. I guess sometimes I miss being young and being able to rely on them for everything," she said wistfully. "Do you ever feel like that?" she asked, watching him closely.

Donovan never talked about his childhood; he talked about everything from after the time Randy and Joe got together but never anything else. She hadn't pushed him to discuss it because it was obvious he didn't want to, but now, if she was going to marry him, she really wanted to know more about him.

Donovan didn't answer for a long moment, but finally shook his head slowly. "Can't say that I do," he said, his voice soft but even. "So where did your family camp? I've heard green valley falls is a really great place." The change of subject wasn't even close to being subtle, but it was obviously not a concern for him.

Jeanie narrowed her eyes at him for a moment, not sure if she wanted to question him further. Finally she answered him. "We camped there a couple of times. We also went up to Potrero Lake—it was very nice there too. So how come you never talk about your child-hood?" she said, throwing the last question in casually, but with a pointed look.

Donovan shook his head. "Jay…"

"Donovan," she said entreatingly, "I know absolutely nothing about you before you became a police officer."

"Why do you need to know about the stuff before that?" he asked, his voice edgy now.

"Why don't you want to tell me?" she asked, surprised at his sudden tension.

"It's not a happy little story, okay?"

"I know about your parents leaving, Donovan, but was it always bad?"

"Yeah, it was, okay," he said, his voice short, almost angry. "Is the interrogation over now?" He stood up. They'd finished dinner a half hour before but had been lingering over wine and dessert.

Jeanie stood too, shocked at the sudden change in him. It was hard to picture the romantic man he'd been only minutes before. Now he was tense and angry, and she could literally feel his defensiveness.

When they got back to the room, Jeanie went into the bathroom. When she came out a few minutes later, Donovan was sitting on the bed. He had kicked off his shoes and pulled the tails of his midnight-blue shirt out of his trousers. He was leaning against the headboard, looking very far away. After a long moment he turned to her. His expression changed from distant to complete desire in a matter of seconds. Jeanie stood in the doorway to the bathroom with nothing on but a smile.

"Wow…" he said, shaking his head slowly.

"Thank you," she replied, walking over to the bed.

"Come here," he said, holding his hand out. She took it and he pulled her to him. She straddled his legs and Donovan sat up, closing the space between them. He kissed her, keeping his hand in hers, as he held her close with his other arm. His kiss was warm and gentle but with a definite hunger behind it, and Jeanie could sense the apology. He continued to kiss her as he caressed her neck.

When they finally parted for a moment, he stared into her eyes. "You are so beautiful," he whispered against her lips.

"I love you," she whispered in response, wanting to get past the tension.

Donovan didn't reply to her declaration. Instead he made love to her, taking his time to excite her thoroughly, making her gasp and writhe as she anticipated his touch. He kissed every inch of her body, heating her way beyond the boiling point and causing her to grasp his shoulders as if holding on for dear life. It was a very sensual union, and it held all the promise their engagement stood for.

Afterward, Jeanie lay in his arms, her head on his chest, her fingers tracing a lazy pattern on the muscles there. "Donovan?" she said softly, knowing she shouldn't ask what she wanted to.

"Hmm?" he murmured, sounding tired but sated.

"What happened?" she asked, her cautious tone indicating she wasn't talking about what they'd just done.

Donovan didn't answer for a long time, but his hand on her back continued its lazy stroking. Finally he sighed. "It was a long time ago,

Jay, and it's not something I want to think about let alone talk about."

"But Donovan—"

"Jay, please," he said, his voice a strong whisper.

"Was it really bad?"

"Yes."

"Will you tell me someday?"

Again he didn't answer right away. Then he shook his head. "Not if I can help it."

Jeanie looked surprised by the statement, staring up at him. He'd told her the truth. He didn't like to think about his childhood. It had been a time of constant terror and he had no desire to relive a moment of it, not even for her.

They were quiet for a while. Donovan knew she was hurt by his unyielding attitude, but he knew he couldn't do anything to change it. It was one issue he wasn't willing to compromise on.

"Do you think your parents will forgive us for living in sin now?" he asked, grinning slightly as he touched the ring on her left hand.

She didn't answer right away, obviously trying to decide if she wanted to stay angry at him because of his obstinance. Finally she grinned and shrugged. "Maybe…"

"Maybe your mom will stop crossing herself every time she sees me?"

"Stop it!" she said, laughing as she shoved at him. "She doesn't do that. Well, only when you're not looking."

"Ah-ha!" he said, holding up a triumphant finger. "She does think I'm evil. I knew it!"

She raised an eyebrow at him. "Well, you are, aren't you?"

"Sometimes," he replied, looking devilish as he pulled her over on top of him. His face grew serious then. "I love you," he whispered. "Can you give me the space I need on the childhood issue?"

"Yes," she said, still looking a little sad. "I just want to know you, Donovan. I don't want to hurt you, I'd just like to understand."

He took a deep breath and then blew it out slowly. "I know, Jay. I just… It's in the past and I really want it to stay there."

Again she looked at him, searching his face as if looking for some clue to what he wasn't telling her about. Finally she nodded, realizing she needed to let it go if they were going to move forward. It nagged at her though. Something so traumatic that he wanted to totally forget it was bound to come out someway, sometime. She didn't know how she would deal with something like that if she didn't even know what to look for. It was a thought that would stay with her for a long time, even in the fun they shared for the rest of the trip. They returned two days before Susan's wedding.

****

Rick walked into his and Midnight's bedroom. To his chagrin she sat up as he approached the bed.

"What are you doing up again?" she asked reproachfully.

"Eating," he said simply, showing her the handful of cookies he carried.

"Eating?" She glanced at the clock on the nightstand. "Babe, it's two o'clock in the morning. People *sleep* at this hour."

Rick sighed, shaking his head. "Not me."

"Richard…"

"Midnight…" he countered in the same tone of voice. "I can't sleep, okay? Do you want me to go in the living room or something?"

"No, I want you to put those down and come to bed."

"So it's you or the cookies?" he asked, grinning as he raised a considering eyebrow.

"Right," she said, watching him with a grin of her own.

"Too easy." He tossed the cookies on the nightstand and climbed onto the bed on all fours, like a predatory cat. He crawled over to her, kissing her sensually on the lips. All the while he hovered over her like a leopard. He kissed her for a long while then moved to rest his head lightly against her shoulder. "I love you," he whispered against her bare skin. He'd been saying it over and over since she'd returned, as if to remind her in case she forgot.

"I love you too," she whispered back as she leaned against the headboard, putting her arms around him and pulling him back with her so his head and torso rested against her. She stroked his bare back and his hair. "You need to sleep, babe," she said softly. "I'm worried about you."

"I'm alright," he said, his voice slightly muffled as he moved to kiss her shoulder.

"How much sleep have you had in the last week?"

"I'm fine, Midnight," he said, not even sure how much he'd actually had.

"Mmhmm," she murmured. Then she kissed his forehead, her eyes showing the worry she felt even if he couldn't see it. "Well, since

203

you're awake anyway, I want to talk to you about something."

"What would that be?" he asked, not moving his head off her shoulder. In truth, it felt really good to lie against her. The scent and feeling of her skin against his cheek and the sound of her heartbeat were so familiar and warm.

"Remember we talked about adopting a child?"

"Yes…"

"Well, I still want to," she said, her tone indicating there was more.

"And…"

"And I know who I want to adopt." She held her breath, waiting for his reaction.

"Okay…" he said, sitting up and looking down at her. "Who?"

"Remember Ricardo?"

Rick nodded. "The boy from the cantina, her son…" He trailed off as he thought again of what the woman had given up to save Midnight.

"Right," she said, biting her lower lip. "I want to adopt him."

Rick looked at her for a long moment, his brows furrowed. "Night, his mother's dead, but not his father."

"His father is in a Mexican prison, Rick. For attempted murder of a police officer, a chief no less. It's not like America—he's not getting out on an appeal or some technicality. He's there for good, or at least until Ricardo's a whole lot older, in his thirties or forties."

Rick nodded. "But what about Montavo? Doesn't his uncle want him?"

"I talked to him again today," Midnight said, looking sad. "He said Ricardo isn't doing very well. He's still despondent over his mother's death, and Montavo says when he does talk, he talks about me." She shrugged. "I guess he's clinging to some happy memory he has from before his mother was killed. Anyway, Montavo can't take care of him. He has school and work and nowhere near enough money to take care of a boy that young, not the way he deserves."

"But we do," Rick said, knowing it was what she was thinking.

"Don't we?"

Rick nodded. "Of course we do, love. I was just finishing your train of thought." He looked contemplative for a moment, then nodded as if making a decision. "We need to talk to Keyla about this."

"I know."

"We'll do it in the morning." Rick lay down and pulled her with him. He took her in his arms, kissing her temple. "If she's okay with it, I am too."

Midnight glanced up at him, surprised with the ease with which he'd decided. Then she grinned mischievously. "That was easy. Should I ask for the summer home in France now too?"

Rick laughed softly. "Do you want a summer home in France?"

Midnight looked thoughtful for a moment, then shook her head. "Nah, I hate French cuisine, nor do I speak a word of French."

"Hired chefs can cook anything you like, and as smart as you are, you'd learn French in a week."

It was Midnight's turn to laugh. "You have too much faith in me. It would take me at least a month to master the language."

Rick laughed again. That was when there was a light knock on their door. The looked at each other and then at the door as Rick said, "Come."

Mikeyla came in. "Are you two awake?"

"Well, we would be now, wouldn't we?" Rick said good-naturedly.

"Sorry," Mikeyla said, having the good grace to at least look embarrassed.

"Come on in," Midnight said, sitting up and reaching for Rick's shirt at the end of the bed. She pulled it over her head. Rick sat up and drew Midnight back to lean against him. "What's up?" she asked.

"Besides you," Rick added wryly.

Mikeyla climbed onto the bed and sat down cross-legged. She looked very young in the oversized Star Wars shirt and black leggings she wore to bed. Her hair was pulled back in a long braid down her back. She did look a lot like her mother, with Midnight's copper-blond hair and petite features. She had her father's deep blue eyes and finely boned face. She was a beautiful girl, something that was very evident even at the age of nearly nine.

"I can't sleep," Mikeyla said in answer to her mother's question.

Midnight glanced back at Rick, narrowing her eyes suspiciously. "Great, a family of insomniacs."

Rick grinned. "That's because you had the nerve to try and get yourself murdered." He looked seriously at their daughter then. "We're still trying to adjust."

Mikeyla nodded, and Midnight looked chagrined. Rick saw it and hugged her close, kissing the top of her head to tell her it was okay.

"Just as well," he said, lightening the mood. "We needed to talk to you anyway, Keyl."

"About what?" she asked.

"Well…" Midnight began. "Your father and I are talking about another child—and before you freak," she said, holding up her hand at the worried look that had crossed her daughter's face, "we're talking about adoption." Mikeyla relaxed instantly and nodded. "We need to know how you'd feel about another child in this house."

Mikeyla thought about her answer for a long minute, then said, "I guess I'd be okay with it. I mean… if the kid's a brat I don't think I'd like it, but if not, it'd be cool." She shrugged.

Midnight glanced at Rick and saw the grin on his face at his daughter's way of thinking. "Well, here's the thing," she said. "We know who we want to adopt, and it's a little boy. He's five years old, and from what I know of him, he's very sweet."

Mikeyla nodded, looking contemplative. "How do you know him?"

"It's the little boy whose mother gave her life to save your mother," Rick said solemnly.

"Oh…" Mikeyla looked surprised. "I thought he was staying with his uncle."

"He is for now, but his uncle is very young and not exactly in a position to take care of a child so young," Midnight said, trying to keep the real need out of the picture; she didn't want to unfairly put pressure on her daughter to approve the decision.

"Okay…" Mikeyla nodded. "But didn't you say he only speaks Spanish?"

Midnight looked chagrined—she hadn't really thought about that. "As far as I know, yes, that's true."

"We can learn Spanish, Keyl," Rick put in. "It'd be good for us, and besides, he'll learn English too."

Mikeyla nodded, as if accepting what he'd said. Midnight squeezed her husband's arm in silent thanks for his support.

"Okay," Mikeyla said finally, her tone upbeat. "When are we going to adopt him?"

Midnight looked at her daughter for a long moment, stunned by her easy acceptance. "It'll take a little while," she said, shaking her head and blinking back the sudden tears in her eyes. "And you're really okay with this?"

"Sure, Mom. You know I've been wanting a baby brother or sister for forever. I can teach him English," she said proudly.

"Yes, you can," Midnight replied, ever surprised by her daughter's spirit.

"I'm gonna go to bed now." Mikeyla stood, yawning. She kissed each of her parents on the cheek then walked toward the door.

"Keyl," Midnight said, making her turn around.

"Yeah, Mom?"

Midnight smiled. "You're a pretty great kid, you know that?"

"Yeah, I know." Mikeyla sounded so much like Midnight herself that Rick laughed as she left the room.

"Got you there, didn't she?" he said as they lay back down.

"Sounded like me, huh?"

"Oh, yes."

"Really think we can do this? Adopting Ricardo, I mean."

"We'll do it, no matter what it takes."

"Could get expensive…"

"If it's going to make you happy, I'd gladly spend my entire trust fund to make it happen."

"Thank you," she said, kissing him on the chest. "I mean for your support in this. I know it isn't going to be easy."

"We'll do it, don't worry. It's the right thing—the powers that be will see that."

Midnight nodded.

Plans for Susan's wedding had continued even when Midnight had been "dead," though Susan had told Warren the day before the funeral that she was planning to change the date. "Why?" he'd asked somewhat accusingly. He hadn't gotten over his jealousy of Christian and Susan sleeping together yet. He likely never would, because he had the distinct feeling Christian was better in that department.

"Warren!" Susan had practically yelled, trying to get through to him. "My aunt is being buried tomorrow. I hardly think now is the time for a wedding, a purportedly happy occasion."

Her words had cut and Warren had backed off. He sensed she would be more than happy to cancel the wedding indefinitely, so he didn't want to push. He'd been beside himself when she was accosted. He blamed Christian and had been sure she would too. They'd talked the day after she returned from Mexico, after she'd spent the night waiting to hear about Christian's condition. She'd been tired and upset, and hadn't really wanted to talk to him, but Warren had insisted.

Since Midnight had returned alive, Warren thought it would be good to keep the original wedding date as planned. Susan had tiredly agreed, too worn out to argue and too worried about Christian to really care what she said at that moment.

Susan had resigned herself to marrying Warren. Things with him had been better since their fight the night he'd hit her. She'd told him about Christian—not everything, certainly not about being in love with the man—but about the sex, and that he'd been there for her during Randy's hospitalization. Warren had been smart enough to apologize profusely for hitting her, explaining that he loved her so much that he hated the thought of another man touching her. He'd been further understanding by saying he realized she'd needed to test the waters a little bit before making a final commitment to him. They'd actually gotten along fairly well during the time Christian had distanced himself. Susan had been angry at Christian's disappearance and decided she needed to concentrate on the stable relationship she had with Warren. He had, after all, shown a jealous streak at the thought of Christian and her together; maybe he wasn't as obsequious as she'd thought. Maybe he would make a good husband—maybe she just really needed to give him a chance.

Christian had turned her head with his incredible looks and his direct and very sexual behavior, but he was certainly not the type of man one would marry and settle down with. Not that it had been an issue; Christian had certainly never indicated he wanted her in any capacity other than as a bed fellow. Hardly a marital state. Susan had decided Christian had been a good learning experience, a chance to get close to the wild side she'd never approached before, but certainly not a way of life.

It was for that reason that she was set to be married the day after

Christian arrived home from the hospital. She hadn't seen him since the night he'd been shot. Her mother had arrived the day after Susan got home and had had her running mad about wedding preparations. Wilson, Susan's father, had arrived the day after that and wanted to have dinner with Warren and his parents and spend time with his little girl. Then her aunts had arrived, and her grandparents were still there, since they'd been there for her uncle during Midnight's absence. Things had been hectic. That night Susan wanted to talk to him, but she had the rehearsal dinner. It was late by the time she got back to Joe's and changed. She walked toward the living room; her mother, her sister—Elizabeth—Joe, Randy, and her aunts, Mandy and Allison, were there, discussing the seating arrangements for the reception. Susan stood in the hallway, listening to it all and feeling overwhelmed.

"You can't put the Terrantins with the O'Hares, Deborah," Mandy was saying. "They'll kill each other. You know old Charles still hates Timothy because of that bad investment. They lost hundreds of thousands in the deal."

"Well, I don't know where else they'll go. I can't fit anyone else on that table—everyone else I have has more than two in their party," Deborah said, sounding tired of the whole thing herself.

"Why don't we just let them sit together and see what happens," Joe said, sounding distinctly like he was smiling.

"Do shut up, Joseph," Allison said, but laughed right after. "You'd just love to see a fight, wouldn't you?"

"Between those two old windbags, you bet," Joe said, laughing too.

Susan listened for a little while longer, then went out by way of the kitchen, walking quickly down the path leading to the carriage house. She knocked lightly on the door, wondering what she was doing even as she did. She heard his voice tell her to come in. Susan pushed the door open and stepped inside. Christian was lying on his bed, bare-chested, a bandage still covering his lower torso. He gave her a sardonic grin, looking a little amused.

"What are you doing down here?" he asked lightly.

"I wanted to come see how you're doing," she said softly.

"Aren't you supposed to be getting ready for the big day tomorrow?" There was more than a little sarcasm in his voice.

"Yes," she said, her tone telling him to shut up. "And now I'm down here seeing how you're doing." There was a lot of moxy in her voice, and Christian couldn't help but smile. If nothing else, she certainly wasn't timid with him anymore.

"So," he said, his grin in place. "Sit down and see how I'm doing."

She did as he said, and reached out to touch the bandage carefully. "Does it hurt a lot?"

Christian shrugged. "Only if I move, breathe too heavy, or think about it," he rattled off.

"Shut up, you," Susan said, measuring her words and grinning at him. "I feel guilty enough about you being shot—I don't need you to make it worse."

"Sorry," he said, sounding anything but. "'Sides, why do you feel guilty? I'm the dumb shit that got in the way of the bullet."

"And the reason for that was?"

"I'm too damn slow?" he asked, his eyes twinkling.

"You're too damn gallant for your own good, is more like it." Then she gave him a serious look. "Thank you," she said softly, her eyes suddenly shining with tears.

"Hey," he said, his visage clouding as he sat up and reached out to touch her cheek. "Don't do that. I got you into that mess—the least I could do was get you out alive."

"No, Christian," she said with a determined shake of her head. "You didn't get me into it—those men dragged me into it. And I was so scared, until you got there—then I knew I was going to be safe."

"I saw that," he said, smiling again. "Pretty sure of me, weren't you?"

"Very sure."

"It gave me a little more strength, seeing that in your eyes," he said, feeling the need to be honest with her. "Truth to tell, I was on edge from the get go, but your obvious calm helped a lot."

Susan nodded, touching his cheek. "I knew you'd take care of me, Christian. I didn't have a doubt in my mind."

"Well, that makes one of us," he said, grinning wryly.

"Stop!" She hit him lightly on the shoulder.

"So," he said, his tone changing, "you pretty sure of what you're doing tomorrow?"

Susan didn't answer for a moment, then nodded. "He's been better since that night he hit me, Christian. I think it was kind of a turning point in our relationship."

Christian nodded, watching her eyes. "And you love him?"

"Yes," she said, as if answering an inquiry instead of a simple question.

213

Christian held up his hands. "Okay, don't shoot," he said, his lips twisting in a sardonic grin.

"Sorry," she said, looking embarrassed at her severity, then sighed. "I guess things have just been really stressed lately. It's beginning to wear… you know?"

Christian nodded. "Yeah…"

Susan canted her head to the side slightly, looking askance at him. "Christian, can I… I mean… would you mind if I stayed down here with you for a while? I'm just so tired of hearing about seating arrangements, place cards, appropriate wedding etiquette, and all that—I could just scream."

Christian held back his smile and nodded, pulling back half the covers so she could slide under. She noted that he wore black sweatpants, his usual attire for bed. Christian lay down next to her, turning carefully on his side to look down at her. "Big wedding, huh?"

"Enormous," Susan said, rolling her eyes. "It all seems to be happening without me, like I'm just part of the whole show—it's very surreal."

"I thought it was supposed to be your big day," Christian said drily.

Susan sighed again. "It is. I just, I haven't really been interested in all this, with everything else that's been happening."

"So postpone it."

"I started to, when we thought Midnight was dead, but now… things are moving forward like some massive machine, with no thought or reason."

"If you don't like the way things are going, Susan, put the brakes on. It's your wedding—your life, for that matter."

"Yes, well, tell that to my father and mother and all three of my aunts, my uncle, my grandparents, not to mention his parents and relatives..." She shook her head miserably.

Christian gave her a long, measured look, then shrugged as if he'd done all he could. "Then don't complain about it."

Susan looked back at him for a moment, her brows furrowing in surprise, but then closed her eyes as if getting it suddenly. "I'm sorry," she said, opening her eyes and blowing out her breath. "I sound so foolish, talking about all this like it really matters. It's just a day in my life—it's not really that important." She waved her hand dismissively. "Let's not talk about it another moment, let's talk about something else. Your mother is here—that must be really nice for you. It's been so long since you've seen her."

Christian grinned at her changing the subject, but nodded all the same. "Yeah, it's good to see her. I guess I didn't realize how much I missed her till I saw her at the hospital."

"I got a chance to talk to her yesterday at breakfast. She adores you, that much is obvious."

"Some people have no taste."

"Oh, please." Susan looked at him slyly. "You know damned good and well that you're adorable, you just want everyone to think you're a pain in the ass."

He smiled. "Thanks."

"No problem," she replied, smiling too. "Actually, she told me you were a very easy child, never a moment's problem. Imagine that."

"Yes, well, we all grow out of childhood, don't we?"

"Some of us," she shot back, laughing as he shook his head.

"Where has this sharp-tongued girl come from? You are not the shy slip of a girl I knew a few months ago."

"Your fault," Susan said, raising her chin defiantly.

"Bully for me," he said, smiling in spite of himself.

"So what were you like as a child?"

"Smaller."

"Christian…"

"Okay, okay…" He smiled again and lay back on the bed. She turned onto her side so she could look at him. "I was pretty easy, like my mum said. I didn't want to be any trouble." He shrugged, glancing at her. "I guess I realized real early on what she'd given up for me, and that every day was a struggle for her. I tried to make it as easy as I could." He made a sour face then. "It didn't last forever though—things got a lot harder as I got older."

"Why?" she asked softly.

He took a deep breath and blew it out, his eyes taking on a faraway look. "As I got older I started growing into my looks—they were more hindrance than help in those days." He saw the question in her eyes. "The guys I went to school with started to see me as competition, and the girls, well, they started comin' round and causing all sorts of commotion about me. It was ridiculous, really. I was the same guy they'd grown up with, but after one summer they all treated me differently."

"You grew up over the break, right?" Susan asked with a knowing look.

"Six inches of height and a lot of muscle, since I had a summer job hauling steel castoff for the mill, and a couple more inches of hair because I was too lazy to get it cut," Christian supplied wryly.

"Oh, brother, you did grow up overnight," she said sympathetically. "So what happened?"

"I learned really early on that I was going to have to defend myself against these other guys, and they didn't always fight fair. That's when I started carrying a knife. I was a fucking kid, fourteen years old and carrying a switchblade for protection. I didn't tell my mother—I didn't want to worry her. Her health had started to deteriorate at that point, and I knew she didn't need any more strain."

Susan nodded, reaching out to touch his jaw, which was tight at the thoughts going through his head. He glanced at her, his eyes softening at the empathy on her face.

"Anyway, the trouble started then. I started getting into fights, and the school started calling home. I intercepted all the messages I could, but eventually my mum found out. It was too hard to explain to her why it was happening, too embarrassing. I just brushed off her questions and told her I was fine, that I'd take care of myself. That's when she worried constantly. 'Course, that wasn't the only stuff going on then. I had my mind on other things..."

"What other things?" Susan asked when he trailed off.

"I'd discovered women... and what I could get from them. What they were willing to do just because I looked good. It was a very powerful feeling. Suddenly I could give a girl a look and she'd practically drop at my feet and beg me to make love to her."

"That's exactly what happened too, isn't it?" Susan asked, with no reproach in her voice.

"Oh yes," he said, not sounding cocky in the least—actually, he

217

sounded a bit chagrined. "It just got worse over the years, and I started to use it to my advantage. That's about the time I lost a lot of faith in humankind and myself."

"I believe that," she said softly. "It allowed things to be too easy for you, didn't it? That's not always the best thing, especially not during an impressionable time like your teen years."

"Tell me about it," Christian said sadly. "You know, I think the worst thing was when I was about sixteen. I had this instructor—she was young, only out of college by about two years, on her first teaching assignment. She took one look at my work in school and failed me. She called me into her office and told me she was failing me because she knew full well I was not living up to my full potential. She told me she'd seen my earlier test scores and she knew I had a good mind, I was just being lazy and doing what little it took to get by. Boy, she wasn't kidding. I was doing exactly what it took to get by—most of my instructors were women and let me slide because of my looks, but not this one. No, this one had a goal—she was going to get me to think and live up to my potential."

"What happened?" Susan asked, seeing the angry, sickened look on his face.

"Well, she started to work with me, and she was harder than hell on me. Calling me out every time I tried to slack off or give less than a hundred percent."

"That's what they all should have been doing."

"Yeah," Christian said, giving her a wry grin. "But at that point I was used to sliding by, and the last thing I needed as far as I was concerned was some fucking optimist messing up my permanent vacation. So I decided to fix it."

"How?" Susan asked, her tone cautious now as she detected the anger and hurt lying so close to the surface. She knew he was telling her something he'd never talked about before, and she wanted to hear it, and help if she could.

Christian glanced at her, seeing the concern in her eyes, and shook his head. "Simple, really," he said contemptibly, naked pain on his face now. "I turned on the charm." He said it as if he were talking about murdering someone.

"And?" she whispered.

He laughed drily. "And it worked. I fucked her, and she passed me." His jaw tightened as he swallowed against the sudden knot in his throat.

"Oh, Christian…" Susan said, shaking her head mournfully. "God, that must have been so tragic for you, to have her give up on you so easily."

Christian shrugged. "It didn't do a lot for my academic career, no. But hey, I guess it was a great segue to my ultimate career, huh? Loving 'em and leavin' 'em, that is."

"No, Christian, it's not your fault that woman had no morals. She should have been shot, or worse," she said vehemently.

Christian laughed. "What's worse than being shot?"

"Being drawn and quartered," she supplied, the beginnings of a grin on her face. She leaned down and kissed his shoulder tenderly. "I'm sorry things were like that for you," she said gently.

"Wasn't so bad," he said mildly. "I got out and never looked back, and moved on to much bigger and better things."

Susan made a face. "Stop being so damned cavalier about it."

He grinned. "Stop being so damned depressed about it, Zan. We can't change it now."

"I know. But I just hate that people used you like that. Why couldn't they see that you have so much more to offer than your looks?"

"'Cause I didn't show them anything else," he said calmly. "I didn't care what they thought, so long as I got what I needed out of them. I let them use me—that was my choice."

"Well," she said stubbornly, "don't do it anymore."

"Why not?"

"Because you're my friend now, and I won't let you."

"Ha, *let me*, hell," he said, his grin widening.

She leaned imperiously over him, her face taking on a haughty look. "Don't make me hurt you, Collins. You're still recovering and all."

"All because you got me shot."

"I got you shot?" she replied, her tone still haughty. "I hardly think your lack of agility constitutes fault on my part."

"Ah, now the truth comes out," he said, nodding knowingly.

"You said so yourself, you got in the way of the bullet."

"Uh-huh."

"Stop it," she said, laughing.

"Laughing at me now, huh?"

She raised her chin. "Never."

"Oh, yes, I'd say so." He touched her chin with his index finger. "Have I told you how beautiful you look tonight?" he asked, his voice lowering an octave.

Susan's breath caught in her throat. "I don't believe so, no," she said, trying to keep her voice light.

"So beautiful." He moved his hand to the back of her neck and gently guided her face down to his, kissing her. Susan responded instantly, her hands going to his chest and gently caressing his muscles. After a few moments Christian dropped his head back on the pillow, sighing loudly. "Can't do this, love."

Susan sighed too. "I know. It wouldn't be right, or fair, or anything near appropriate."

"Must be appropriate," he said, grinning sardonically and raising an eyebrow at her.

"I come from a very proper family, you know," she said, raising her own eyebrow.

He rolled his eyes. "Lord, don't I know it. 'Cept your uncle—I hardly think Rick qualifies for proper."

Susan laughed. "I think you're right on that account." She looked thoughtful then. "Actually, my little sister isn't exactly proper either. She's been kicked out of a number of private schools for outrageous behavior."

"Yeah?" Christian looked impressed. "She comin' to town?"

"She's here, Christian," Susan said, then narrowed her eyes at him. "And she's too young for you."

Christian didn't look put off. "How young would that be?"

"She's seventeen, Christian Joseph Collins. Don't. You. Dare."

Christian laughed at her tone. "Is that a threat, Ms. Endicott?"

"Yes, it is."

He grinned. "'Fraid I'll corrupt her?"

"Ha! Not bloody likely!" she said, using one of his favorite terms. "She may even be able to teach you a thing or two."

"I have to meet this one," he said, looking for all intents and purposes enthusiastic.

"And I told you, no," Susan said tightly, though she was grinning.

"Hey." He gave her a cool look. "After tomorrow night you'll be a married woman—I'll have to replace ya. What better than someone from the same family?"

"Christian!" she said, truly alarmed this time.

Christian laughed, shaking his head. "God, you're still so damned easy!"

Susan narrowed her eyes, then slapped him on the arm. "And you are such a scoundrel!"

"Uh-huh," he said, smiling proudly. "I think you know I'd never do that…"

"Yes, I suppose I do," she replied, shaking her head at his sense of humor. "You really are a cad! Making me think that…"

Christian grinned unrepentantly.

They talked long into the night about all kinds of things, most of them trivial. Eventually they both fell asleep.

Before dawn the next morning, Christian woke to the sensation of lips on his neck. He stirred, his body responding before his mind even woke fully. Opening his eyes, he saw Susan watching him. Her eyes were searching his, her lower lip between her teeth.

"I just—" she began softly, but his lips on hers stopped her. His kiss was soft but devouring, and within moments her body was on fire. He slid his hands over her clothes, dragging her shirt upward to touch her bare skin hungrily.

"God, Zan..." he murmured against her lips. "I want you, so fucking much."

"Yes... yes," she whispered, her lips leaving his to travel down to his neck. Christian gasped as her teeth grazed his skin. Then he was removing her shirt, tossing it aside and tugging at the button on her jeans and pulling them off as well. He ran his hands over her body, touching her breasts, caressing her skin, making her writhe and moan. "Christian," she said, her voice aching with desire. "Please... please, make love to me. I need you, I want you one last time. Please..." Her voice was a desperate beg, and Christian couldn't have ignored her even if he'd actually wanted to.

His body slid into hers, making them both groan. It had been a long time, and Christian had actually forgotten how good it felt to be inside her. They moved together, touching and tasting each other but taking their time. It was their last time together—they wanted it to last. When they finally reached their climax together they cried out, holding on tight to each other as they rode the wave of passion and then floated back down to earth. Afterward, Christian lay over her, trying to catch his breath, his lips against her neck, his breath warm on her skin.

"I don't know if I can live without this," he said softly, his mouth next to her ear.

Susan closed her eyes, having been thinking the same thing moments before. She knew she was doomed to a life of mediocre love-making. She was fully aware of the fact that had she never been with Christian she wouldn't have known what she'd be missing. It was as if fate were getting her back for cheating on Warren in the first place. If she hadn't strayed, if she hadn't slept with Christian even though it was so wrong, she wouldn't be in the position of giving up probably the best sex she would ever experience in her lifetime.

They slept again for a while then, and when they woke they made love again. Afterward, though, Susan knew she had to get back to the main house, or her mother and sister would be looking for her. She certainly didn't want them to find her in bed with Christian. She didn't want her uncle going after Christian again because of her, or something he saw as a slight on his family. In reality, Rick was very proper when it came to his family's reputation.

Later that day, Christian found himself driving Deborah around for some last-minute things she needed to do; everyone else was too busy to help. Deborah noticed that he was very quiet. She knew he'd been shot a few days before, and she'd been uneasy about him over-exerting himself so soon, but he'd assured her that he needed to get out of the house for a while.

Deborah had heard from Joe about her daughter's participation in Christian's redemption in Mexico. She had also heard about Susan's suspected on again, off again relationship with Christian. She was surprised that her daughter had chosen someone so jaded to sow her wild oats with. But she was pretty sure Susan had probably decided Christian Collins was too much for her. She wondered if Susan had decided Warren was "safer."

"So what do you think of all this?" Deborah asked, looking over at Christian.

Christian didn't answer for a long moment. "Are you talking about the wedding?"

"Yes."

Christian shrugged. "Glad I'm not payin' for it," he said simply.

Deborah laughed. "I should say not. It's costing a fortune." Christian nodded, taking a drink from the can of soda in his hand. Deborah gave him a measured look, then asked, "What happened between you and my daughter?"

He took another drink, wishing remotely that it was something a lot stronger than Pepsi. Then he glanced at Deborah and gave her a half-grin. "What happened between you and me?" he asked, his tone saying she should have known that.

Deborah nodded. "I'm assuming it was more than once though," she said speculatively.

Christian gave a short laugh. "It was more than once in the last twenty-four hours," he supplied sardonically.

"Oh my…" Deborah was surprised despite herself. "So you have been seeing her for a while?"

"Seeing her?" Christian repeated, saying the words as if she'd cussed.

"I mean you've been with her over the last few months," Deborah replied, trying to use the right words to describe a relationship she didn't really understand.

"I've had sex with her, yes." Christian knew he was being inflammatory, but wasn't willing to say more about his and Susan's relationship.

"So you're saying you have no feelings for her?" Deborah asked, surprised by his detached attitude.

"I care about her," he said, but didn't sound like he felt compelled to convince her of that statement. He shrugged. "But she knows what she's doin', marryin' Warren. She knows about him."

"What do you mean, knows about him?"

"I mean about him hitting her."

"He hit my daughter?" Deborah asked, her tone suddenly sharp.

"Yeah." Christian nodded. "I took the fall for that one, though."

"Why?" she asked, aghast.

"Your brother's kind of protective," Christian said placidly.

"Yes, but why didn't you tell him it was Warren and not you?"

"Long story," he said, waving it away, then saw the worried look on Deborah's face. "I don't think it's a habit he's into—don't worry about it. He got pissed off at her because she told him she'd slept with me. She said he was jealous."

Deborah shook her head. "Yes, but…"

"Deborah, he won't do it again."

"How do you know?"

"Because he knows I'll kill him if he touches her again."

Deborah looked at him for a long moment, again surprised by his words. "And yet you'll let her marry him?"

Christian laughed. "*Let* her? Deborah, Susan's a big girl. She knows what she's doing."

"But, Christian…"

"She has to make her own decisions. It's her life."

Deborah looked at him pointedly. "Maybe she just needs a better offer."

Christian looked back at her for a moment, then shook his head with a short laugh. "I don't think so. That's not my thing."

"But you could stop her."

"Deborah," he said caustically, "I don't want to stop her. I want her to make her own decisions about her life. She can't depend on other people to make her happy. And if she depends on me, she'll be miserable."

Deborah looked back at him for a long moment, then sighed, nodding. She understood what he meant, and she also knew he was right. If Susan didn't learn to make her own decisions and change the direction of her life, if she didn't like the way it was going, it was her own fault if she was unhappy. It was just very difficult to see her making what Deborah was sure was a mistake.

CHAPTER 7

That evening, the crew turned out at Joe's to get together before the wedding. Susan had invited all of her aunt and uncle's "gang." It was her feeling that they were all part of her extended family; some of them had been involved in her rescue, and the rest had been very supportive of her and her uncle during her aunt's absence. It had been a comfort to have them as friends, and thus she felt they deserved to be invited.

She knew it would drive her father insane, since he'd never liked the "seedy" side that his brother-in-law had brought into the family. He'd never really liked Midnight or what she did for a living. Wilson had always felt that Rick had married beneath him and would live to regret it someday. On the other hand, Susan had loved her aunt from the moment she'd laid eyes on her.

She still remembered the wedding she'd attended. It had been Rick and Midnight's as well as Randy and Joe's, and it was beautiful. She had adored Midnight and thought that she wanted to be like her aunt, but it was hopeless. Susan had never had the confidence Midnight possessed, nor the direct manner. She knew that if she were more like Midnight she wouldn't be allowing things to carry her along as they were.

Susan knew that her aunt would never have married a man she didn't really and truly love. If she were her aunt, though, she could have brought even a man like Christian Collins to his knees. As it was, she had gone to him the night before her wedding and begged him to make love to her one last time. How pathetic could one get, she wondered as she sat in the dressing room at the church that evening.

She'd spent the day moving as if in a dream, doing what she was told. Sitting patiently while the hairdresser arranged her honey-blond waves into an intricate braid of seed pearls and baby's breath. Sitting more patiently as the makeup artist worked away and the manicurist did her nails. Somewhere along the way, Susan began thinking that she wished she was the type to drink. She remembered all the times Christian had gotten drunk when things were tense, and she wondered if it would help her now, but she was too afraid to find out. Instead she thought constantly of Christian, the way he had kissed her that morning, the way his arms had felt around her, his chest against her cheek when she'd awoken. At one point while she was sitting under the dryer at the salon, she closed her eyes and allowed herself to think of the more intimate things. She thought about the feeling of his body over hers, the taste of his skin, the warmth of his hands on her body, and the sound of his voice in her ears as he reached his climax. The thoughts alone made her long for him again. She knew she was going to go crazy.

By that evening, she felt an insane desire to run out of the church. She knew it was last-minute jitters—hadn't she already decided that marrying Warren was the best thing to do? Hadn't she gone over and over it in her mind? It wasn't like Christian had ever made any overtures of commitment; he'd never indicated any interest in anything but sex. That was not a relationship, she told herself firmly. Even if it was incredible.

She stood and went to the floor-length mirror, pulled out a tube of lipstick and began to apply it. She looked herself over again. She wore a gown of silken antique ivory lace. The bodice was fitted, and the top was off the shoulder in an elegant version of a peasant-style blouse. A spray of pearls gathered the three-inch ruffle of lace at the center of the top and allowed for just a hint of cleavage. The skirt flared from her petite waist and fell in a long silken train behind her. The ivory color of the lace set off her gold-toned skin perfectly, as well as enhancing her deep blue eyes and honey-blond hair. The makeup artist had used mauve tones to highlight her almond-shaped eyes and make their intense sapphire color almost glow. Her naturally high cheekbones were set off with a dusty mauve blush, and the lipstick she was applying was a deeper tone of the same color. She'd had the hairdresser leave part of her blond waves down, in some inane deference to Christian's preference of her hair loose. It was a stupid, adolescent thing to do, but she'd done it anyway, causing the hairdresser to reassess the way she'd arranged the veil, which was a crown of pearls and silk flowers that came to a V in front.

She heard the door open and was just thinking that it seemed a little early for her father to be coming to get her when she glanced up in the mirror. And there he was, Christian Joseph Collins, standing in the doorway to the dressing room, looking very devilish in all black. He was watching her, his light blue eyes locked on hers in the reflection. Susan didn't turn around. She'd been thinking about him so much that day that she was sure she was only imagining him there, and if she turned around, he'd disappear. He stepped inside and closed the door, and in three long strides stood right behind her. She stared up at him as his eyes traveled over her reflection.

"Jesus Christ, you look beautiful," he said, awed. She felt his hands on her waist then, as he bent his head to kiss her bare shoulder. She closed her eyes at the feeling of his lips on her skin.

After a long moment and a fight to regain her composure, she turned to look at him. "What are you doing here?" she asked, keeping her voice calm.

He grinned sardonically down at her. "Just wanting to see if you're still goin' through with this." He gestured to her dress. "Guess you are, huh?"

"Yes, I guess I am," she replied, a little more sharply than she'd meant to. She was angry with his casual tone, and the way he could tell her how beautiful she was one moment then hassle her the next.

Christian looked pleased that he'd managed to raise her hackles. Then he shook his head slowly. "Big mistake…"

"No one's given me a really good reason not to marry Warren," Susan retorted angrily.

"Do you love him beyond all reason?" Christian asked, his expression telling her he already knew the answer.

"No," she replied simply, but her own expression told him she didn't think that mattered.

"That's a really good reason not to marry him."

"Sometimes that kind of love takes time," Susan replied haughtily.

"Yeah?" He looked surprised. Then, without warning, he stepped forward, causing her to back up into the mirror. His mouth came down on hers in a hotly sensual kiss. His tongue parted her lips and slid inside to touch hers, tasting her hungrily.

When their lips parted, she was breathing heavily, holding

tightly to his shoulders. His look was cool as he raised an eyebrow at her. "If I can get you this hot ten minutes before you marry another man, don't you think you might be making a mistake?"

"It's purely physical," she said contemptuously.

Christian was about to answer when the door opened again. It was Susan's father. His eyes widened at the man standing in front of his daughter in such an intimate fashion.

"I say, what's going on in here?" he demanded.

"Nothing," Susan said, giving Christian one more narrowed look as she moved away from him. Christian stared back at her, an expression of calm acceptance on his face. Susan turned back to the mirror to reapply the lipstick Christian had kissed off, glancing at him as she did. Christian's forefinger rubbed at his lips as if trying to remove the impression of hers—or to remind her again of the kiss, which it did.

Susan walked over to her father, feeling Christian's eyes on her the entire time, but she staunchly refused to look back at him. Wilson was still glowering at Christian, but the younger man was oblivious. They left, and Christian leaned against the wall, his expression thoughtful. He had tried to make his point, but obviously she wasn't ready to hear it. What else could he do? She wanted to marry the geek, let her do it. *To hell with her*. With that, he walked out of the dressing room and toward the church doors.

Rick, Midnight, Mikeyla, Joe, Randy, and the rest of the gang sat in the pews, waiting for the wedding to start. Rick and Joe were next to each other, making jokes about lightning striking them for being in a Catholic church again. Midnight and Randy kept putting in their comments about chastity being a good form of absolution and confession being good for the soul. Both men denied the suggestions resoundingly. Dibbins, who sat next to Randy, agreed on that, and Spider put in a comment about Dibbs having trouble abstaining from anything with three women after him. Everyone got a good laugh at that. There were many angry looks in their direction from the upper-crust English and American society types, even though Joe and Rick were from the same set. The gang didn't seem to notice or care; they'd long since accepted that they would always stand out in a crowd, regardless of who that crowd was.

"I can't believe I have to sit through an entire mass," Joe said, shaking his head miserably.

Midnight leaned forward to look at her partner. "What do you mean, an entire mass? How long are these bloody things?" she asked, using English slang easily after so many years of being married to an Englishman.

Joe looked at Rick. "What, about an hour and a half?"

Rick nodded. "Yeah, sounds about right."

"Longer than our wedding?" Randy put in, leaning forward too.

Joe rolled his eyes. "God, nothing could be longer than that was!"

"Hey!" Randy said, punching him in the arm.

"Yeah!" Midnight shoved at Rick so hard his shoulder bumped Joe's. All four of them laughed. "Is it really that long?" Midnight asked then, sighing.

"Unfortunately." Rick's grin was intact as he put his arm around his wife and kissed her on the forehead.

A little while later the music started, and then Susan came slowly down the aisle. She did look beautiful, if a bit anxious.

"She looks nervous," Midnight said to Rick.

"Weren't you when we got married?" he whispered.

"Yes, I guess so…" She shook her head. She still didn't like the idea of Susan marrying Warren, but Rick had been adamant about it being the right thing. Midnight had talked to Deborah that day, and Deborah had told Midnight about her conversation with Christian. Midnight wanted to slug the young Englishman for being so goddamned impossible. But she knew he was right; Susan needed to learn to speak for herself and not rely on everyone else to talk for her.

The ceremony proceeded, and Midnight found that Joe and Rick were right—it was a painfully long mass. An hour and a half had passed when Rick nudged her. "They're actually getting to the wedding part now," he said, aware she'd been letting her mind wander. He knew his wife well; she'd been thinking of all the things she needed to do when she got back into the office the following week.

Midnight trained her mind on the front of the church and tuned in to what the priest was saying.

Susan felt extremely weary after all the talking in the mass. She was thinking she shouldn't have let Warren's parents make that decision when she heard a distinct creak from the back of the church. She sensed him there before she glanced back and saw him. Christian stood at the back of the building, leaning indolently against the door he'd just come through. He was watching her, his head canted just slightly to the side, his light blue eyes narrowed as if he were trying to read her thoughts. Shaking her head slightly, she turned her attention back to the priest. If Christian had decided to come to the ceremony, fine.

Susan listened as the priest talked about the sanctity of marriage and how important such a union was in God's eyes. He turned to Susan then and spoke to her; she watched him as he said the words she'd been waiting to hear.

"Do you, Susan Victoria Endicott, take Warren Rider to be your lawfully wedded husband, for richer, for poorer, in sickness and in health, forsaking all others and giving yourself only unto him, till death do you part?"

"I…" Susan began, her voice catching in her throat. She sensed the sudden tension in the church. The priest's words came back to her. *Forsaking all others, giving yourself only unto him…* Oh God… Suddenly her voice wouldn't come—she couldn't finish the acceptance.

She was about to nod numbly when Christian's voice, suddenly right behind her, said, "Don't."

There were outcries from the congregation, and people started to talk even as Susan turned to Christian. He stood there staring down at her, his light blue eyes seeing right through her.

Rick started to stand—Joe's hand on his arm stopped him. "Don't make me hurt you, man," Joe said seriously. "You know this is the right thing."

Rick looked at his friend, his eyes narrowed, but Midnight's voice chimed in. "He's right, Rick."

The rest of the gang nodded affirmation, getting to their feet as if to back Christian up, and that was their full intention.

Susan still stood speechless, staring up at Christian. Warren stepped forward then, breaking the silence.

"What the hell do you think you're doing?" he demanded.

Christian's gaze flicked to him. "I think I'm stealin' the bride," he replied, his tone just as arrogant, then looked back at Susan. "Come with me, Zan. Don't do this—you don't love him."

Susan swallowed convulsively, unable to believe this was happening. "I…" she began, still not able to find her voice.

Warren grabbed her arm roughly, pulling her to him. "Don't do this, Susan, I'm warning you."

"And I'm warnin' you," Christian said darkly, curling his hand over the other man's wrist. "Get your fucking hand off her, or I'll break it."

Warren stared back at him for a moment, obviously trying to decide if Christian was capable of it, then finally released Susan's arm.

Christian held the other man's wrist for an extra moment, leaning in to tell him, "You ever touch her like that again, and I'll kill you." Warren looked like he didn't doubt him for a moment.

Christian turned back to Susan, his eyes searching hers. "You love me, don't you," he said. It wasn't a question.

"Yes," Susan breathed, beginning to tremble with the strain of the moment.

"Then come with me, now," Christian whispered. Then he lowered his head, putting his lips next to her ear. "I love you." She gave a soft cry. Without another word, Christian took her hand, gave Warren a peremptory nod, and led her toward the back of the church.

Most of the people gathered were on their feet by now, and Wilson moved to block their way. Dave Dibbins put a warning hand on his shoulder. "I don't think you want to do anything, man," he said evenly.

"No, I don't think you do," Tiny said, moving to the man's other side. His sheer size coupled with Dibbins' dangerous expression were enough to keep Wilson from continuing forward.

It was Rick and Joe that made it to the back of the church in time to head Susan and Christian off. Christian held Susan's hand tightly, keeping her just behind him, his expression challenging Rick. "I'm taking her out of here," he said, his tone low, his stance aggressive. "Even if it means coming through you."

Rick looked thoughtful for a minute, glancing at Joe, who gave him an "I told you so" look, barely concealing his grin. Rick stood back and gestured for them to pass with a flourish.

Christian nodded and looked at Joe, who held his hand out. Christian clasped it tightly for a moment as Joe clapped him on the shoulder and said, "Bold move, man." It was obvious from his tone that he admired his cousin's audacious behavior.

An hour later, Susan and Christian sat on a quiet beach. He'd driven around aimlessly for a long time, still holding her hand tightly. Finally, he'd headed toward the beach, finding a secluded spot near some large rocks just above the surf. He didn't know it was the same spot many of the people he knew and respected came to to sort out their thoughts. He took his jacket off and put it around Susan as she sat on the steps above the rocks. Then he sat down behind her, his long legs on either side of her, and leaned back against the stair behind him. He put his arms around her and pulled her back against him, nuzzling her hair with his lips. They'd been silent since they'd left the church; it was as if neither of them knew what to say.

"I'm sorry I let you get that close," Christian said, his lips right next to her ear. She felt him shrug. "I guess I had to really see that you were going to do it, before the idea had a chance to make me really crazy."

"Crazy?" Susan asked softly.

"Yeah," he said, grinning. "Crazy enough to break up a wedding in front of all those people. Some of whom carry guns for a living."

Susan laughed quietly. "It was a rather brash action," she said, not sounding the least bit put out by it.

"Yeah, well…" He curled his lips in a sardonic smile. "I don't do things halfway."

"You could have told me that you love me last night," Susan pointed out reasonably.

"I wasn't sure I did last night. Seeing you today, and knowing you were about to become some other man's wife, was what let me know for sure."

"How?"

"It made me mad as hell."

Susan nodded. "Crazy."

"Right."

"Of course…" Susan said, embarrassment creeping into her voice. "I guess I could have told you that I love you back when I knew it as well."

"And when was that?" he asked, narrowing his eyes at her.

"Back when Randy was in the hospital." She looked chagrined that it was so long ago. "Remember that night we went over to Donovan's? I knew then that I loved you, because you understood how I felt about Randy being hurt. Warren didn't understand, but you held me and made me feel safe, and I knew I loved you for that."

Christian nodded. "So why didn't you tell me?"

"Would you have been happy to hear it?"

Christian was contemplative for a moment, then shook his head. "I probably would have pushed you away twice as fast."

"That's what I thought."

"But you could have told me last night."

"I could have…" She ran her hand over his arm in introspection. "But by that time I had decided that marrying Warren was the right thing to do all around."

"Right thing to do?"

"In terms of all the plans that had been made, the arrangements, the money spent, the 'responsible' thing to do."

"But you didn't love him."

"No, but I thought I did before I got involved with you." She shrugged. "I figured you just turned my head with your incredible looks and the vulnerable side that you didn't like to show… I guess I wanted to be different for you, and I thought that was what drew me to you. It was an impossible dream that I could be with you, and I thought that was why I wanted you."

"Was it?" he asked, raising a jet black eyebrow.

"No, it's because I'm in love with you, and I want to be with you," she said, her tone slightly chiding.

"So you were willing to live your life with a man like that to be proper?" Christian said disbelievingly.

"I didn't want to disappoint anyone."

Christian gave a short laugh. "I think there's no avoidin' that now."

Susan shrugged, dropping her head against his shoulder. "I don't care anymore. I just want you."

Christian craned his neck to look down at her. "Just want me, huh?" he asked, his voice lowering an octave.

"Yes," she whispered.

He kissed her then, his lips possessing hers totally. He reached up to caress her neck as she turned to get closer to him. They kissed for a long time, enjoying the thought that they were finally together. When their lips parted, she looked up at him, her eyes searching his.

"Would you really have fought my uncle?"

"Yes."

"But before, you wouldn't fight him. Why?"

"Before, he was justified." He shrugged. "Well, to my way of thinking, anyway. I couldn't fight back then, but today… I was taking you with me and he wasn't going to have anything to say about it."

"He didn't stop you," she pointed out.

"No, but he was thinkin' about it."

"He's just worried about me—he thinks it's his job."

"Yeah, well…" Christian let his voice trail off, as if to say he didn't think so.

"So what happens now, Christian?" Susan asked, finally voicing the question that had been on her mind since they left the church.

He was silent for a long time, then shook his head. "I don't know for sure, Zan. This is all new for me. And I have to tell you, it scares the hell out of me to think about what I just did." He looked down at her, straight into her eyes. "All I know is that I love you, and I couldn't let you marry that asshole."

Susan nodded, understanding his reasoning but not sure what it meant. She figured she'd just have to wait and see. All that really mattered to her right now was that she was with him, and he was willing to admit that he loved her.

After the quick end to the wedding, it had been decided by the gang that they needed a party anyway. Joe's house was immediately elected as the most logical place. Everyone stopped off to pick up beer and other assorted liquor and then made their way to Joe's. Joe, Rick, and Randy sat in the kitchen as Midnight made more margaritas.

"I think it was the coolest thing I've ever seen," Midnight said, giving Rick a pointed look.

"Yeah, real cool," Rick said sulkily. "Do you know how much that wedding cost?"

"Oh Jesus Christ, Rick!" Joe said, rolling his eyes. "Wilson's got more fucking money than God—serves him right to have to waste a little of it."

"Besides," Randy put in, "none of that dismisses the fact that Susan obviously loves Christian."

"Hmph," Rick grouched, looking sullen.

"Oh, stop it!" Midnight threw an ice cube at him. "You are so impossible sometimes. They love each other—doesn't that count for anything?"

"Yeah, yeah," Rick said. "But I didn't hear him sayin' he'd marry her."

"So?" Joe made a sour face. "He don't have to marry her to make her happy."

"Oh, you just wait, Sinclair," Rick said, nodding knowingly. "When Kat gets older and the guys start comin' round."

"Oh, shut the hell up, Debenshire!" Dibbins said, coming into the kitchen.

"You!" Rick pointed an accusing finger at Dave. "You're the worst of all. How many fucking girlfriends do you have now?"

Dave rubbed the bridge of his nose with his forefinger, looking ever so slightly abashed. "Uh… three…" He grinned widely then.

"See?" Rick said, looking back at Midnight. "See, your own people—sluts, all of you!" He was laughing by this time, as was everyone else in the room.

"So, uh," Dave said, "I got two questions. Are the margaritas ready yet, and does anyone know where those kids went?"

"No, and no," Midnight replied, grinning as she started the blender.

"Okay…" Dave nodded before turning around and walking out of the kitchen.

"Where did they go?" Midnight asked.

"Who knows…" Joe grinned, realizing he shouldn't speculate in front of Rick lest he drive his friend even more crazy.

Josephine wandered in. "So what did my son do?" she asked,

raising an eyebrow at the four people in the kitchen. It was obvious where Christian got the habit from.

"Well," Joe said hesitantly. "He sort of broke up a wedding…"

"How?" Josephine asked, shocked.

"He stole the bride." Rick's smile was a little on the frosty side.

"Good lord," Josephine said, touching the crucifix that hung around her neck.

"Yes, well," Midnight began, giving her husband a vile look, "what Rick's not saying is that he's in love with her and she with him. It was actually a good thing."

"But you don't look happy about it," Josephine said, looking at Rick.

"Well…" Rick began, feeling like a bit of an ass then. "I just— the woman he ran off with is my niece, and I guess I'm a little over-protective of her."

"And my son isn't exactly marriageable material, is he?" Josephine said evenly, though her eyes narrowed slightly.

"I, well…" Rick felt distinctly like he was being scolded by his own mother at that moment, even though Josephine was only a couple of years older than him.

"What my husband is trying to say," Midnight said, her grin wide, "is that he's worried about Susan getting hurt. Christian has kind of played the field here, and we don't really know how he feels about her."

"Susan?" Josephine said. "Isn't that the young woman whose life my son saved?" Again the eyebrow went up, and her tone was very definitely chilled this time.

"Uh…" Joe shook his head at Rick as if to say, *Dumb shit.* "Yes, she is the woman whose life he saved."

"And that doesn't constitute some sort of serious emotion to you people?" Josephine asked disbelievingly.

Midnight canted her head to the side, throwing her husband a look. "You're absolutely right, Ms. Collins. We have no right to question Christian's motives. He saved her life and he obviously cares about her."

"Damn right I do," Christian said from the doorway. Susan stood next to him, beaming.

"Hey!" Midnight moved to hug him warmly, and then Susan.

Christian looked at Rick, seeing the man's wary expression and realizing he wasn't fully convinced of his intentions. After a long hesitation, Rick walked over, extending his hand. "You better make her happy."

"I'll do my best," Christian said, sounding anything but intimidated. Rick looked back at the younger man, surprised by his lack of reverence but noting the determined look in his light blue eyes as well.

Christian hugged his mother. She kissed him warmly on the cheek. "You love this one, don't you?" she whispered softly, recognizing the look on her son's face.

"Yes," he answered without hesitation.

Josephine nodded, then turned to Susan. "If my son gives you any trouble, you tell me. I'll box his ears for you," she said warmly as she held her arms out to the young woman.

Susan laughed softly as she hugged Josephine. "I think there'll be plenty of opportunities," she said when they parted, and glanced at Christian, who pointedly looked up at the ceiling. "I'm going to go change," Susan said then, gesturing to her wedding gown. "I think this is a little formal for the type of party going on here tonight." She headed down the hallway to her room.

Midnight knocked on her door a few minutes later, walking in and sitting down on the bed as Susan dressed.

"So?" Midnight asked expectantly.

"So…" Susan said, glancing at her aunt. "I love him and he loves me, and that's about as far as it goes right now."

"Is that enough for you?"

"For now, yes. It's more than I ever expected with him." She sat down on the bed with her aunt. "I love him, Midnight, so much. He's not what everyone sees—he's so much more. He's a good man, he just lets everyone think he's cold and distant. But you know that, don't you?"

"Yes, I could see that right away. He's pretty great."

"Yes…"

"We just don't want you to get hurt."

"I know. But being with Warren wasn't what I really wanted—I just didn't think I *could* have what I wanted."

"And you wanted Christian."

"Yes."

Midnight nodded, accepting what Susan was saying.

A few minutes later they walked back out to the party and found Rick, Joe, Tiny, Spider, Dave, Donovan, Kana, and Christian getting set to do a tequila shot together. The rest of the women in the room watched with amused grins or outright smiles on their faces. They'd all found out a little while before that it was kind of an engagement party as well, celebrating Donovan and Jeanie's pending nuptials.

"Okay," Joe said, holding up a hand and grinning at the faces around him. "What exactly are we drinking to?"

"To getting drunk," Spider said.

"To the public at large," Tiny added.

"To the guy that invented tequila," Dave put in, grinning.

"To the guy that grew the limes to go with the tequila," Donovan called.

"To the guy that grew—is it grew? Anyway, to the guy that gave us the salt to precede the tequila and the lime," Rick said, sounding a little far gone already.

"Good one, Debenshire," Midnight said sardonically as she walked up to them. "Pour me one too, Sinclair." She held the shot glass aloft. "To getting my partner back, even if I had to die to do it." She grinned rakishly. "And to my niece for catching the man she *really* wanted, even if she had to cost her parents an enormous amount of money to do it." She turned to Deborah, who stood in a nearby doorway, and rolled her eyes dramatically. "To Donovan and Jeanie, who finally got their shit together long enough to get engaged." Her gaze fell on Donovan and Jeanie, who both looked embarrassed. "And furthermore, to my ever loyal members who, as usual, came through when I needed them most. I love you guys, and no matter what Joe says about you, you can keep your jobs forever." She laughed as many eyes turned on Joe and he held his hands up defensively. "Raise your glasses, boys and girls, because you have before you the best of the best, the greatest of the greatest, and my very best friends."

"Oh, hell, it's always the same toast," Joe said, grinning wryly as he held his glass higher. "To FORS."

Everyone did likewise, and the whole room, even the non-members, cried out, "To FORS!"

You can find more information about the author and series here:

www.sherrylhancock.com

www.facebook.com/SherrylDHancock

www.vulpine-press.com/midknight-blue-series

Also by Sherryl D. Hancock:

The *WeHo* series follows a group of women from Los Angeles as they navigate the ups and downs of love, life, work, and everything in between.

www.vulpine-press.com/we-ho

The *Wild Irish Silence* series. Escape into the world of BJ Sparks and discover how he went from the small-town boy to the world-famous rock star.

www.vulpine-press.com/wild-irish-silence-series